W9-BRR-873

Lords
of
Passion

Also by Virginia Henley

"Smuggler's Lair" in *Lords of Desire*

Also by Kate Pearce

Raw Desire

Simply Forbidden

Simply Insatiable

Some Like It Rough

Simply Shameless

Simply Wicked

Simply Sinful

Simply Sexual

Also by Maggie Robinson

Mistress by Marriage

"To Match a Thief" in *Improper Gentlemen*

Mistress by Midnight

Mistress by Mistake

Lords *of* *Passion*

VIRGINIA HENLEY
KATE PEARCE
MAGGIE ROBINSON

Maggie Robinson

KENSINGTON BOOKS
http://www.kensingtonbooks.com

KENSINGTON BOOKS are published by

Kensington Publishing Corp.
119 West 40th Street
New York, NY 10018

All Kensington titles, imprints, and distributed lines are available at special quantity discounts for bulk purchases for sales promotion, premiums, fund-raising, educational, or institutional use.

Special book excerpts or customized printings can also be created to fit specific needs. For details, write or phone the office of the Kensington Special Sales Manager: Attn. Special Sales Department. Kensington Publishing Corp., 119 West 40th Street, New York, NY 10018. Phone: 1-800-221-2647.

Kensington and the K logo are Reg. U.S. Pat. & TM Off.

ISBN-13: 978-0-7582-7156-3
ISBN-10: 0-7582-7156-5

First Brava Books Trade Paperback Printing: December 2010
First Kensington Books Mass-Market Paperback Printing: November 2012

10 9 8 7 6 5 4 3 2 1

Printed in the United States of America

Contents

Beauty and the Brute

VIRGINIA HENLEY

Chapter One

My feet are freezing! Lady Sarah stepped down from the carriage and hurried into Caversham Park Manor. A servant helped to remove her cloak and boots and handed her a pair of velvet slippers. "Thank you so much. Is Mother in her sitting room?"

"Yes, dear, she's waiting for you."

Sarah walked quickly, hoping the fire was blazing bright in her mother's parlor. She curtsied as she had been taught to do. "I hope you are well, Mother. I was so surprised when you sent the carriage to school for me. Are my Christmas holidays starting early?"

"They are indeed, Sarah." Margaret, Countess of Cadogan, held a rustling paper in her hand. She gave her slim, pale daughter a critical glance. "I've had a letter from your father in The Hague. Don't stand so close to the fire," she said impatiently. "Do sit down; I have something important to tell you."

Sarah curled her toes inside her slippers.

"Your father wants us to join him in The Hague."

"When?" asked thirteen-year-old Sarah, her eyes as big as saucers. She had never been farther than her school in Reading.

"We are to take ship immediately. It is wonderful news. I will be able to spend Christmas with my family in the Netherlands."

"So it is Father's Christmas present to us," Sarah said in wonder.

Her mother did not tell Sarah about the other *Christmas present* he had in store for her. It would be far better for her daughter to learn of it when she arrived at the Court of Holland. That way, Sarah would have no option but to accept it gracefully.

Thirty miles away in Oxford, eighteen-year-old Charles Lennox, Earl of March, slapped his female companion on her bare buttocks. "Wake up, Fanny. It's time you got the hell out of here. I'm due to attend class in less than an hour. It'll take me that long to wash the stink of strumpet off my nether regions."

The buxom lass sat up in bed and swung her legs to the floor. "There's no need to hit me, m'lord. Is it a class that teaches manners?"

"Cheeky wench! Watch your mouth if you want to enjoy my favors again. I know a dozen females eager to share my bed."

Fanny picked up her petticoat from the rug and quickly moved out of his arm's reach.

"That's because you have royal blood in your veins.

They want to see if you're as good in bed as your ancestor, King Charles II," she taunted.

"I'm longer, both in size and endurance," Charles drawled.

"Ha! Nothing like blowing your own horn."

"I'm not likely to do that when I have wenches like you to do it for me."

Suddenly the door to his room opened, and his tutor, Henry Grey, hurried inside. He addressed the plump female struggling into her smock without looking at her. "Better wrap up warmly—it's freezing out there."

"Henry, old son, what brings you here at such an early hour?"

Grey waited until the girl left before he brandished an envelope. "A letter from your father. It's marked *URGENT.*"

"Then open the damn thing and read it to me."

Grey pulled back the curtains and slit the wax seal with his thumbnail. He scanned the letter quickly and conveyed its message. "His Grace wants to see you in The Hague. He orders you to take ship immediately." King George I had recently appointed the Duke of Richmond ambassador to the Netherlands.

"At last!" Charles whooped. "My college days are over. How bloody fortuitous that my father and I agree that a well-rounded education should be based on the Grand Tour. I couldn't ask for a better Christmas present!" He climbed out of bed. "Pack our bags, Henry. I shall go and bid a fond farewell to that insufferable swine, the dean. Then I shall demand a refund of next term's tuition from the skinflint treasurer."

The Hague, Holland
November 28, 1719, three days earlier

"Damnation, Cadogan, you've the devil's own luck. You've won every hand we've played for the last sennight." Charles Lennox, Duke of Richmond, pushed his chair back from the gaming table and wiped his brow. "Stap me! I'm wiped out—you've had the lot!"

General William Cadogan glanced at his darkly handsome opponent. He was the illegitimate son of the late King Charles II, who had impregnated his mistress, Louise de Keroualle. "Would you like me to tally up, Your Grace?"

Richmond waved a negligent hand. "By all means, let me know the damage."

The dashing Irish general didn't take long. He had a damn good idea of what the duke had wagered and lost in their endless games of *écarté*. The duke was a heavy drinker, which was the main reason for his losses. The general set the seven score cards down on the table, one for each night they had played. "I tot it up to a little over ten thousand guineas."

"What?" Richmond howled. "Are you jesting?" By the benign look on Cadogan's face, Charles Lennox knew he was serious. He downed the glass of gin sitting before him. "I don't have it. You'll have to accept my marker."

The men sitting at the table, who had been observing their deep play, began to murmur. Richmond flushed darkly. A gentleman always paid his gambling debts. His shrewd mind quickly inventoried his assets. Land was out of the question—the aristocracy accumulated property; it never relinquished it. Besides, the Earl of

Cadogan already owned the hundred-acre Caversham estate on the outskirts of Reading.

Horses were the next thing Richmond thought of. His family seat, Goodwood, at the foot of the South Downs, had a racing stable of Thoroughbreds. The thought of parting with his horses made him feel physically ill.

He looked across at General Cadogan. "You have a daughter, I believe."

"I do, Your Grace. Her name is Sarah."

"How would you like to make Sarah a countess? My son, the Earl of March, is without a wife." Lennox believed no man could resist such a magnanimous offer.

But the Earl of Cadogan, who was Marlborough's top general, and largely responsible for Britain's victories in the War of the Spanish Succession, was a shrewd negotiator. That was the reason he had been given the diplomatic duties concerned with resettlements among Great Britain, France, Holland, and Spain.

"My daughter, Lady Sarah, has a dowry of ten thousand pounds. If I gave you my daughter and her marriage settlement, I would have to pay you ten thousand instead of *you* paying *me* ten thousand." He raised his hands in appeal. "It doesn't fly, Your Grace."

"Charles is heir to my Dukedom of Richmond and all the estates that encompasses," Lennox pointed out. "Lady Sarah could become a duchess." *Surely it's not necessary to remind you that we have royal blood?*

"A marriage between my daughter and your son, and heir, could be the solution."

Cadogan paused for emphasis. "Without the marriage settlement, of course."

"Curse you, general. You're not negotiating with the enemy here!"

"Since we are civilized gentlemen, I propose a compromise, Your Grace."

"Let's split the difference," Richmond suggested. "Your daughter's hand in marriage along with a dowry of *five thousand*."

The other men at the table leaned forward in anticipation of Cadogan's answer.

"Done!" The general's reply was heartfelt. He raised his hand to a servant. "Drinks all around. We must toast this historic union."

The Duke of Richmond raised his glass. "Here's to you and here's to me, and if someday we disagree, fuck you, here's to me!"

All the gentlemen roared with laughter and drained their glasses.

"I shall send for my daughter immediately."

"And I shall summon my heir," the duke declared.

"The *Green Lion* is a lovely name for a ship," Sarah exclaimed as they boarded at the Port of London.

"I only hope our cabin is warm. This is a dreadful season to be crossing to the Netherlands," Lady Cadogan said with a shiver.

"I'm glad I'm wearing my woolen dress and cloak. This is so exciting!"

The pair was shown below to their cabin, and when their trunk arrived, it took up most of the space between the two bunks.

"Such cramped quarters," the countess complained.

"It's a good thing we will be arriving before dark tomorrow. But at least the cabin is warm."

"Oh, I think we are under way." Sarah grabbed hold of the bunk rail as the vessel swayed. She was bursting with excitement. "May I please go up on deck and watch as the *Green Lion* navigates through the Thames?"

"If you must, Sarah. But when the ship approaches Gravesend, you must come below decks immediately. Daylight will soon be gone, and the wind will be so fierce, it could easily blow you overboard," her mother cautioned her.

The grave warning did not deter Sarah; it made her more eager to go up on deck.

"Thank you, Mother. I'll be careful."

Sarah climbed the stairs that led onto the deck and pulled her cloak tightly about her. She watched the docks recede slowly, but soon lost interest in looking back. She much preferred to look ahead and made her way to the very front of the vessel. She stood in wonder as the banks of the river widened. She breathed deeply, filling her lungs with sea air, as if the smell of tide wrack were the elixir of life.

She lifted her face to the cold breeze as she heard the gulls and terns screaming overhead. *What an exciting life to be a sailor!* Sarah stood enraptured as the ship reached the estuary and headed out to sea. She became aware that the light was fast fading from the day, and the moment the ship sailed into the North Sea, the wind whipped her cloak about and she remembered that she must go below.

The fierce wind was against her as she lowered her head and began to run. Suddenly she collided with someone, and the impact knocked the breath out of her.

"You clumsy, idiot girl! Watch what you're about for Christ's sake."

Sarah paled as she stared up into the furious face of a young man. "I'm . . . I'm sorry, sir," she gasped.

"Sorry, be damned!" He blocked her way. "You haven't the brains of a bloody baboon, barreling down the gangway like a loose cannon."

"I have to get below—I promised Mother."

"We all want to get below decks to a warm cabin, damn your eyes."

"You are frightening the girl, Charles. Let her pass," Henry Grey said quietly.

Charles Lennox grudgingly stepped aside. "The witless girl needed a lesson. I hope you remembered to bring that bottle of rum. It's colder than a whore's heart tonight."

When the Countess of Cadogan and Sarah stepped from their carriage at the Court of Holland, a liveried attendant ushered them inside. Margaret's father had been Chancellor of the Court before he retired, and the servants showed her great deference.

When they arrived at the suite of rooms that had been assigned to General Cadogan, he flung open the door and welcomed them warmly.

"Margaret, my dear, I hope your voyage wasn't a rough one."

"It was tolerable. December is no month to be at sea."

"It was an absolute necessity, my dear. We couldn't let an opportunity like this slip away." He looked at his young daughter and gave her a hug. "Were you seasick?"

"No, Father," she said breathlessly.

"That's my girl. Take off your cloak and let's have a look at you."

Sarah removed her cloak and bonnet. She smoothed her hands over her flattened hair. "I must look a fright."

"Nay, child. The wind has put roses in your cheeks."

Sarah blushed with pleasure at the compliment.

William raised his eyes to his wife. His daughter's figure was slight and her face extremely pale. "I hope you've brought her a decent dress to wear tomorrow."

"You gave me such short notice, there was no time to have a new gown made. In any case, it's cold. A woolen dress will suffice."

"Have you told her?" William asked.

"I thought it best to wait until we arrived. You may have that pleasure, my lord."

Told me what? Sarah went very still. She had an ominous feeling that her mother was being sarcastic. She doubted that *pleasure* would be involved. She couldn't find the words to ask, but the apprehensive look in her eyes questioned her father.

"We'll wait until after dinner," he said heartily. "Sarah looks like she could use some food. There's nothing like a thick broth to warm the cockles of your heart. After dinner, Sarah and I will have a private chat."

"I'll go and unpack." She sensed that her parents had something to discuss that concerned her. Something was in the air, and she took refuge in the short reprieve.

When she lifted the lid of the trunk that had been delivered to the bedchamber, she stroked her hand over the rich material of her mother's gowns. One was purple velvet, embroidered with gold, and another was black, quilted brocade decorated with crystals.

Sarah carefully lifted them from the trunk and hung them in the wardrobe, along with two other day dresses and the lovely whalebone panniers that went beneath. Her own clothes had been packed on the bottom, and as a result were slightly creased. As well as flannel petticoats and knitted stockings, she had brought only two dresses. One was oyster-colored wool with a cream frill around the high neck, and the other was gray with fitted sleeves that ended in white ruffles around the wrists. She wished that she had panniers to hold out her skirts. They would help disguise how thin she was, but her mother had decreed that she was still too young for grown-up fashions.

Sarah hung her dresses next to her mother's and sighed with resignation at the contrast between the rich, fashionable gowns and her own plain attire.

Since the hour was late and the ladies had been traveling for the past two days, the trio ate dinner in Cadogan's suite. Tonight for some reason Sarah's appetite was nonexistent.

Her mother gave her a critical glance. "You must eat more. You will never fill out if all you do with food is push it about your plate."

Her father changed the subject. "What are you learning at school?"

"Latin," she said softly.

"Latin? What the devil good will Latin do you?

Surely French would be better for a young lady of fashion."

I don't feel like a young lady of fashion. "We say our prayers in Latin."

"I wager you have some uncharitable names for the nuns."

Sarah's eyes sparkled with mischief. "We call them the *Sisters of the Black Plague.*"

Cadogan threw back his head and laughed. It tickled his Irish sense of humor. "By God, I warrant they teach you not to spit in church, and very little else." He bent close.

"I think a change of schools is in order. What d'you say, Sarah?"

"Oh, I would love it above all things."

When they finished eating, the earl gave a speaking nod to his wife and she excused herself so that her husband could have privacy for the chat with his daughter.

Cadogan led his daughter to a chair before the fire and sat down opposite her. "The time has come when we must think about your future, Sarah."

She nodded but made no reply, knowing there was more to come.

"I have no son, so I want the very best for my daughter." He paused to let his words sink in. "For some time now I have been searching for a suitable match for you. I would never consider any noble of a lower rank than my own."

Sarah's blue eyes widened. *You are talking about finding a future husband for me.*

"Not only must he be titled, he must be heir to wealth and property."

You married a lady from the Netherlands. I hope you don't look for a match for me here. She clasped her hands together tightly. *I want to live in England.*

"I have been offered a match for you that surpasses all my expectations. It is an undreamed-of opportunity that will raise you to the pinnacle of the aristocracy. A premier duke of the realm has asked for your hand in marriage for his son and heir."

Sarah sat silently as questions chased each other through her mind. *Who? Where? When?* But most puzzling was *why?*

William Cadogan's face was beaming. "The Duke of Richmond is offering marriage with his son, Charles Lennox, the Earl of March." He leaned forward and patted her hand. "Sarah, my dear, you will be the Countess of March, and the future Duchess of Richmond."

"I . . . I can't believe it," she murmured. "Are we to be betrothed?"

Her father waved a dismissive hand. "You are to be *wed,* not betrothed!" He loosened his neckcloth. "Fortunately, Richmond and his son are here at The Hague."

"So we will be able to meet each other and see if we suit?" she asked shyly.

"Of course you will suit! The marriage contracts have already been drawn up. You will meet each other at your wedding . . . tomorrow."

Sarah was stunned as a sparrow flown into a wall. *"Tomorrow?"*

Chapter Two

"Only the thought of starting my Grand Tour has sustained me through the rigors of the nightmare journey to get here. Holland is as cold as the balls on a brass monkey. I'd like to go straight to Spain, then sail the Mediterranean all the way to Constantinople, Turkey. At the moment I crave sunshine, and look at Grey here, he's pale as a corpse."

The Duke of Richmond poured his son and his tutor measures of gin. "Scotch whiskey does a better job at warming the blood, but gin is the best Holland has to offer. My apologies, gentlemen."

Charles did not miss the mockery in his father's voice.

"So—you're done with Oxford, are you? Absorbed all the culture and knowledge that august seat of learning has to offer, I presume?"

"The university is all very well, especially the cricket, but it cannot broaden the horizons and equip one for life as the Grand Tour must surely do."

"Have it all planned out, do you?" the duke enquired.

"Absolutely. I've thought of nothing else for the past year. After Turkey, there's Athens, Venice, Rome, Spain, Portugal. I might skip Germany and take in the Balkans. With the letters of reference and introduction to the royal houses and the envoys you will provide, I warrant it will take the best part of three years."

"To say nothing of the letters of credit drawn on the Bank of England I will provide," Richmond said dryly.

Charles swallowed nervously. "Well, that goes without saying, Father."

"Remind me again—what it is you intend to study in the great cities of the world, besides drinking, gaming, and whoring?"

With tongue in cheek, Charles replied, "I intend to follow in your footsteps, of course." He paused for emphasis and then continued. "I shall study language, art, architecture, geography, and culture."

"Mmm, do you suppose you could spare time from getting pissing drunk and acquire some filial gratitude, a modicum of deference, and a few manners while you're at it?"

"Things you acquired from your father, no doubt."

"My father had impeccable manners and a great deal of charm. He also had shrewd common sense along with his sensuality. You could do worse in a role model."

"Thank you for your advice." He finished his gin. "It's all settled then? I don't want to hang about wasting time. When may I leave?"

Richmond smiled. "You may leave anytime you please, after tomorrow."

"Tomorrow? What's going on tomorrow?"

"You're getting married, Charles."

"What?" His dark brows drew together. "Have you taken leave of your senses?"

"I have arranged for you to marry. The ceremony will take place tomorrow."

"Who am I to marry, pray?"

"Lady Sarah, the daughter of the Earl of Cadogan, Marlborough's top general."

Charles jumped to his feet. "I won't do it!" he shouted.

Richmond shrugged. "Suit yourself, my boy. No wedding, no Grand Tour."

"Margaret, surely you packed something for Sarah that is more flattering than this gray dress. She looks like she's wearing an institutional uniform," Cadogan complained.

Sarah smoothed the folds in the gray skirt and felt rather forlorn.

"Go and put on your other dress, Sarah," her mother admonished her. The countess was gowned in her rich purple velvet with gold leaves embroidered on the stomacher.

When his daughter left the room, Cadogan said, "You had better move to the London residence and enroll Sarah in an elite finishing school for ladies. She needs classes in music, dancing, and all the social graces. She must learn how to attract a gentleman and hold him in the palm of her hand. By the time the young Earl of March returns from his Grand Tour, she should be an accomplished lady of fashion who can hold her own, not only at Court, but in all aristocratic, high-class society."

Sarah returned wearing the oyster-colored gown with the cream frill around the neck. Her pale blond hair and alabaster skin blended in with the shades of her dress, and it would have been charitable to say she looked like a colorless stick.

The general masked his despair and reminded himself that his daughter had gentle manners and a sweet amenable disposition. Upon occasion he had even caught a glimmer of his own Irish humor, despite Margaret's efforts to stifle any spark of droll wit.

"For privacy, the nuptial vows are to be exchanged in the Earl of Richmond's suite. As ambassador to the Netherlands he has the most luxurious chambers in The Hague." He checked the time. "You had better take Sarah there now, and I will make sure the Anglican cleric is on his way."

The duke's personal manservant opened the door to Richmond's apartment. Charles was standing before the fireplace, in conversation with his father and the ambassador's legal secretary. Both father and son were richly garbed in brocade coats and satin breeches as befitted the significant occasion. When the ladies entered, the duke welcomed them with a warm smile.

"Countess Cadogan, do come in, and please be at ease."

Charles glanced at the countess, then his eyes swept back to the door expectantly. A full minute went by while he waited impatiently. He glanced back at his father. "Where the devil is she?"

Richmond extended his hand. "I believe this is Lady Sarah, the bride-to-be."

Charles stiffened as he stared in disbelief at the girl who stood beside the splendidly gowned countess. His eyes moved down from the crown of her head to her spindly ankles, then back up to her pale, pinched face. "You surely don't expect me to marry this dowdy chit of a girl!" He looked down his aristocratic nose at the rail-thin creature. "She's flat as a board—how old is she?" he demanded.

The Countess of Cadogan's lips tightened at the young earl's insulting remarks, but she bit her tongue rather than retort with words that might offend the Duke of Richmond.

Sarah blanched, and a white, bloodless circle appeared about her mouth.

Richmond gave his son a fierce look that would have felled a less arrogant youth. He pressed a powerful fist into the small of the groom's back and propelled him forward. "Lady Cadogan, may I present my son, Charles?"

Margaret did not smile but sketched what barely passed for a curtsy.

"Charles Lennox, at your service, my lady," Richmond's son said through his teeth.

Sarah stood, stiff as a stick of wood, and stared. She recognized the bully who had cursed at her on board the *Green Lion*, and icy fingers clutched her heart. *This cannot be real; I must be having a nightmare. Surely my parents don't want this monster to be my husband?*

The door opened and Earl Cadogan came into the chamber accompanied by the Anglican cleric. Sarah took a step toward her father, as the hope that he would save her lifted her heart. "Father, I want to go home," she pleaded.

"And so you shall, my dear. You are so young, you will be a wife in name only. Once you have exchanged your wedding vows, your bridegroom is embarking on his Grand Tour, and you are returning to London to attend an academy for ladies."

Sarah's hope shattered and left her feeling hollow and abandoned.

Her father took her arm and led her forward.

The Duke of Richmond forced his son to stand beside her.

The minister stood before them and intoned an abbreviated version of the *Solemnization of Matrimony*. The vows they exchanged were forced. When Sarah opened her mouth and gasped, it was taken as consent. Charles was silent for a long, stretched-out minute. When his father thumped his spine, he gave a surly, *"I will,"* then added, *"against my better judgment and at my father's insistence."*

"Who giveth this woman to be married to this man?"

Sarah stood, numb with shock, as her father actually gave her to Charles Lennox.

A gold wedding ring was produced and placed on Sarah's finger.

"Those whom God hath joined together let no man put asunder. I now pronounce that Sarah and Charles be man and wife together."

Cadogan and Richmond were congratulating each other, both relieved that the marriage was all right and tight and legal.

"You are an *ugly* little chit," Charles murmured cruelly.

"You are a *brute,*" Sarah whispered. "I hate you!"

During the course of the next three years Lady Sarah experienced a metamorphosis. She underwent a striking physical change as her body matured and filled out in all the right feminine places. Her breasts became high and full, her waist tiny as a wasp, her hips rounded, and the curve of her bottom drew envious female glances and lustful, longing looks from all the males of her acquaintance.

Her long honey-blond hair had a tendency to curl and lent itself to all the latest fashionable and intricate Georgian styles. Her porcelain skin and generous mouth needed only a touch of rouge to give her face the beauty of an English rose. Golden lashes fringed large blue eyes, the deep shade of Persian sapphires. Her slim fingers, delicate ankles, and long legs that had once given her the appearance of an ungainly colt now lent her a fluid grace that was exceptional.

Sarah had always been intelligent, and the lessons she learned in deportment, music, classical poetry, dancing, and riding gave her a polish of sophistication she had not possessed at thirteen.

The five thousand pounds her father had saved from her dowry were put into an account in her name at the Bank of England. As a result, Sarah's wardrobe was extensive. Her taste in clothes was impeccable, and she learned exactly which shades, styles, and fashions flattered her delicate fair coloring.

Out from under the influence of her controlling mother, her natural Irish wit began to bloom, and as a titled, married woman she enjoyed a great deal of freedom. Since her mother preferred living at Caversham Park Manor, Sarah resided alone in London at the Cadogan town house, and by the time she turned sixteen, she was on the guest list of every social hostess.

Sarah's hand went to her throat as she read a note inviting her to afternoon tea.

"What is it, m'lady? Not bad news I hope?" Molly asked. Sarah had elevated the Irish girl, whom her father had employed as a servant, to lady's maid, and companion-confidante.

"I expect it is. This invitation is from the Duchess of Richmond, my mother-in-law. I've seen her at Court, but I've always managed to avoid her."

Molly rolled her eyes. "May she rest in peace . . . soon."

Sarah laughed. "That's such a wicked thought, but vastly amusing." She sobered. "I don't suppose I can evade her any longer. It's more or less a summons. Help me choose something appropriate to wear."

"D'you want to make her grass green with envy, or d'you want Her Grace to loath and detest you?"

"Well, neither, actually. I would like her to realize what a fine marriage prize the Richmonds have gained. A lady who is far superior to their insufferable son and heir."

"One look will tell her their *git of a sodding son* is no fit match for you."

* * *

That afternoon, Sarah knocked on the door of Richmond House in Whitehall and was admitted by a liveried majordomo. She was wearing a day dress of sapphire blue lawn that matched her eyes. The contrast of the dark tone showed off her golden hair that was upswept and threaded with narrow loops of blue satin ribbon. Sarah was confident that she looked her best, and it helped her mask her apprehension.

She followed the servant to a large sitting room where an older woman and a younger lady stood when she entered. To her surprise the majordomo announced her formally.

"The Countess of March, Your Grace."

The Duchess of Richmond stepped forward. "Welcome, my dear. May I call you Sarah?" The dark-haired lady smoothed the silver strands at her temple and smiled.

"Yes, please do, Your Grace." Sarah made a deep curtsy.

The older woman reached out her hand and raised her immediately. "It is not necessary. Please let's not be formal with each other, Sarah. This is my daughter, Anne. Our meeting is long overdue. Forgive me for not inviting you sooner."

Lady Anne Lennox stepped forward with a warm smile and embraced Sarah. "You are so lovely. Mother and I are overjoyed that you are both beautiful and graceful."

"Thank you," Sarah said breathlessly, amazed that they were so friendly.

"Do sit down," the duchess invited her. "Anne, ring for

tea." She moved to a sideboard that held a decanter and glasses. "I hope you like Madeira?"

Sarah nodded. She did enjoy sweet wine, though she hadn't expected to be drinking it in the afternoon. She took the glass and sipped daintily.

"I can see you are a little apprehensive," the duchess said, "and I admit that Anne and I do have an agenda."

"Two agendas," Anne corrected her mother.

Sarah swallowed half her wine, and felt her blood warm.

"The Duke of Richmond returned from The Hague last year. Of course you met him at your wedding."

A picture of the swarthy duke came full blown to Sarah, and she shuddered.

"My husband is suffering from ill health."

"Oh, I'm sorry," Sarah murmured politely.

"He has brought it on himself, with a lifetime of drink and dissipation," the duchess confided to her. "Still, it is my duty to return to Goodwood and look after him."

Sarah had heard rumors that Richmond had mistresses and at least one bastard. She drained her wineglass and set it down.

"So that's where my daughter's agenda comes in," the duchess explained. "You are a married lady, and Anne's sister-in-law. Could we possibly impose upon you to act as chaperone for the Season? She has so many social invitations, but since she is unwed, it would be improper for her to remain in London unless you take her under your wing."

Sarah laughed. *I'm only sixteen, how can I take on the role of matron?*

"I'm nineteen," the dark-haired beauty admitted. "If I miss another Season, I'll be considered an old maid. Do say we can be friends. I'll try not to behave scandalously."

"Oh, dear, if that's how you intend to behave, we shall have a dull time of it."

Anne joined in her laughter. "Thank you, Sarah. I can see we'll be like two peas from the same disgusting pod!"

"I thank you, too. I am most fortunate in my daughter-in-law." A maid brought in a teacart, complete with finger sandwiches and petit fours. "Thank you, Jane. I'll serve."

Sarah ate sparingly. She was confident that she and Anne would get along well, but she was a little nervous about what the Duchess of Richmond would ask of her. The three ladies sipped their tea, and when she was urged to take a petit four, Sarah could not resist the pink one, decorated with candied violets.

At last the duchess spoke up. "I don't want my son to follow in his father's footsteps. The duke married me because I had an income of twelve thousand pounds a year. In truth, it was a marriage of convenience. My father jumped at the chance of a connection with *Ye Royal Family*. We were not in love, and Richmond thought it his right to take mistresses and produce by-blows." She paused and looked beseechingly at Sarah. "I want you to make your husband fall in love with you."

Sarah choked on the pink petit four. "We are separated." *Thank God.*

"Charles is returning to London this summer. My husband and I had a letter from him last week," the duchess informed her.

This summer? Christus, it's already May. I cannot endure the thought!

"I know it is unfashionable for a husband and wife to have tender feelings for each other, but I desperately want my son to be happy, and after seeing you, I am confident you will have no trouble luring him to fall in love."

I hate Charles Lennox. I don't want to make him happy. I want revenge!

"I think Sarah is up to the challenge," Anne declared. "With her beauty and wit, she'll bring *Champagne Charlie* to his knees in no time."

Bringing the brute low would go a long way to settling the score and give me a measure of satisfaction. Sarah made up her mind in less than a minute. She looked at the duchess and then smiled. "I'll do it!"

Two days later, Lady Anne invited Lady Sarah to a Court function at St. James's Palace. "I'm so glad you accepted my invitation. My aunt is the widowed Duchess of Shrewsbury. Adelaide is Lady of the Bedchamber to the Princess of Wales. You will adore Princess Caroline. She loves to dance and gamble. She is the glittering sun of the Royal Court around which all the lesser stars circle."

When the young beauties arrived at the palace, Anne introduced her to her aunt. Sarah made a graceful curtsy.

"Oh, la, save your curtsies for Princess Caroline, my dear."

Sarah tried not to stare at the opulent breasts of the dowager duchess that threatened to overflow her décolletage.

Anne whispered behind her fan, "Adelaide is King George's mistress."

Sarah whispered back, "She has two outstanding qualifications for the post."

They made their way to the ballroom where the Princess of Wales was dancing with her fifteen-year-old son, Frederick. When the dance ended, Caroline greeted Anne, who introduced her sister-in-law to the princess.

Prince Frederick bowed before Sarah. "Would you do me the honor, my lady?"

The princess laughed. "It seems you have made a conquest, Sarah. Since you are a married lady, I'm sure my son will be safe in your experienced hands."

It was soon evident to Sarah, however, that she was not safe from Freddy's hands. When the dance ended, Sarah found Anne in the company of a handsome male.

"Allow me to introduce the Earl of Albemarle. He is Lord of the Bedchamber to King George. This is my sister-in-law, the Countess of March." Anne gave him a seductive glance. "I playfully call him William van, since so many gentlemen of my acquaintance are called William."

Sarah greeted him warmly and guessed that the handsome male with the thick blond hair was the reason Anne had come to Court tonight.

After the dance Anne satisfied Sarah's curiosity. "His name is William van Keppel. He was Baron Ashford in the County of Kent, but when his father died two years ago, he became the Earl of Albemarle." She confided, "William van is very amorous, but I hold him at arm's length."

"Until he comes to heel?" Sarah asked with a wink. "That is a good strategy, to beckon him with one hand and hold him off with the other." *I shall remember that ploy when my beast of a husband returns.*

Charles Lennox, Earl of March, had undergone his own metamorphosis during his three-year Grand Tour of Europe's major cities. By the time he turned twenty-one, the earl's physical changes had been dramatic. He was taller, his shoulders and chest broader. His face now had a sculpted, chiseled leanness about it, and the sun had burnished his skin.

Charles's transformation on the inside had been even more dramatic. Sickness had taught him compassion, when his tutor Henry fell ill, and it had taught him gratitude when he had caught the virulent contagion that brought him close to death. Henry Grey, who had barely survived, in turn had nursed Charles back to health. Though it had been a slow and painful process for both, the experience brought with it much needed maturity and made Charles a far better man.

For years he had anticipated visiting Constantinople which had once been the capital city of the Roman Empire. Because of his royal connections, he was invited to Topkapi Palace. He marveled at its opulence and was intrigued by the Sultan's seraglio. But later when he explored the Harbor of the Golden Horn he was horrified at the hordes of child beggars who swarmed the streets.

As his travels took him to the major cities of Eu-

rope, he began to notice more and more the insur-
mountable contrast between rich and poor. In the slums
of Athens, Rome, and Madrid it was commonplace for
starving children to die in the street. The six months
that Charles and his tutor spent in Paris, living among
the artists of the West Bank, gave him a true appreciation of painting. But the sheer numbers of child prostitutes of both sexes from the Parisian slums made him
feel revulsion toward the French.

Charles realized how fortunate he was to have been
born to privilege and wealth. He was appalled at the
way he'd taken his parents' indulgence for granted and,
before he returned to England, wrote to his father and
thanked him for providing him with an Oxford education that had culminated in a three years' Grand Tour.

Chapter Three

Richmond House, Whitehall, London, England
June 1722

"I'll unpack my own clothes, Henry. You have enough to do emptying your own trunks." Charles Lennox had given the servants instructions to have the crates and boxes that would soon be arriving brought upstairs to his wing of the house.

"I intend to keep them packed, my lord. With your leave, I'll be returning to Oxfordshire tomorrow."

"Henry, since we have shared our lives on a daily basis for the past three years, it is preposterous to call me *my lord* simply because we've returned to London. I hope you consider yourself my friend."

"Then speaking as a friend, I've had enough of cities for a while. I'd like to return to Oxford. I shall need to find scholars to tutor."

"How thoughtless of me. Of course you will want to go home. But, if you are willing, I'd like you to return. I shall need a business secretary to handle my affairs, and I can think of none who would measure up to your standards, Henry."

"Thank you, Charles. I am honored to accept your generous offer. I'll return to London in a fortnight, if that is convenient."

"Perfectly convenient. Tonight, we'll go out on the town and celebrate our homecoming."

The majordomo arrived. "I'm sure some of your clothes will need pressing, my lord. And if you intend to stay in London, perhaps you'd like to choose one of the footmen to be your valet."

"Excellent idea, Soames. Both Henry and I will need our evening clothes pressed. We are off to the Kit Cat Club."

"That will be rather difficult, my lord. It closed two years ago."

"Really? Then I warrant it will have to be the Star and Garter on Pall Mall. I assume my parents are at Goodwood?" The Sussex house was the seat of the Dukes of Richmond.

"Her Grace was here recently but returned to Goodwood to care for the duke. Lady Anne is in residence, however," Soames informed him.

"My sister is residing here alone?" Charles drew his brows together. "She didn't by any chance marry recently, did she?"

"No, my lord. Though Lady Anne is much in demand."

"She's out and about at the moment, I take it?"

"She is, my lord. She accepted an invitation from the Princess of Wales."

"An invitation to St. James's Palace, no less? My sister is apparently moving in Court circles these days."

"Yes, and no, my lord." Soames took the black evening clothes from Charles.

"Prince George and Princess Caroline have moved from St. James's Palace and taken up residence at Leicester House, which is now the center of social life in London. King George and his son are not on the most convivial of terms."

Charles laughed. "You are a master of understatement, Soames."

"Thank you, my lord. I'll have these pressed right away."

"Are you enjoying Leicester House, Highness?" Sarah set down her dessert fork and placed her linen napkin, embroidered with a gold crown, beside it.

"Yes indeed. St. James's is like a mausoleum these days. I love having my own household where I am free to do whatever I wish." Caroline signaled a footman.

"Leicester House is far more luxurious than the old palace," Anne Lennox remarked.

"Exactly," Caroline agreed. "And the Prince of Wales is free to have his own courtiers here, without the king raving that anyone paying us court will no longer be considered a friend of his." She told the footman that they would take their wine to the card room.

Prince Frederick jumped up immediately to hold Lady Sarah's chair while she stood up from the table.

The Princess of Wales glanced impatiently at her eldest son. "Why don't you go and join the gentlemen?"

"While they drink each other supine? I much prefer the company of the ladies."

"I think you mean the company of the Countess of

March, to be specific." Princess Caroline glanced at Sarah. "You have made quite a conquest, I warrant. Would you mind if Frederick joins us for a game of Faro?"

"I would be delighted if His Highness would join us," Sarah replied.

Flattered that Sarah always called him *Highness,* he followed her like a lap dog.

The prince offered to be banker and dealt the cards from the dealing box. Princess Caroline, Anne, and her aunt Adelaide were experienced gamblers compared with Sarah, who had never played cards before she came to London; yet Sarah began to win. Finally Prince Frederick was accused of cheating on Sarah's behalf, and amid laughing protestations and denials, the ladies decided they had had enough gaming.

"Why don't we go to the theater?" the Princess of Wales suggested. "I would love to see Fletcher's comedy, *The Woman Hater.*"

"Oh, that sounds wonderful. I've never sat in the Royal Box before," Sarah declared.

"I have." Anne rolled her eyes. "Everyone in the audience watches the box more than they watch the actors onstage. It is absolutely divine!"

"Hello, William." Charles greeted his old college friend and glanced at Henry. "No sooner do I walk through the door of the Star and Garter than I meet Viscount Rialton. I don't know if you remember my tutor, Henry Grey? We've just returned from the Continent."

"Hello, Charles. I never would have recognized you. Three years is a long time, and things change. I'm no longer Viscount Rialton . . . I'm now Marquis of Blandford."

"My condolences on the loss of your grandfather, William. I take it that since Marlborough had no son to inherit his title, Parliament has given it to his daughter."

"Yes, strange as it seems, my mother Henrietta is now the Duke of Marlborough, and I am Marquis of Blandford through her." William raised an eyebrow. "Shouldn't you be spending your first night back in London with your wife?"

The warmth left Charles's face. "Bite your tongue, Blandford. It's a marriage in name only. My wife is a child and likely residing at Caversham, where she belongs."

"Sorry." Blandford ordered them drinks, and the three men moved to one of the gaming rooms. "Here's Hartington. I swear the Star and Garter would collapse if William wasn't here to prop it up."

"Hello, March, how the devil are you?" When the three friends were together they used their titles, because Blandford and Lord Hartington were both named William.

Charles introduced Henry Grey to Hartington. "We're just home from the Grand Tour and, to be perfectly honest, damned glad to be back in London."

"It's great to see you again. Sit down. Perhaps you'll bring me luck." Hartington glanced ruefully at his dwindling pile of counters.

"Your pockets are to let, as usual." Blandford stated the obvious.

"My pockets and everything else. I'm in debt over my head to my cousin, the Duke of Bedford. He keeps telling me the only way out is marriage."

"Since you're next in line to the Dukedom of Devonshire, you should be able to attract a wealthy heiress," Charles remarked.

"Bedford's financial adviser, who's rolling in it, has an unwed daughter. Tell me, March, you have a marriage of convenience. How do you stomach it?"

"I don't. The marriage took place three years ago, and that's the last I saw of her, thank God. She has my name, and that's all she'll ever get."

Hartington and Blandford exchanged a speaking look.

For the next hour the friends played baccarat. The first dealer was Hartington, who lost everything to Blandford. Charles offered to be the next dealer, and he, too, lost to Blandford. Thankfully Henry Grey broke even.

"If it's true what they say, that *gambling is the wine of life,* you should be pissing drunk by now, Blandford." Charles pushed the counters toward his friend.

"I've had enough," Hartington declared in disgust. "Marriage is becoming inevitable, I'm afraid. Let's get out of here."

"Where shall we go? I promised Grey here an evening's entertainment."

"How about seeing a play?" Henry suggested, hoping for a smattering of culture.

"Just the ticket," Hartington agreed. "I won't lose a fortune at the theater."

Blandford laughed. "*The Woman Hater* is playing at the King's Theatre in the Haymarket. How bloody apt is that for all of us?"

"We should form a club," Hartington suggested.

Charles shook his head. "There'd be too many vying for membership!"

When the quartet arrived at the theater, the curtain had already gone up, and in the darkness they managed to find four seats together in one row. The comedy dealt with the gender question and tried to fathom which was the morally weaker sex. It was a farce, laced with bawdy wit, and the four men found it hilarious. They found the *Chastity Test,* which produced hoops of laughter, particularly entertaining.

At the intermission when the curtain came down and the lights went up, they, along with the other members of the audience, gazed about to see whom they knew. The Princess of Wales and her elegantly dressed friends occupied the Royal Box, and all eyes were upon them.

"Charles, there's your sister, Lady Anne." When Blandford looked at his friend, he saw that he was staring up at the Royal Box as if mesmerized.

Blandford looked at Hartington and surreptitiously pointed to the box and then to their friend. The two cleared their throats, which brought Charles out of his trance.

"Whomever is that lovely creature sitting next to Princess Caroline?" he murmured.

Blandford and Hartington exchanged an amused glance, and when it dawned on them that the Earl of March had no idea that the lady was his wife, they made a silent pact to keep quiet in hopes of milking the devilishly amusing situation for all it was worth.

"No idea," Blandford said, "but isn't that your sister, Lady Anne?"

Charles glanced briefly at his sister and nodded impatiently, then his eyes were drawn back to the beauty with honey-blond curls whose porcelain complexion was like cream and roses. "Excuse me, gentlemen," he said absently, and arose from his seat.

He went upstairs and made his way to the Royal Box. A servant dressed in royal livery stood guard outside the door.

"Excuse me." Charles reached out toward the door, and the guard blocked him.

"I'm sorry, my lord, the Princess of Wales is occupying the box tonight." The royal servant looked into the dark face of the tall, imposing gentleman with the saber-sharp cheekbones and gathered his courage to stand his ground.

"Step aside," came the curt command.

"My lord, I dare not disobey my orders. The princess does not wish to be disturbed. I'm sure you understand."

"Rubbish! My sister, Lady Anne Lennox, is attending Princess Caroline. Allow me to pass."

"The interval is over—the second act is about to start."

Charles took a threatening step toward the guard and saw a pleading look come into his eyes. "If I let you pass, I would be dismissed immediately, my lord."

The Earl of March stepped back. "Of course. I understand your predicament." He turned and went back downstairs to his friends. Though the curtain had gone up, Charles never glanced at the stage. The theater was once more shrouded in darkness, yet he focused his full attention on the Royal Box. *Who is she?*

The lady had an innocent beauty that called out to all his senses. Yet he had seen her wipe tears of mirth from her cheeks at the droll entertainment presented onstage. This only added to the lady's allure. *What man doesn't desire a laughing female in his arms?* In the shadows, his imagination took flight. He became fixated with a deep need to possess this perfect English rose.

When the play ended and the actors were taking their curtain call, Charles excused himself again and made his way upstairs. He did not approach the Royal Box but stationed himself at the top of the stairs, knowing the royal party must pass this way.

In a short time, he heard the laughter of the ladies as they emerged from the box. First came Princess Caroline and her lady-in-waiting, who was his aunt Adelaide. They were chattering about the play and didn't even look at him.

Behind them came a tall youth with Charles's sister Anne on one arm and the unknown beauty on the other. Anne didn't seem to recognize him, and he simply stood and gazed at the lovely young lady who was even more beautiful close up. For one moment she focused on him, and her sapphire blue eyes looked into his, then she spoke to her companions and moved on.

Charles followed them at a distance as they went downstairs into the theater lobby.

The fashionable beauty attracted as much attention as the Princess of Wales, and was greeted familiarly by numerous gentlemen as well as older ladies. *She seems to be the toast of London. Who the devil can she be?*

Blandford, Hartington, and Henry Grey joined him. "Did you learn the identity of the captivating creature?" William asked.

"Not yet," the earl declared, "but I intend to rectify that within the next five minutes." When he looked up, the royal party had disappeared. "Bloody hell, I've lost them. Thanks for nothing!"

"What are friends for?" Blandford drawled.

"With friends like you, I don't need sodding enemies." Charles saw the amusement in his companions' faces and knew he was the cause of it. They thought it hilarious that a female had taken his fancy to such a marked degree. "Come on, Henry, let's go home. Sufficient unto the day is the *snickering* thereof."

Blandford called after him, "There's a reception at Marlborough House tomorrow night. We'll see you there."

"Goddamn it, why have these wooden crates been left in the entrance hall?" Charles demanded as he walked through the door of Richmond House. "If we'd been three sheets to the wind, we could have killed ourselves."

Anne appeared at the top of the stairs. "Well, well, look what the wind blew in. I suspected the prodigal son had returned when I saw all this claptrap piled in the hall."

Charles glanced up at his sister. "Ah, you are just the one I want to see." He took the stairs two at a time.

She stared at the man who stood before her, taking in the wide shoulders and the sun-burnished face. Then she said slowly, "You were at the theater tonight. Why the devil didn't you say something, Charles?"

"I'm saying something now," he said impatiently.

Henry Grey sidled past the siblings and bade Charles good night. He could have been invisible for all the notice they took of him.

"Who was the lady sitting with you in the box tonight?"

"Princess Caroline, of course. Who else would be sitting in the Royal Box?"

"I'm not an idiot, Anne. I know the Princess of Wales when I see her."

The corners of Anne's mouth went up. "You used to be an idiot, Charles." She turned, walked into the sitting room, and poured herself a glass of wine. "Don't tell me you were converted on the Road to Damascus?"

"I truly appreciate your brilliant wit, Anne, but I'm serious. I want to know the name of the beautiful young female who was with you tonight."

She gazed at him from beneath her lashes, trying to gauge whether or not her brother was being facetious, as was his habit when he was younger. She decided to put him to the test. "I don't know who she is . . . a friend of Caroline's I presume."

"Hellfire, you must know her name at least!"

Anne was suddenly convinced that her brother hadn't the faintest idea that the beauteous Sarah was his own wife. She realized instantly that the situation was deliciously entertaining. "I didn't quite catch her name when we were introduced, and we didn't get a chance to speak because Prince Frederick monopolized her all evening."

"That tall, gawky youth was Prince Frederick?"

Her glance swept him from head to foot. "Yes, isn't it amazing the transformation that can take place in three years' time?" She sipped her wine thoughtfully. "Did you bring me a treasure from some far-off decadent city?"

"You always were a greedy little witch."

Anne clapped her hands. "You really have been converted. You used to call me *bitch,* not *witch!* Don't tell me you have a newfound respect for the opposite sex?"

Charles smiled at his sister. "Was I really such an insufferable swine?"

"Yes." She laughed, accepting the hug he offered. "And I don't believe for one minute the leopard has changed his spots."

He looked down at her and waggled his black eyebrows. "Tell you what. I'll give you the treasure I've brought you—when you find out the beauty's name."

"That's blackmail," she protested.

"Merely a bribe." He gave her a knowing smile. "In my experience, nothing works better with a woman."

"He's back!" Anne said breathlessly as she hurried into the breakfast room at the Cadogan town house the next morning.

"Who's back?" Sarah was surprised at the early visit from her friend.

"Charles. Your husband!"

Sarah dropped the fruit knife she was holding and went pale. "Are you sure?"

"Of course I'm sure. He was at the theater last night. He was standing at the top of the stairs when we left the Royal Box."

Sarah's hand went to her throat. "I didn't see him." Her thoughts went back to the theater. "The only male I saw had a powerful build and dark chiseled features."

"That's him! I didn't recognize him, either. He arrived at Richmond House shortly after me. His physical appearance has changed dramatically."

Sarah swallowed hard. *The man I saw looked dangerous.*

Anne sat down and helped herself to a scone and strawberries. "He's completely changed."

Yes . . . he's taller, older, and more powerful. But I warrant he's still a brute!

"Here is the most divinely amusing part . . . he begged me to find out your name! One look and Charles was smitten. Oh, Sarah, it will be like taking bonbons from a baby to make him fall in love with you. He's halfway there already."

Sarah opened her mouth in dismay and closed it again. She pushed her plate away. Her appetite had vanished like snow in summer.

"I told my brother I had no idea who you were. But of course, that will whet his appetite. Charles even tried to bribe me. He told me he would give me the present he brought me when I found out your name. It's such a famous jest!"

"Yes. Priceless."

Anne finished her strawberries. "Are you sure I'll be welcome at Marlborough House tonight? I didn't receive an invitation."

Sarah looked at her blankly for a moment, lost in thought. Then her friend's words penetrated. "Of course. The Dowager Duchess of Marlborough has the reputation of a dragon, but it is completely undeserved. Actually she's my godmother. I've known her all my life; my mother named me for Sarah Churchill. When I was a child I often visited Blenheim Palace."

"Wasn't your father one of Marlborough's top generals?"

"Yes, before the war my father and Marlborough had a friendly competition over which garden was superior, the one at Caversham Park Manor or Blenheim Palace."

"I hear the dowager duchess is filthy rich."

"Yes, when the duke died last month, he left her over a million pounds."

"Her grandson, the new Marquis of Blandford, paid court to me last year. I should have encouraged him," Anne declared wickedly.

"William tried to chase me with a frog when I was a little girl. I wasn't the least bit afraid. I remember pulling his hair and making him take the frog back to the pond."

"Will Blandford be there tonight, do you think?"

"I expect he will. Lady Marlborough has formally adopted her youngest granddaughter, Lady Diana Spencer, and is introducing her to society tonight."

"I must wear something alluring. Will you call for me tonight?"

I'm not coming to Richmond House. "W . . . why don't you meet me at Marlborough House? I'll give you my invitation to get you inside. I'll wait for you in the grand foyer."

"Where the devil are you off to tonight?" Charles looked with disapproval at the low décolletage of his sister's peach-colored gown. "You know, Anne, I don't think it's proper for you to go gadding about London without a chaperone. I don't know what Mother can be thinking to let you live here alone."

"But I don't live here alone. My *married brother* is in residence at Richmond House."

His dark eyes glared coldly. "You're being deliberately offensive. Where are you going?"

"I'm off to Marlborough House. The dowager duchess is giving a reception tonight."

His features turned speculative. "You don't suppose a certain young beauty will be attending, do you?"

"Anything is possible," she said innocently.

"By an amazing coincidence, I, too, am attending the function at Marlborough House this evening. I will escort you."

Anne bit her lip to stop herself from laughing.

The Earl of March stepped from the carriage at Marlborough House in Pall Mall and helped his sister, Lady Anne, to alight. He told the coachman to return at midnight.

The majordomo who took Anne's invitation had so much heavy gold braid on his livery, Charles murmured, "How the devil does the poor sod stand upright?"

Anne laughed. "Your humor is decidedly irreverent."

The main floor foyer was packed with guests, and the staircase was filled with people ascending to the ballroom. "Seems everyone and his *sister* are here tonight."

Anne ignored the barb. "They're eager to rub shoulders with the latest millionairess."

"Or insulted. The old girl's a bit of a termagant . . . rules with an iron hand."

"Men think dominance is their prerogative."

"It is . . . it's God-given," he said smoothly.

Anne slipped away from him to greet the Earl of Albemarle. She was both surprised and delighted that William van was here tonight. Perhaps she could use her friendship with Blandford to make him jealous.

Suddenly, Charles went still. There on the stairs was the lady who had dominated his thoughts to such a degree last night that he had dreamed about her. He turned to the gentleman standing next to him. "Excuse me, do you know the name of the lovely lady in green? The one carrying the ostrich feather fan?"

The older man looked at him with a condescending smile. "You must be new to London. The young beauty is the toast of the town. She is the Countess of March."

Charles stared at the man, wondering if he was making fun of him. He raised his eyes to the staircase in disbelief. He felt stunned, as if a stone wall had fallen on him.

Chapter Four

"The jig is up, Anne. You will take me to meet your friend *now.*"

She looked into his unsmiling face. "So, you learned her identity. You must admit, Charles, it was vastly amusing that you didn't recognize your own wife."

"Hilarious to you, perhaps, but not the least bit funny to me. She was a child when we married . . . a very *plain* child."

"And you're licking your lips that the ugly duckling has turned into a graceful swan."

Charles propelled his sister across the ballroom until they were standing before the exquisite lady with the honey-blond hair, gowned in pale green tulle.

"Sarah, may I present my brother, the Earl of March? Charles, it gives me pleasure to introduce the Countess of March."

"The pleasure is mine, Lady Sarah." He bowed, then took her hand to his lips and kissed it with reverence.

Sarah wanted to snatch her fingers from his, but

summoned up the courage to examine him. She had to look up since he was a good deal taller than she was. His eyes were dark brown and, above them, his black brows were strong and well defined. His cheekbones were sharp; his mouth sensual, his face deeply tanned against the contrast of his snow-white linen.

"It is indeed, my lord." She lowered her lashes and languidly wafted her fan.

"You must call me Charles."

"I cannot bring myself to do that, my lord, until we are better acquainted. We are strangers."

"That is something I intend to rectify in short order. If I have my way, we will soon be on intimate terms."

Sarah reminded herself that she had vowed to make him fall in love with her. She gathered her courage and raised her lashes. "Do you usually get your way, my lord?"

"Always." His voice was deep and smooth, his eyes as seductive as pools of dark, liquid chocolate.

"Perhaps I shall prove the exception to the rule, my lord."

"Is that a challenge, my beauty?" he murmured.

He's so self-assured, and more than a little arrogant. Sarah shuddered.

Charles smiled into her eyes, letting her know he had seen her reaction to him.

Blandford joined them. The marquis made no effort to mask his amusement. "Well, well, it is extremely refreshing to see a man escort his own wife to a party. Lady Anne, it's lovely when a family is close."

"Grow up, Blandford," the earl admonished his friend.

Though he tried, William couldn't keep the laughter

from his face. "Come, let me introduce you to my grandmother and my cousin, Lady Diana, the guest of honor tonight."

Blandford led the small group to the Dowager Duchess of Marlborough, who sat like an aging queen upon her throne, reigning over her subjects. Before he could speak, Sarah dropped into a curtsy.

"Hello, Your Grace, I am so happy to find you in good health."

"Sarah, my dear, I am *flourishing.*" Her glance flicked to her grandson. "Blandford, be sure to take care of Lady Sarah tonight."

"No need, Grandmother. Her husband will do the honors. Allow me to present my friend, Charles, Earl of March."

Sarah Churchill fixed the dark noble with a stare that almost pinned him to the wall. "So, you are the brute who caused my goddaughter such great unhappiness when they forced you upon her three years ago?"

"I had no say in the matter, Your Grace. The marriage was arranged by our fathers."

"Mmm, to settle some shameful gaming debt, according to the rumors I heard. I have a low opinion of the male sex. When I lost my dearest daughter Anne a few years ago, her degenerate husband Sunderland wed a fifteen-year-old trollop before my daughter was cold in her grave. Men, it seems, like to warm their beds with young flesh." She raked the Earl of March with disapproving eyes. "When Sunderland dropped dead two months ago, I celebrated the occasion. I have legally adopted my youngest granddaughter, Lady Diana. I will make sure she is matched with a husband who is worthy of her." Her look told Charles she considered him unworthy to draw breath.

Fourteen-year-old Lady Diana Spencer smiled and gave the Earl of March a flirtatious glance from beneath her lashes, before she sketched him a curtsy.

Charles did not return her smile. "My wife is precious to me, Your Grace. I intend to take very good care of her."

She fixed him with a gimlet glare. "Hmph! See that you do. Your father Richmond's marital fidelity left much to be desired."

Blandford bit his lip. "Grandmother, allow me to present Lady Anne Lennox, the Earl of March's sister."

"Is this the gel you were chasing after last year? The one who got away?"

Blandford flushed, and it was Charles's turn to be amused at his friend's discomfort.

Lady Anne stepped forward and curtsied. "I am delighted to meet you, Your Grace. My friend, Lady Sarah, speaks so highly of you."

"And I am fond of her in return. March, make sure you treat Sarah like a lady. Ah, I hear the music starting. Blandford, you may partner Lady Diana in the first dance."

The Earl of March bowed before his wife. "Lady Sarah, may I have this dance?"

She hesitated, but she knew it would be a breach of etiquette to rebuff him. When he held out his arm, she placed her hand upon it. He led her into the minuet, which was the most popular dance of the day. It was a stately dance with a slow pace.

"Did you know the minuet was designed for courtship?

It requires disciplined body control that looks effortless. Similar to the movements that lead up to making love."

Sarah blushed. "Designed for courtship? You are making that up." She dipped beneath his arm and sank into a curtsy.

"The lady dips low so that the gentleman is offered a glimpse of her breasts, which the corset displays to perfection." He deliberately looked into her décolletage.

Her blush deepened. Charles placed one leg before the other and made a courtly bow. "This movement clearly shows off the male's legs, clad in tight breeches and stockings. 'Tis said a gentleman leads with his calves, and a lady leads with her bosom."

"You shouldn't say these suggestive things, my lord," she said breathlessly.

"Between a man and his wife, nothing is forbidden, no matter how suggestive."

"We are man and wife in name only, my lord. And I suggest that *everything* is forbidden until you have wooed and won me."

"I cannot begin my wooing until you stop saying *my lord*. I want you to call me Charles. I want to hear the sound of my name on your lips."

"Ah, my lord, I cannot."

"Try," he urged. "You have such delectable lips."

The tip of her tongue came out and licked her full bottom lip.

His dark eyes focused on her mouth. "You are teasing me, Sarah. When you do that my imagination takes flight. I think of all sorts of uses to put your tongue and lips to."

Sarah wanted to flee, but he held her fast in the dance. She had no idea what he meant, but she knew it was something intimate. It took her a few minutes to catch her breath when the music ended, but she knew it wasn't the dance that took her breath away, it was Charles Lennox, her newly returned husband.

When he insisted on partnering her again in the next dance, she examined him more closely. *He is nothing like the graceless youth I wed three years ago. That young brute couldn't get away from me fast enough. Now it seems he cannot get enough of me. If I play my cards well, it shouldn't be too difficult to take my sweet revenge.*

This time the dance was a courante. "There is something heartfelt in this music," he murmured, "a longing on which hopes are built."

He's extremely attractive in a dark, devilish way. Perhaps I will enjoy settling the score.

When the dance ended, Charles thanked her and asked Lady Diana if he could partner her. Sarah saw that Blandford was about to ask Anne to dance, but Albemarle beat him to the quarry and led her sister-in-law onto the dance floor.

Blandford smiled at Sarah. "I'd ask you to dance if Charles wasn't so possessive of you, my lady. He's quite capable of planting me a facer. Jealousy is such an unattractive quality in a man."

Sarah smiled. "In a husband I think it is delightful. Why don't we see if we can make him miserable?"

"Well, he just sent me a forbidding look. As a good friend, I suppose it is my duty to rub salt in his wound." He gave the lovely girl he partnered an appraising glance. "I am amazed that the scrawny child I chased with frogs has turned into such a beauty. 'Tis said the Countess of March is the new toast of London."

"Nonsense, after tonight, Lady Diana Spencer will be all the rage."

"She will if our grandmother has anything to do with it."

Sarah laughed. "The Dowager Duchess of Marlborough certainly gave March his orders, and told him to treat me like a lady, but I very much doubt that he will."

Blandford bent to speak in a confidential murmur. "He is quite besotted with you, Sarah. He will jump through hoops for you. I swear it was love at first sight."

"Mmm, second sight perhaps," she said dryly. "It was *hatred* at our true first sight, on both our parts I might add."

"I am delighted that you have both changed your minds."

"Whatever makes you think that?" she asked without a trace of mockery.

Blandford looked longingly at Anne who was dancing with Albemarle. "Do you think Lady Anne would let me escort her to the supper room?"

"William van is quite mad about her. He will give you a run for your money."

When it was time for supper, Charles separated his wife from all her other admiring dance partners, and from that moment on never left her side.

Anne remarked to her brother, "You are behaving

like a dog with a bone. Take care you don't make a cake of yourself, Charles."

"Look to your own behavior, my dear. Setting one suitor against another is acting like a *cocktease*. If you are not careful, I shall pack you off home to Goodwood."

"The Earl of March preaching morals. How bloody ironic!"

He grasped the glass of champagne she was holding and took it from her hand. "You've had enough to drink, Anne. I believe it is time to leave." Charles turned to Sarah. "I shall escort you home."

Sarah bade the Dowager Duchess of Marlborough good night and thanked her for her lovely hospitality. A footman brought her cloak, and she and Anne, accompanied by the Earl of March, went downstairs and climbed into Lennox's carriage.

The carriage set off from Pall Mall, and after a few minutes, Sarah glanced from the window. "This isn't the way to the Cadogan town house."

"No, it is the way to Richmond House in Whitehall," Charles said.

"But you said you would escort me home," Sarah protested.

"Richmond House is your home," Charles pointed out. "My home is now yours."

"I cannot live with *you*." Sarah began to panic. "Stop the carriage!"

"Where else would a wife live, but with her husband?"

Sarah opened her mouth to revile him with every insulting name in her salty vocabulary. Then her inner voice cautioned her. *You catch more flies with honey*

than with vinegar. Nevertheless, she had no intention
of becoming his wife in the true sense of the word. At
least not until the time was ripe, and of her choosing.

"I shall insist upon my own private bedchamber."

Charles smiled. "I wouldn't have it any other way,
sweetheart. Did I not promise to woo and win you?"

When they arrived at Richmond House, Anne gave
Sarah a knowing wink and excused herself immediately. Charles took his wife upstairs to his own private
wing. He opened a door and led her into a spacious
bedchamber that was furnished luxuriously. She glanced
about nervously and her eyes fell on an adjoining door.

"If this bedchamber adjoins yours, I won't sleep
here."

He opened a drawer in the night table beside the
wide bed and produced a key. Then he took her hand,
placed the key on her palm, closed her fingers over it,
and then kissed her hand. "Oh, she of little faith," he
teased.

"There are two doors," she pointed out distrustfully.

"This key locks them both. Sleep tight, my beauty."

The moment he left, Sarah lost no time turning the
key in both locks. She sank down on the bed, relieved
that he had told her the truth. She realized she had
nothing to sleep in, so after she removed and hung her
gown in the wardrobe, she took off her corset and stockings, and decided to sleep in her petticoat.

The bed was wider than any she had slept in before,
and she worried she would never get used to it. She
thought about Molly, who would be worrying about
her not coming home, and Sarah decided she would go
and get her Irish lady's maid first thing in the morning.
Her decision made, she fell asleep almost instantly.

* * *

Sarah opened her eyes and screamed as the bed-clothes were lifted from her and thrown on the carpet, revealing her only in her undergarment.

"Come on, sleepyhead, the day is awasting," Charles cried.

"You devil! How did you get in here?" she demanded, crossing her arms across her breasts to protect them from his laughing, bold brown eyes.

Charles held up a key and waved it about with glee.

"But you gave me the key and I locked both doors!"

"Credit me with some intelligence, my beauty. I possess more than one key."

"You, sir, possess an overabundance of arrogance. How dare you?"

"Sarah, my love, I'd dare anything where you are concerned." He sat down on the end of the bed and gazed at her.

"You lecherous swine, why are you staring at me?"

"Because I'll never have enough. I want to learn everything about you. I want you to lift your lashes so I can gaze into your Persian sapphire blue eyes. I want to see you laugh until the tears roll down your lovely cheeks. When you get angry I want to see your fire and hear you spit curses at me. When I pull off your covers, I want you to fly at me, pull my hair, and roll about the bed with me . . . Sarah, you are only sixteen, I want to play with you!"

She saw that he was wearing tall boots and tight black riding breeches. The white linen shirt contrasted with his sun-bronzed face and neck. He was so attractive, her heart skipped a beat. *I'm supposed to be teas-*

ing and tempting him. The wicked devil has turned the tables on me.

"Hurry and dress. I want to take you riding."

"I have no clothes, other than the gown I wore last night. I have to go to my house and pack my things and get Molly, my lady's maid."

"Rubbish! I want you to be spontaneous. Anne will lend you a riding habit, or you can wear a pair of my breeches." He rolled his eyes. "I can just picture your round arse in tight black riding breeches."

"Go! If you leave me, I will ask Anne to lend me some clothes."

"I'll give you ten minutes. If you're not ready by then, I'll strip off your petticoat and dress you myself." He held up ten fingers and headed to the adjoining chamber.

Sarah knew he was perfectly capable of the outrageous antics he threatened. She jumped off the bed, snatched up her stockings and corset, unlocked the bedroom door, and went in search of Anne.

She found her sister-in-law reaching for a tray so she could eat her breakfast in bed.

"I need a riding habit," Sarah said breathlessly.

Anne pointed to her wardrobe. "My boots may be a bit too large for you. I have *Ye Royal Family* feet," she said between mouthfuls of toast.

"Save me some breakfast, please. I have no time to get my own. The devil wants to go riding and has only given me a few minutes to get dressed."

"Don the habit, then come sit down and eat. Let the mountain come to Mohammed. Surely you know better than to go running when a man beckons."

Sarah put on her corset, drew on her stockings, and

began to laugh. "You are right. Whatever was I thinking?" She sat down on the bed and helped herself to some food.

Anne went to the wardrobe and brought out a fuchsia-colored habit. "This shade of purple will be glorious on you."

The door flew open and Charles strode in. "Your time is up, and here I find you filling your face. I warned you, Sarah."

He picked her up and put her over his shoulder clad in only stockings and corset. He grabbed the riding habit from his sister's hands, picked up the boots, and swept out the door with his kicking and protesting wife. Charles carried her back to her bedchamber and set her feet to the carpet. He then proceeded to finish dressing her, managing to stroke his hands over every inch of her luscious curves.

When he was done, his powerful hands held her fast as his eyes swept over her with appreciation. "The sparks of anger in your eyes have turned you into a blazing beauty, and your curses are music to my ears. You are in a passion, and it delights me."

Sarah took a deep breath. "My fury excites you!"

"You have no idea, my beauty."

She, too, felt excited and knew Charles was the reason why. *Is it because his hands caressed my limbs, or because he aroused my temper? Perhaps he aroused more than my anger. Perhaps my own body is betraying me.* "You are a devil!"

"Let's be devils together." He sat her on the bed and knelt before her. Then he lifted the hem of the riding habit and rolled his eyes wickedly as her legs were revealed.

Sarah bit her lip to keep herself from laughing at his antics, but she couldn't hold her amusement inside. She threw back her head and shook with mirth.

Charles lifted her foot and slid the riding boot onto her leg. Then he did the same with the other one. This time, however, his hands continued sliding up her thigh until they stroked the bare flesh above her stocking. "Smooth as silk," he whispered.

Sarah stopped laughing and drew in a swift breath as a frisson of arousal spiraled up inside her. He bent toward her, and she thought he was going to kiss her, but when his lips were a mere fraction from hers, he swept her up in his arms again and carried her from the room.

When they got to the top of the staircase, he turned around, threw his leg over the banister, set her before him between his thighs, and wrapped his arms about her beneath her breasts.

"No!" she gasped as she felt his hard cock press into her soft bum.

"Yes!" he cried as they slid down the long polished banister and shot off the end, landing in a tangle of arms and legs. "Good thing I cushioned you."

"Cushion? You are hard as a rock."

He nuzzled her ear. "Sweetheart, you have no idea."

Sarah had a damn good idea. She began to laugh. She realized she had no defenses against the playful devil and knew she would concede control to him, for the present. If she didn't, Charles would take it anyway.

In the stable, when he lifted her into the sidesaddle, once again his hands lingered on her waist, rekindling the frisson of arousal that spiraled up into her breasts. Charles mounted his own horse, and together they rode sedately through St. James's Park and then crossed over into Hyde Park.

There were many riders on Rotten Row. This did not fit in with the earl's plans. "This way, Sarah." He cut through some trees and his companion followed his lead.

Finally they came to a long open stretch of lush green grass. "Have you ever ridden hell for leather? Have you ever experienced the rush of pleasure from riding full out?"

When Sarah shook her head, Charles let out a whoop and dismounted. He fastened the reins of her horse to a tree and lifted her from the saddle. He carried her to his own mount and unceremoniously hiked her skirt up to her thighs. He lifted her by the waist. "Put your legs astride. You'll get few thrills riding sidesaddle."

The minute she obeyed him he mounted behind her and took the reins. One touch from his heels and his black hunter took off in a mad gallop. As the wind rushed past them, he whispered in her ear. "Can you feel the exhilaration? Don't you love new experiences, Sarah? There's so much I long to teach you. In my arms there is no limit to the peaks of excitement we can achieve." He bit her earlobe and pulled her back so her soft bum cushioned his cock. "Ride with me to the stars, and I'll let you taste heaven."

Charles turned his horse, and without slowing the pace, they raced back to where he had tethered her mount. He vaulted from the saddle and held up his arms in invitation.

She knew without a doubt that he was enamored with her, but she wanted more. She knew a need to enslave him. In that moment, Sarah felt empowered. She did not hesitate, but flung herself down into his waiting arms. Her eyes were filled with a wanton enticement, her laughing mouth luring him to take whatever he desired.

Charles took her down to the lush grass and rolled with her until she was above him in the dominant position. With her mons pressed into his cock, he brought her down until his lips brushed against hers.

At that moment a pair of riders emerged through the trees. The lady's horse shied at the couple in the grass. With the man's help, the lady got her mount under control and the pair stared in disbelief.

Though Sarah struggled, Charles held her tight against him, their intimate parts melded together, as he laughed up into her eyes.

"Whatever will they think?" she muttered as shame turned her cheeks to flame.

"There can be no shame between man and wife," Charles said as the pair of riders galloped off.

Her eyes glittered with blue sparks. "Not for one moment did they think we were married. Husbands don't roll their wives in the grass in compromising positions."

"This husband does." He captured her mouth in a kiss that was so sensual, her breasts and her woman's center began to ache with longing.

Chapter Five

When they returned to Richmond House, Charles unsaddled Sarah's horse for her. "I'll see you at dinner tonight."

She refrained from asking him where he was going. Men hated wives who questioned their comings and goings. "I'll need the carriage to transport Molly and some of my clothes."

"*All* your clothes. From now on you will reside at Richmond House . . . with me."

"Yes, my lord."

"Tonight, I shall persuade you to call me Charles, or die trying."

Anne joined Sarah for lunch. "I don't need to ask if you enjoyed your ride. Your face has a vibrant look about it. When a woman looks like you do, it's usually because a man she desires is paying court to her. I can tell you are making progress."

Sarah laughed softly. "I have him eating out of my

hand." *'Tis the other way about. Stop deceiving your-self.*

"Albemarle has invited me to take a carriage ride this afternoon. I shall tear a page from your book, Sarah, and tempt him to desire me above all others."

"Are you sure he's the one you want, Anne? Has Blandford lost his attraction?"

"William is all very well, but he gambles too much for my taste. My own father is addicted to gaming, and he hasn't been the ideal husband. And then there's Blandford's mother, Henrietta, who is now effectively the Duke of Marlborough. She likes to rule the roost and would surely impose her will on a daughter-in-law, if Blandford could ever be brought to the altar."

"I warrant you're right. Her mother Sarah, the dowager duchess, has always had a soft spot for me, but she does rule her family with an iron hand." She remembered how strict and straight-laced her own mother had been. *Being married gives me the freedom I love. The only fly in the ointment is being saddled with a husband . . . an amorous one to boot.* Sarah smiled a secret smile.

After Anne left, Sarah pondered her situation. A full-blown picture of Charles came to her, and she had to admit to herself that his physical appearance was potently attractive. His bold, dark eyes told her he wanted her, and she had no doubt he was the kind of male who took what he wanted. *The sun has bronzed his face and neck. I wonder if his chest and broad shoulders are also tanned?* She took a deep breath. *Stop it this moment! You will never get your revenge if you don't take control of your silly female fancies!*

Anne's words about gambling came back to her.

Since the Duke of Richmond was addicted, it was highly likely that his son was no different. *Ye Royal Family* traits of going into debt to pay gaming debts, and acquiring a bevy of mistresses, had probably been passed down to Charles.

She remembered the humiliation she had suffered in The Hague when they had exchanged their marriage vows, and her resolve hardened. *Don't let his physical attractions blind you. This is a dangerous game you are playing. You must be the winner, and Lord Bloody March must be the loser!*

"This is a grand mansion," Molly declared. "Even the servants' quarters have posh furniture." She hung up the last gown that remained in Sarah's trunk. "I'll ring for a footman to shift this. Have you noticed how attractive the male servants are?"

Sarah laughed. "It's likely the livery. Females can't resist men in uniform."

Molly winked. "It's what's *under* the gold-buttoned breeches that counts."

"Dinner is served later here, at seven o'clock rather than six."

"Jaysus, me belly will think me throat's been cut by seven." Molly brightened. "I'll just go along to the kitchen and ask that big bloke in the white hat if he's got anything to satisfy my cravings. If you don't ask, you don't get!"

That night when Sarah arrived in the dining room, Charles was there before her. He held her chair for her and then his hands touched her shoulders in a brief caress.

"Thank you, my lord."

He gave a theatrical sigh. "You've forgotten my name again."

When Anne arrived, Sarah asked, "Did you have an enjoyable ride?"

"I did, Sarah. I feel as if I'm on the brink of success."

"I warrant it would be polite to include me in your conversation."

"I'm a Lennox, Charles. I wasn't aware politeness was in our vocabulary."

"You would do well to emulate Sarah. Nothing captivates a man more than a sweet smile and a gentle manner."

"Save perhaps a *seductive* smile and a *saucy* manner," Anne contradicted.

"And this has brought you to the brink of success? With whom, may I ask?"

Anne bit her lip. "If you must know, the Earl of Albemarle is pursuing me."

"With an intention to marry?" Charles asked bluntly.

"How dare you suggest otherwise?" Anne demanded.

"*Seductive* and *saucy* behavior prompt me to suggest otherwise." He glanced at Sarah. "In a wife that would be deeply desirable; in an unwed young lady, it would be fodder for gossip. As a matter of fact I was in Albemarle's company this afternoon. He is a wealthy man who could have any woman he fancies. If you don't behave like a lady, he'll never propose marriage." Charles turned his attention to his wife, effectively dismissing Anne.

"Were you able to transfer your clothes and your lady's maid this afternoon?"

"Yes, my lord. Molly believes Richmond House is a step up in the world."

He smiled. "And do you share her opinion?"

"I share her Irish sense of humor," she teased.

"I love to watch you laugh—among other things."

Sarah set down her fork. "I fail to see any enjoyment in watching me eat."

"You have such dainty manners, I am fascinated. When you taste something delicious, the tip of your tongue comes out to lick your lips. When you sip your wine, you savor it, as if it were ambrosia."

She picked up her fork and resumed eating. "I'm not a goddess, come down from Mount Olympus, my lord. I am merely a woman."

He looked into her eyes. "You are not yet a woman in the full sense of the word, Sarah. That pleasure still awaits you."

Her pulse quickened, and her cheeks were tinted pink. To cover her shyness, she licked her lips. Then they both laughed at her reaction to his words.

Anne finished her food quickly and threw down her napkin. "Since I am *de trop,* and you have eyes only for each other, I shall relieve you of my presence."

"Thank you," Charles murmured without taking his eyes off his wife. The moment Sarah finished her wine, he lifted the decanter and refilled her glass. When he handed it to her, their fingers met.

"After dinner, would you like to see some of the things I brought back from my travels? I have all sorts of artifacts, jewelry, paintings, and such. Perhaps we can find a gift for you. What do you like?"

"I like art, my lord."

"So do I. An interest in art is something we have in common. I'm avid to learn more about you, Sarah. Anne's only interest was a gem encrusted bracelet."

"I've never had jewels, my lord."

"I shall rectify that. Tonight," he added.

When the food was cleared away, they finished their wine as Charles told her about his travels. She emptied her glass and he held out his hand. "Let's go upstairs."

Sarah placed her hand in his, and he led her to his private wing of Richmond House.

He opened the door of a large room that was filled with crates and boxes. He found a stool for her and went down on his knees to pry the wood from a crate that held paintings. He lifted them out, one at a time, and stood them against the walls. "I acquired these in Paris. Tell me what you think. Be honest!"

The first painting was of men and women in fashionable clothes and wigs, dancing in a garden. It was by an artist named Watteau. "I don't care for it," Sarah declared. "It looks like the idle rich. They all look bored, and the presentation is too theatrical."

"I bought it to remind me just how decadent the rich are in France. The chateaus are opulent and the fashions ridiculous, while the masses subsist on bread."

"Oh, I like that painting of villagers dancing at a fair. Their clothes are shabby, but the joy on their faces is real."

"Yes, the artist is Nicolas Lancret. I believe he'll be famous one day."

Sarah glanced at another painting. "Is that a portrait of you?"

"It's King Charles II when he was a young man. I

can't make out the artist's name, but I bought it for Goodwood. I'm sure my father will enjoy it."

"I've only ever seen portraits of when the king was an older man. Your resemblance to this one is amazing."

"Is that a compliment, Sarah, or an insult?"

"It's a compliment. You should be proud to be the grandson of a king."

"He was beloved by many, though he certainly had his faults. But he readily admitted to them, which was part of his charm, I warrant."

You can be rather charming yourself, when the spirit moves you, but I doubt you will ever admit to your own brutish faults.

Charles opened another crate and lifted out two paintings.

"I absolutely love that one! It must be a painting of Venice."

"Yes, this is the Grand Canal." He pointed out a building on the right. "That's the Doge's Palace. The artist isn't well known yet in England. His name is Canaletto. Would you like this painting, Sarah?"

"I would love it! Thank you so much."

He got up from his knees and took her by the hand. "Come with me." He led the way to his own bedchamber and took her out onto the balcony. "The view from here across the Thames reminds me of that Venetian scene. See, there's enough light left in the dark sky to see the white dome of St. Paul's. I'd like a painting of the river and the buildings from this vantage point. It won't be like this forever. Things change."

She was caught up in his enthusiasm. "Do people change?"

"I'd like to think I have, Sarah."

He moved close and dipped his head and she thought he would kiss her.

Instead he took her back inside. She watched him open a lacquered chest that held items of jewelry. Charles pulled out several trays. "Take your pick, my beauty."

She stared at brooches, bracelets, and rings, all set with precious gems. Her eyes fell on a necklace of rubies and she craved it immediately. "Are you sure?" she whispered.

"Absolutely. Consider it a wedding present, my love."

"I'm particularly partial to rubies." She remembered hearing it from the heroine in a play at the Court last winter, and uttering the words made her feel both giddy and wicked.

Charles picked up the necklace from its velvet tray, lifted her hair, and fastened it around her neck. He swept her up and set her down before a cheval glass. "Your beauty puts the rubies to shame," he murmured in her ear before he kissed it.

"Thank you, my lord," she said breathlessly.

"There are ear bobs to match, in there somewhere. Call me Charles and they are yours. You have wooed me into a giving mood. Will you be generous with me, Sarah?"

She hesitated for the pleasure of making him wait. "Perhaps . . . Lord March."

He longed to hear the sound of his name on her lips, but refused to show his disappointment. If she wanted to play a teasing game, he would accommodate her. Charles dipped his head and this time captured her mouth in a possessive kiss.

She clung to him as she felt her knees turn to water. Then she gasped as he swung her up into his arms and carried her into the adjoining chamber. He set her down in a chair beside the bed. "Good night, Sarah." He went out and closed the door softly.

She blinked into the darkness. *What just happened?*

When she heard a low knock on the door, she smiled and opened it expecting to see Charles. She was surprised when Molly bustled in and proceeded to light the lamp.

"I'm here to help you undress. I put your nightrails in the middle bureau drawer. I imagine you want to wear the sheer one to drive him barking mad."

"No, a silk one will be fine." *Oh, lord, Molly thinks I'll be sleeping in his bed. After the way he kissed me, I expected it, too. Perhaps he's being a gentleman and is showing me consideration.* She almost laughed. Charles Lennox was the most inconsiderate brute in the world. More than likely the kiss had been a pretense. *He isn't panting after me at all. At least, not yet. But he will!*

Molly undid her corset strings, and Sarah took a deep breath as the tight garment dropped away. "If I were you, m'lady temptress, I'd keep the rubies on. The color matches the jewels at the tips of your breasts."

As Sarah slipped on the white silk garment, she recalled Molly's words from earlier:

You don't ask, you don't get. "Thank you for your help, Molly. Good night."

She crossed the chamber and stood before the adjoining door trying to get up her courage to behave outrageously. *If I want the upper hand, I must take it.* She turned the knob and let the door slowly swing open.

Charles turned his head toward the door and threw the shirt he had just removed onto a chair. Framed in the doorway with the light of the room behind her, he could see the outline of her body through the silk. Exultant anticipation surged through him, and his arousal stretched the tight material of his breeches. "You've come for the ruby earrings."

"No, my lord. I've come to return the ruby necklace." She reached up to unfasten it.

"Don't!" The command was sharp. "Come, let me do that."

She glided toward him, and when she stood before him, she turned her back and lifted her hair so he could find the clasp. She felt his lips brush the nape of her neck, and she shivered. "Take it off."

His arms came around her and his palms cupped her breasts. He bent his lips to her ear. "I don't want to take it off. I like the feel of your skin through the slippery silk." His possessive hands slid down over her belly, then back up to her breasts. He pulled her body back against his.

"I . . . meant . . . take . . . off . . . the . . . necklace," she said breathlessly.

"No, you didn't, Sarah. You wanted me to see you wearing it. You know I am *particularly partial* to beautiful things." His hands again caressed her belly, but this time they went lower and stroked over her high mons. Then he turned her and held her at arm's length so he could look his fill. Her nipples stood erect from his fingers toying with them, and he could see a hint of their pretty color through the white silk.

Her glance moved down his neck to the muscled expanse of his chest. She reached out and ran her finger-tips across his ribs. "I have my answer," she mused.

Charles shuddered at her touch. "Answer?"

"Your body is bronzed by the sun."

His hands slid down the silk until he cupped her bum cheeks. "I'm curious about your body, too. Let's explore them together, sweetheart."

He lifted her against him and walked to the bed. He pulled back the covers and laid her against the sheets. Then he sat down on the edge and removed the remainder of his clothes. "Open your eyes, Sarah. How can you satisfy your curiosity if you don't look? How can you satisfy your longing if you don't touch? How can you satisfy your hunger if you don't taste?" He slid into bed beside her, and leaning on his elbow hung over her.

She raised her golden lashes slowly.

He thought her dark blue eyes looked like deep pools of tropical water. His fingertips traced the curve of her neck and feathered across her delicate clavicle below the necklace. His throat ached at her fragile loveliness. She was so trusting; he wished he could erase his shameful behavior when they had met at their wedding.

He bent his head and kissed her softly; their eyes met, and he held her gaze as he licked her lush lower lip, then slid the tip of his tongue inside her tempting mouth. His kiss deepened, and his palms stroked over her breasts through the slippery silk. His fingers toyed with the tips of her breasts until they ruched into hard little jewels. Then his hands swept the nightgown from her shoulders and lifted her bare breasts so that his hungry mouth could lick and taste her creamy flesh.

Charles captured her fingers in his and brought them to his naked chest. He trailed them down his ribs and across his taut belly. When they brushed against his hard erection she tried to pull her hand away, but he would not release it. With his other hand he reached down to the hem of her silk nightrail and slowly drew it up over her thighs. Then he inched it higher to reveal the honey-blond curls between her legs.

Sarah caught her breath in anticipation of what was to come. She was amazed at how gentle he was and at the adoration his heavy-lidded eyes lavished on her.

With her fingers in his, he stroked them over her mons. Then he inserted her fingertips into her woman's secret place. She gasped in protest as he guided them to stroke the bud inside her sheath, making it tingle and swell, and in spite of her modesty, Sarah began to enjoy the erotic sensations that spiraled and spread into her core.

He moved her fingers in a tantalizing rhythm that aroused a frisson of desire. It built into a bubble of need that suddenly burst and brought her a sensation of pleasure she'd never experienced before.

He took her fingers to his mouth and licked their tips, tasting her woman's essence.

Sarah was both shocked and bemused at this intimate gesture. *Is he satisfying his hunger by tasting me?*

He released her fingers, and his hands began to caress her thighs. "Your skin is lustrous as alabaster. Caressing your bare flesh is far more pleasurable than touching you through silk." He threaded his fingers through the golden curls, then slid two fingers into her slippery sheath.

He paused until she got used to the fullness inside

her and then began to thrust them in and out, slowly at first, then increasing the rhythm until she quickened.

"Charles," she cried as she climaxed.

He watched her face as her eyes became dreamy and her mouth softened, inviting his kiss. His lips found hers, drinking in her sweetness as if it were rare nectar.

Charles enfolded her in his arms, feathering kisses along her brow, nuzzling his lips against the sensitive spot where tiny golden tendrils curled about her ear.

Sarah fell asleep in the warmth of his embrace. In the morning when she stirred, her body sensed his withdrawal. She opened her eyes and found she was alone in the bed.

She turned her head, and there on the pillow lay the ruby earrings. *Are they a gift, or are they a reward for obeying his demand that I call him Charles?* She thought about their intimate interlude in his bed and smiled a secret smile. "I received far more than I gave," she whispered, "and I'm not talking about jewels."

When Sarah arrived in the breakfast room, Charles and Anne were already there. He got to his feet immediately, held a chair for her, and dropped a kiss on her curls. He smiled into her eyes when he saw she was wearing the ruby earrings.

"In all conscience, I should go to Goodwood and visit my parents," Charles told her. "Do you think you could find it in your heart to accompany me, Sarah?"

"Your mother was most gracious to me. Of course I will come." She hid her apprehension about visiting the Duke of Richmond. "You can take the painting you bought for your father."

"I'm coming, too," Anne declared. "Father won't dream of railing at me when he has you to savage, dearest Charles."

"Coward."

"I am not a coward, I'm simply following the rules of Society. As an unmarried lady I cannot remain in London in the absence of my married brother and his adored wife."

"It's up to Sarah. Can we put up with the baggage, my sweet?"

A mischievous devil inside Sarah prompted her to say something outrageous. "Oh, if we must, but it will mean we won't be able to make love in the carriage."

The adoring look Charles gave her told Sarah that he enjoyed her wicked humor.

Chapter Six

The travelers reached Chichester in late afternoon. "I've never been here before." Sarah gazed through the coach window at the lovely stone houses in the walled town.

"There's Chichester's famous cathedral," Charles said, pointing to the spire. "We'll be at Goodwood in just a few minutes."

The town disappeared and the carriage rolled over the South Downs. Sarah knew that Goodwood House was an estate of more than a thousand acres. When the horses stopped, Anne alighted and went inside to announce their arrival. By the time Charles and Sarah ascended the front steps, the Duchess of Richmond was in the foyer to greet them.

"Welcome home, darling."

Charles's arms went about his mother. He swung her around, kissed her cheeks, and gently set her feet to the carpet. He frowned with concern at how much she had aged in the years he'd been away. "You've lost weight. Are you feeling well, Mother?"

She waved away his words. "I'm an old lady. You mustn't worry about me." She turned to Sarah. "My dear, you are absolutely blooming. I'm so glad you've arrived in time for dinner. This is a lovely surprise."

"Goodwood is such a beautiful, ancient manor, Your Grace."

"Charles, take your wife up to your bedchamber; I'm sure she wants to get out of her traveling clothes after being in the carriage all day." When the duchess saw Sarah's hesitation, her smile faded. "Forgive me, perhaps you prefer separate chambers?"

Sarah couldn't bear to disappoint the duchess. She was so eager for her son to be in love with his wife. "Of course we don't prefer separate chambers."

Charles took her hand and squeezed it, grateful for her generous response.

Sarah experienced a pang of guilt at her deception. It melted away when she remembered she would soon have to be civil to the Duke of Richmond. She followed a footman with her luggage up the grand staircase. All at once she felt long fingers encircle her ankle. She kicked her foot backward, annoyed that Charles would touch her intimately in public. When she heard him chuckle, her anger increased. She followed the servant into the spacious bedchamber and waited in silence until the footman put the luggage down and left.

"You are most courageous to enter my den of iniquity."

Sarah turned and gave him a hard push. "You devil!"

He fell onto the wide bed. "For shame—can't you wait to seduce me?"

"I didn't want to disappoint your mother by asking

for separate chambers, but that doesn't mean I will share your bed. You, my lord, can sleep on the floor!"

"If you think I will allow you to go back to *my lord-*ing it, you are sadly mistaken."

He rose from the bed and loomed above her.

"Allow? Allow? Don't use that forbidding tone with me, Lord Bloody March."

She watched his face change. His features turned dark and dangerous. For a moment she feared he might strike her. Then she saw him clench his fists to gain control of his temper. He bowed coldly and left the room.

Sarah sank down on the bed with shaky legs as she gathered the remnants of her courage. *Don't you dare back down. Keep the upper hand or you will be lost, lost.* Sarah began to argue with herself. *Pitting yourself against him is not the way to seduce a man. If you want him eating out of your hand, you must tempt him with ambrosia.*

She occupied herself by unpacking their clothes and hanging them in the large wardrobe in the adjoining dressing room. Then she washed and changed her gown. She chose a deep rose taffeta that rustled invitingly with every step. As a finishing touch, she decided to wear the ruby earrings he had gifted her with only this morning.

When she left the chamber, she was unsure which way to go, because Goodwood was so vast. Then she spied Anne at the end of the hallway.

"This way, Sarah. I want a private word with Mother before dinner."

"Are you sure you want me to join you?"

"Of course I do. I have no secrets from you."

They found the duchess in her sitting room. Charles was in the library with his father, and she was enjoying a quiet moment away from her demanding husband.

"Anne, Sarah, how lovely you both look. Come and join me."

"I have some exciting news, Mother. William van Keppel, the Earl of Albemarle, is courting me. I think he's on the verge of proposing marriage."

"That would be a wonderful match, Anne. Did you know that William was born at Whitehall Palace and his godmother was the late Queen Anne? He's now Lord of the Bedchamber to the king, I believe."

"Yes, we were introduced at Court by Aunt Adelaide. He inherited his father's wealth. William owns Ashford Manor in Kent and also property in Lancashire. If he asks me to become the Countess of Albemarle, I intend to accept. I expect Father will be negotiating a marriage contract soon."

"Ah, that might pose a problem." The duchess looked worried.

"What do you mean?"

"Your father is much debilitated. You'll see for yourself at dinner." She bit her lip. "It's the effects of drink, of course. A lifetime of over-indulgence has left him befuddled and argumentative. He has a man of business to look after his affairs because he's incapable of conducting them himself. The poor fellow is browbeaten on a daily basis." She lowered her eyes. "His Grace of Richmond has become an embarrassment."

I feel a great deal of sympathy for her, but none at all for that swine Richmond. I remember his arrogance at The Hague. He wielded authority over everyone, and none dared to disobey his orders.

Sarah glanced at Anne and saw that she had gone pale, as if all her fine plans had been ruined. Then she heard a loud, querulous voice and knew she was about to come face-to-face with her detested father-in-law.

The Duke of Richmond, leaning heavily on a walking stick, swept heavy-lidded eyes over his son's wife. "Well, well, Cadogan's gel turned into quite a fancy piece. Your objections have been silenced, I take it?"

"Lady Sarah is a wife to be cherished. And far more than I deserve." Charles held out his arm to his father. "Shall we go in to dinner?"

Richmond shoved his son's arm away. "I don't need help. I'm not an invalid!"

Charles masked his impatience and spoke pleasantly. "Of course not." He held out his arm to his long-suffering mother and led her into the magnificent dining room. Anne and Sarah followed. Once his mother was seated, he held his wife's chair.

Richmond's loud voice dominated the conversation. His once handsome face now lay in ruins. He showed little interest in the food, but drank continually between inappropriate comments and attempts at humor. His laughter brought on fits of coughing. He began arguments with his wife and then his daughter, which Charles skillfully deflected. By the end of the first course, the duke was in his cups and almost incoherent.

By the end of the meal, he had fallen asleep and had to be roused by his manservant who half-carried him to his bedchamber, which of necessity was located on the main floor.

Charles escorted the ladies to the drawing room. "Is he poured into bed every night?" When his mother nodded, he asked, "Is he receiving medical attention?"

"Yes. The doctors say there is nothing more they can do for him. Since he only has a few months left, they deem it cruel to deprive him of his comforts."

"Do these doctors spare a thought for you? You look worn out, Mother."

"I shall manage. I've no idea the state of his affairs. Would you have a word with his long-suffering secretary, Charles?"

"Of course. You may safely put your concerns aside. I see how matters stand and will take care of it."

"You have taken a weight off my shoulders. I'll go up to bed, if you'll excuse me?"

Anne jumped up. "I'll take you upstairs, Mother."

When they left, Charles looked at Sarah. "I am so sorry you were exposed to such a display. I wish you could have experienced Goodwood under different circumstances. Let me show you the picture gallery."

Sarah smiled. "I'd love to see it." She was relieved their spat was forgotten.

The Long Gallery was a sight to behold. Charles took her hand and smiled down at her. "Thank you for wearing the ruby earrings. It was extremely thoughtful of you to want to please me."

He led her slowly down the ornate chamber, explaining who was in each portrait. Every duke and duchess, every earl and countess who had served at the Courts of the Stuart kings lined the walls. There were paintings by Van Dyke, Holbein, and Hilliard.

Each time they came to a beautiful lady in a stylish gown, Sarah paused to appreciate the painting. "Oh, this is your grandmother, the Duchess of Portsmouth. She is a black-eyed beautiful enchantress."

"Yes, one glance and Charles was in love. I didn't

think such a thing was possible until I saw you sitting in the Royal Box at the theater."

Sarah smiled a secret smile and moved on to the next paintings that included family groups with children and dogs. "These portraits are a history lesson come to life."

"My great-grandfather, King Charles I, was the greatest art connoisseur who ever sat on the English throne. I would like to have your portrait painted, Sarah. I want your delicate beauty captured and displayed for future generations."

His compliment took her breath away, and in spite of her resolve she was charmed.

"Your portrait should hang here, Charles. You are the future Duke of Richmond."

"There's one of me." Charles pointed to the far wall.

"But that was obviously done years ago. It doesn't resemble in any way the man you have become. Now you are tall, and broad shouldered, and bronzed by the sun, and—" She stopped. *And so physically attractive you make my pulse race each time I look at you. When you draw close the breath stops in my throat, and sometimes when you touch me I want to scream with excitement.*

Charles drew her hand to his lips and kissed her fingers. "Flattery, begod!"

She quickly changed the subject. "These horse paintings are wonderful."

"They are rather superb. The artist is John Wootton. In the morning, we'll go to the stables. The Richmond horses are legendary; their bloodlines famous. Goodwood has its own racetrack. For years it drew the nobility and the cream of Society like a lodestone. It's hard to believe now, but my father's hospitality was once unsurpassed."

"I'd love to see the horses."

"Good. We can saddle up, and perhaps we can ride hell for leather."

His words evoked her memories of their romp in the grass.

"Let me take you upstairs."

Sarah's cheeks were warm, her skirts rustling with invitation, as he led her from the gallery. By the time they arrived at his bedchamber, his *den of iniquity* as he'd referred to it, her heart was fluttering.

Charles dropped a kiss on top of her curls. "I need to consult with Digby. The estate's business affairs have been neglected, and I shudder at the mess my father's personal affairs must be in. I'm sorry to leave you on our first night at Goodwood, Sarah, but I must put duty before pleasure."

Alone, her pulses slowed and she had the honesty to admit that she was disappointed.

Sarah asked herself why, but the answer wasn't so easy. She grudgingly admitted that her physical attraction to Charles was growing but flatly denied any tender feelings for him.

She glanced about the luxuriously furnished chamber, and a large tapestry caught her eye. She walked across the room to view it up close and realized it was a priceless Gobelein. It depicted a king and his courtiers enjoying a picnic in a garden. The flowers were so vividly real that Sarah imagined she could smell their scent.

The chamber was decorated in black and gold. She ran her hand over a pair of lacquered cabinets and was curious about what they held. The cabinet doors opened to reveal sliding shelves. When she pulled them out, each shelf held drawings and pencil sketches, as well as written notes on sheets of parchment. Sarah sat down on the floor and looked at each one.

There was a theme that ran through the drawings. They depicted children, all poor, some begging. Many were sketches of King Charles II at various ages, but all showed him surrounded by urchins and handing out coins. The artwork was exceptionally fine, and she wondered who the artist could be.

She read the notes on the parchments and found them to be anecdotes of the king who could never resist the plight of ragged, hungry children. There were notes about which were the poorest sections of London, and they listed the names of the streets that were derelict. The contents of the cabinets were touching; the drawings tugged at the heartstrings. Sarah felt as if she had intruded on something private. She carefully put everything back the way she had found it.

She undressed, put on a pink nightrail, hung her gown in the dressing room wardrobe, then returned to the bedchamber. Before she climbed into bed, she removed her ruby earrings and put them on the nightstand.

Sarah lay thinking about the contents inside the lacquered cabinets. Charles hadn't occupied this bedchamber for at least three years, and she had difficulty connecting the brutish youth he had been back then to the sensitive collection she had discovered. Yet in her heart of hearts she believed the drawings had been done by Charles. She drifted into a light sleep and hours later was awakened by the sound of a door closing.

"You stayed awake for me. You are far more sweet and thoughtful than I deserve. It's past midnight."

She had turned the lamp down low. She watched him undress, and when he removed his shirt, she saw how the glow turned his skin to shimmering golden bronze. *If you but knew it, you are far more handsome than the kings from whom you are descended.*

Charles slipped into bed naked and pulled down the sheet so he could gaze at her clad in the pink silk. "You look like strawberries and cream." He licked his lips. "I want to devour you. Where on earth shall I begin?"

Sarah curled her toes.

"So be it," he said, moving down in the bed. He lifted her foot to his lips, dropped a kiss on each toe, then took them one at a time into his mouth and sucked. When he traced the arch of her foot with his fingers, it tickled and she began to laugh and squirm. His palm stroked up over her calf, and when his lips trailed kisses along the inside of her bare thigh, she suddenly stopped laughing and drew in a swift breath.

He blew on the pale tendrils that covered her mons and then he lowered his mouth and dipped his tongue inside her. Her shock that he would do such a thing soon gave way to intoxicating sensations that made her arch into his wicked mouth.

"Mmm, perhaps not strawberry but cherry," he teased. "Whatever the flavor, it is exactly to my taste." He thrust in his tongue again, curled it about her bud, withdrew it all the way out, then plunged all the way inside her sugared sheath.

"Charles!" She arched and writhed, threaded her fingers into his black hair to hold his head captive between her thighs, then cried out her pleasure at the new, enthralling vibrations of desire that spiraled up inside her and made her shiver with need.

Charles was enthralled with her reaction to his lovemaking. He had resolved to go about her sexual initiation slowly so she would receive only pleasure in their first encounters. Sarah was extremely young and innocent, and he vowed to control the wild passion she aroused in him until her desire stirred her natural female sensuality.

He raised his head and gazed at her. "You are beautiful in your arousal, sweetheart." He moved up beside her and gathered her into his embrace.

Her fingers traced his dark brow and sharp cheekbone. Then she offered up her lips for his mouth's possession. She shivered as she tasted herself on his tongue. Sarah admitted to herself that she was physically attracted to this powerful, dark male who had suddenly come into her life. The contrast between this man and the callow youth she had been forced to wed was striking. *Don't be beguiled by his handsome face and amorous attention, for he will doubtless follow in his father's dissolute footsteps, her inner voice warned. But I see no reason why I shouldn't enjoy my awakening sensuality while I lure him to lose his heart.*

He feathered kisses into her hair, enthralled by her taste and her scent. Then tenderly, he turned her in his arms so that he could tuck her head beneath his chin. He knew he had lost his heart to his wife, and it filled him with happiness.

Sarah awoke early, sensing that she was alone in the bed. Charles emerged from the dressing room in riding breeches, and she remembered he was taking her to the stables this morning.

A tap on the door was a servant with a breakfast tray for two. "I ordered this last night, so we could ride early."

She laughed as she looked at the great amount of food. "I'll never eat all that!"

"I hope not," he teased. "Most of it's for me. Go and put on a riding dress, and I promise not to devour everything."

Sarah donned her emerald green habit and twisted her hair into a chignon. She pulled on her leather riding gloves and then began to remove them when she emerged from the dressing room and saw the food.

"No, don't take them off. I'll feed you." He picked up a crisp rasher of bacon and held it to her lips. Then he fed her toast followed by a sausage. He poured her a mug of fresh-brewed ale and lifted it toward her mouth.

"I never drank ale for breakfast before."

"There's a first time for everything, Sarah. It's bracing and will give you courage to ride like the wind." He tipped the mug, inducing her to open her mouth.

"You devil! You give me no choice."

Charles slanted a dark eyebrow. "As Countess of March, you will have to learn how to imbibe and keep up with *Ye Royal Family.*"

In a show of bravado, she drained the mug and licked her lips.

"Well done! Come, the day is awasting."

The Goodwood stables were vast. Sarah had never seen so many horses under one roof in her life, not even in the royal stables. The minute the pair entered, half a dozen youths crowded around Charles, all laughing and talking at once.

He guessed each young groom's name. He got them all correct and they cheered.

"They were just little nippers the last time I saw them," he told her.

She hid her surprise that they welcomed him so warmly.

"This is my beautiful wife, Sarah. I know you will serve her well." He chose a pair of horses for them, but the stable hands insisted on saddling them. Charles acquiesced and took her hand. "Let's take a look at the Richmond horseflesh."

They slowly walked down row after row of stalls that held glossy Thoroughbreds. There were mares, stallions, and geldings, along with fillies, colts, and newborn foals. Charles spoke to the head groom. "I'm glad to see that the stables are well run, and the breeding has been prolific. Good job, Logan. I'm taking over the management of Goodwood, so if you have any concerns you can address them to me from now on."

"Thank you, Lord March. It's good you are back in England."

Charles led the pair of saddled horses from the stable. "It's a good thing your skirt has a long slit up the side. It will allow you to ride astride." When he lifted Sarah into the saddle, he rolled his eyes with pleasure at her exposed legs clad in long boots.

He mounted his own horse, took her reins, and led her from the stable yard. "I'm taking you to the South Downs. You've never experienced anything like it."

They cantered side by side until they reached the

Downs, which were on Goodwood land. Charles grinned at her. "Ready? Set . . . Go!"

They set off on a wild gallop across the rolling Downs. The turf was thick and green beneath their horses' hooves; the billowing clouds in the blue sky above them shifted constantly. And the lapwings soared high as their bird cries carried on the light breeze.

They rode neck and neck in a race that was immensely invigorating. At the end of their five-mile gallop, Charles allowed her to win the contest. "You beat me!"

Sarah turned and rode back to him. "Not fair and square . . . why did you let me win?"

"For the sheer pleasure of it, my beauty. I wanted to watch your honey-blond hair stream behind you like a banner, and watch your lovely round bottom bounce." He reached over, lifted her from her saddle, and deposited her between his muscled thighs. His lips brushed her ear. "I'd like you to ride me like that."

The pictures his words conjured in her mind were wickedly shocking, but at the same time they were provocative, and her imagination took flight so she could see their naked bodies joined together with her astride him in the dominant position.

When his hands came up to cup her breasts, she took delight in rubbing her bum against his hard erection. *I'm cockteasing and enjoying his every groan!*

Charles slid his hand inside the slit of her riding skirt, and his fingers played among her curls until she was wet. "I'm pussy teasing," he murmured. When she gasped with pleasure, he chuckled. "I think I'll keep you in a constant state of arousal from now on. Your newfound sexuality thrills me to my core."

After their ride, when he lifted her from the saddle, he let her body slide down his until her feet touched the ground. When they mounted the steps that led into the manor, he caressed her bottom. Upstairs when Sarah changed from her riding dress, he helped her, managing to touch and stroke every intimate part of her body.

For the remainder of their stay at Goodwood, Charles never entered a room without drawing close, caressing her cheek, and brushing the back of his hand across her breast. His fingers toyed with her curls; his lips kissed her ear and murmured love words.

Sarah smiled a secret smile. *Charles is besotted with me. He's on the brink of falling in love. When he tumbles, I'll spring the trap.*

Chapter Seven

Sarah and Anne bade good-bye to the Duchess of Richmond and climbed into the carriage. Charles elected to ride one of the Thoroughbreds back to London.

"My brother has taken over from Father. He told me that from now on he would be handling the family's affairs, business and otherwise."

Sarah glanced through the carriage window and caught her husband's eye. When he winked at her, she knew it was a hint and a promise of tonight's bed play. She lowered her eyelashes, pretending she was feeling shy. She knew it enchanted him.

"He doesn't discuss business matters with me." Sarah sounded disappointed.

"He told me that Albemarle must come and ask him for my hand, if William wants to marry me. Charles, not Father, will negotiate the marriage contract."

So, he will be handling the money from now on. "Do you know how much your dowry is, Anne?"

"Five thousand . . . perhaps ten. Whatever it is, I

warrant Charles won't part with the full amount. If he has the family trait of being habitually in debt, Champagne Charlie is bound to be acquisitive when it comes to money."

"Why do you call him Champagne Charlie?"

"I should think that's obvious. It's because he imbibes too much, like our father."

"I've never actually seen him drunk." *Oh, Lord, don't start defending him, Sarah. He is the enemy.*

"Well, he certainly drank too much his last year at Oxford. He and his friends were in a continual champagne fog. He got sent down once for being drunk and disorderly."

Sarah's brows drew together. "Like father, like son, I expect."

"Henry, I wasn't expecting you for another week, but I'm damn glad you returned to London early. We have a great deal of work to do."

"Oxford turned out to be less hospitable than I expected," Henry Grey admitted.

"Sarah, come and meet my friend. When we embarked on my Grand Tour he was my tutor. By the time we returned he was my dear friend and confidant. Henry has agreed to become my secretary. Henry, this is my lovely wife, Lady Sarah."

Henry Grey bowed. "It is my honor to meet you, Lady March."

She inclined her head. "Mr. Grey." *You were with Charles Lennox aboard the* Green Lion *when he treated me savagely.* "I'll have Soames prepare a suite of rooms for you, Mr. Grey. If there is anything I can do to make you more comfortable, please don't hesitate to ask." *I intend to make you my ally, Henry Grey.*

When she left the library in search of Soames, she found him with Anne.

"Look at these roses, Sarah. They just arrived from St. James's Palace. Albemarle sent them to welcome me home. The card says he missed me intolerably, and he's sent me an invitation to a Court reception at the palace tonight."

Soames held a stack of envelopes that had arrived while Sarah was away. He handed her two and kept the rest. "These are for Lord March, my lady."

"I, too, got an invitation to the palace. Let's go up and decide what we'll wear."

"Sarah, I need your help. Tell me which gown will make me irresistible."

"Anne, you are irresistible no matter what you wear."

As Anne opened her wardrobe to display her gowns, Sarah opened her second envelope. "Oh, my parents are in London! They came up at the invitation of King George. They'll be at St. James's Palace tonight."

"When did you last see them?"

"A little more than a month ago, at the Duke of Marlborough's funeral."

"Ah yes, your father was a renowned general. It must be wonderful to have a father who isn't an embarrassment."

"Still, I'm glad he's not often in London. Now that he's retired, he spends his time improving the gardens at Caversham Park." *I'll never forgive him for forcing me to marry Charles Lennox.* Sarah quickly changed the subject.

"I think you should wear this primrose yellow gown. It's an extremely flattering color for someone with dark hair. The skirts will rustle invitingly, and you can tuck a couple of the yellow roses Albemarle sent you into the décolletage."

"Sarah, you are so clever in knowing what will attract the opposite sex."

"I've made a study of it," she said dryly.

"Molly, I believe I'll wear my pale lavender gown tonight."

While Sarah's maid was helping her don the gown, Charles entered their bedchamber. When he signaled that he wanted to be alone with his wife, Molly withdrew quickly.

"I have something that will make you the envy of all the ladies at Court." He opened the jewel cabinet and took out a necklace. He came up behind her, smiled at her reflection in the mirror, then looped the black pearls twice about her neck. "They make your skin look like alabaster."

Sarah admired the black pearls against her throat. "They make me look beautiful."

"No, you make the pearls look beautiful."

His deep feelings for her were clearly written on his face, and Sarah experienced a pang of guilt for taking presents from him when she did not return his feelings. "I'm going to the Court function with Anne."

"I'll be along later."

Sarah was surprised. "I didn't know you intended to go."

"There is no place like the King's Court for conducting business, my love. Wealthy nobles gather like flocks of sheep waiting to be fleeced."

"My parents will be there tonight."

He lifted her hair and kissed the nape of her neck. His eyes met hers in the mirror. "I've already stolen their treasure."

When Sarah and Anne arrived at St. James's Palace, the first thing they did was make their curtsies to King George I. "I'm willing to bet Aunt Adelaide is here tonight, though, of course, His Majesty won't have his mistress sitting on a throne next to him," Anne jested. "I can't wait to meet your parents, Sarah."

"You won't have to wait. They are here before us." She led Anne over to a couple across the chamber. "Hello, Mother. I'd like to present my sister-in-law, Lady Anne, who has become my dearest friend."

"Lady Cadogan, I am delighted to meet you."

When Anne curtsied to her mother, Sarah knew her mother would be flattered that the Duke of Richmond's daughter would show her deference.

"I'm happy that the two of you are good friends. Sarah, where did you get your magnificent black pearls?"

"They were a gift from my husband," she said quietly, and looked at her father. "It gives me pleasure to present my sister-in-law, Lady Anne Lennox."

Cadogan made a leg and brought Anne's fingers to his lips.

Anne dipped her knee and smiled. "I've been wanting to meet England's greatest general for some time."

"The honor is mine, my lady."

Anne's smile widened. "Sarah has told me all about

your glorious gardens at Caversham Park. She tells me they put the gardens at Blenheim Palace to shame."

Cadogan laughed, pleased that his daughter had praised his skills to Anne.

"Please excuse us," Sarah murmured politely. As the friends moved away, Sarah said, "You have made a conquest of my father. He will be your slave forever." She raised her eyes and saw the Earl of Albemarle across the chamber. "There's William. I scent another conquest in the air."

The earl spied Anne and immediately came to greet her. Sarah melted into the crowd, giving the couple the privacy they would need for an intimate conversation.

She joined the Dowager Duchess of Marlborough, who had brought her granddaughter, Lady Diana Spencer, to Court. "Your Grace, how lovely to see you. Did you know my parents are here tonight?"

"Ah, under happier circumstances than the last time we met." The duchess scanned the crowd. "Where's that husband of yours? In some gaming hell, I shouldn't wonder. With Blandford, unless I miss my mark."

I wonder if she's right? "I believe he had some business to attend to. The Earl of March said he would be here later."

The old duchess tapped Sarah's arm with her fan. "Funny bloody business, I warrant. A guinea says that Blandford and March arrive together."

When Sarah saw the glowing look on Anne's face, she guessed what had put it there.

"William has asked me to marry him, and I said *yes!*" Anne searched the crowded room with her eyes. "Has Charles arrived yet?"

"I'm afraid not, but he should be here soon, it's getting late."

"Off gambling with Blandford and his friend Hartington, no doubt."

That's what the Duchess of Marlborough said. "Speak of the devil." Sarah nodded toward the ornate doors, where Charles had just entered. Her eyes narrowed when she saw that he was indeed with Blandford.

Charles, who had eyes for none but his wife, walked a direct path to her.

Sarah refrained from asking where he'd been, but Anne demanded to know.

"We were at Devonshire House, bolstering poor old Hartington's courage. Seems he is about to embark on a journey to the altar."

"Who is the lucky bride?" Sarah asked dryly.

Charles's eyes glittered with amusement at her sarcasm. "An heiress, Lady Katherine Hoskyns. Her father is a wealthy businessman who advises Hartington's cousin, the Duke of Bedford."

"Bedford must have asked Hartington to pay off his gambling debts," Anne declared.

"You've hit the nail on the head," Blandford confirmed. "I cannot envision a more degrading reason for marriage than to settle a gaming debt."

Sarah blanched at his thoughtless words. "Marriage must be in the air," she said brightly, trying to mask the humiliation she felt.

Charles, who had been watching Sarah, looked at his sister and raised his brows.

Anne nodded happily. "The Earl of Albemarle is about to ask you for my hand."

Blandford's shoulders slumped with dejection.

Anne said wickedly, "Don't feel badly. My brother will give you advice on how to become irresistible to a lady."

Blandford snorted and took his leave.

Charles slipped his arm about Sarah for a brief hug. "Excuse me, I'll be right back."

Sarah watched him as he sought out the Earl of Albemarle, who was attending the king. The three men conversed briefly, then Charles returned to her side.

"That didn't take long." Anne looked anxious.

"We can hardly thrash out a marriage contract at a Court function. Albemarle and I have arranged to meet privately." He took his wife's arm. "Why don't we ask your parents to join us in the supper room?"

"I'll come, too. I was too nervous to eat earlier. Now I could eat a horse."

Charles offered his other arm to Anne. "Considering the king's frugal ways, perhaps equine hors d'oeuvres are on the menu."

On the brief carriage ride from St. James's Palace to Richmond House, Sarah thought about how jovial her parents and Charles had been. Her reserved mother had been almost kittenish responding to her son-in-law's attention, and the camaraderie between her father and Charles grew with every drink they quaffed.

"Sarah, I envy you your father," Anne said wistfully. "He has such a military bearing and is highly regarded at Court. Our father has become an embarrassment."

"Anne, I forbid you to think unhappy thoughts," Charles chided. "You are about to become a countess."

He captured his wife's hand and squeezed it. "And countesses are irresistible." He put his lips to Sarah's ear. "Some more than others, of course."

"I want to be married as soon as possible."

Charles laughed. "Now that you've hooked him, you don't want the poor devil to wriggle off the line. What do you mean by soon?"

"The end of the month, or certainly no later than the first week of July."

"Such haste may be fodder for gossip," he teased.

"I shall be the Countess of Albemarle. What the devil do I care?"

When the carriage stopped, Charles helped his sister and then his wife to alight. Sarah was surprised when he took her in his arms for a long kiss. When he finally released her, he said, "Don't wait up for me." Then he got back into the carriage.

"Where the devil is he off to?" Anne said from the front steps.

"He didn't tell me."

Anne shrugged. "Must have private business to conduct."

Funny bloody business, I warrant.

Sarah followed Anne upstairs. She told her sister-in-law how happy she was for her and bade her good night.

"Oh, Molly, you waited up for me."

"It's only just gone midnight. You'll need help with your corset, unless *His Nibs* claims the honor."

"*His Nibs* won't be home until later. I'll sleep in my own bedchamber tonight."

"Good thing you hung on to the pearls for safe-keeping."

"Molly, why do you assume he's gone to a gaming hell?"

"I'm giving him the benefit of the doubt. They're the only places open all night, other than brothels."

As Sarah lay abed, her imagination played havoc. She hoped that Charles wasn't in some gaming hell, racking up losses and going into debt, borrowing from his friends. *What the devil do I care?*

Her thoughts then wandered in another direction. *When he's besotted with me, why would he sleep with a whore?* Doubt crept in. *Charles has never consummated our marriage. I don't satisfy his needs.* Sarah thumped her pillow. *What the devil do I care?*

It was hours before she finally drifted off to sleep. When she began to dream, she was back at school in Reading. Two things that were hard to endure had marred those years: the cold and the loneliness. Sarah curled her toes and drew up her knees.

The dream ended, and when she opened her eyes, she realized that she was shivering. Sarah felt lost and vulnerable in the wide empty bed. She feared falling asleep again in case the dream returned.

She slipped out of bed and padded over to the adjoining door. She hesitated for long minutes as she gathered her courage to join Charles in his warm bed. Sarah turned the knob and let the door swing open. The first light of dawn was coming through the tall windows. It showed her that his chamber was empty; his bed had never been slept in.

Her heart sank. Then she raised her chin and straightened her shoulders. *What the devil do I care?*

* * *

Sarah was late going down for breakfast, but even so, she arrived before Anne, who came into the room yawning.

"I had the most dreadful dream. William and I had just exchanged our wedding vows when Father suddenly began shouting and arguing. He'd been drinking and couldn't be controlled. A fight broke out, and Charles had to restrain him from choking the Prince of Wales."

"Is someone taking my name in vain?" Charles arrived. He was bathed and shaved and wearing fresh linen. "Good morning, my beauty." He dropped a kiss on his wife's curls and sat down. "I got home late and didn't want to disturb you."

"Where did you go?" Anne asked pointedly.

"I returned to St. James's Palace. Albemarle and I had unfinished business, if you will recall. We came to terms over your marriage contract, and he'll be along later today to sign it. We hit it off famously. I'm delighted we will be brothers-in-law."

Sarah wasn't sure she believed him. *Surely that didn't take all night.*

Charles smiled at her. "Your father was amazingly magnanimous. When I mentioned Richmond's health problems, he suggested we hold the wedding at Caversham Park Manor. He said the gardens were in full bloom and that Lady Margaret would be in her glory entertaining our noble guests."

Anne jumped up from the table and threw her arms about her brother. "Oh, thank you, Charles. Sarah, I told you I envied you your parents. It would be a nightmare to have the wedding at Goodwood. And now our problem is solved!"

Sarah glanced at her husband. *Your problem is solved; mine remains.*

"There's so much to do!" Anne had asked Sarah to be her matron of honor, and they were making a list of people who would expect to be invited to the wedding. A modiste, who had made elegant gowns for Sarah, was coming today to measure Anne for her wedding gown. Midafternoon Albemarle arrived, and Charles took the earl and Anne to the library to sign the marriage contract.

Anne accompanied William to the door when he departed. The betrothed couple kissed good-bye and promised to see each other at Leicester House that evening. Then Anne rushed to find Sarah. "Look at my ring! I can't wait to show it off tonight. Princess Caroline will be grass green with envy when she sees the size of my diamond."

That evening when Sarah went upstairs to dress, she found a pair of sheer black stockings embroidered with violets lying on the bed. Her lips curved with delight; she'd never seen embroidered stockings before.

"Molly, I believe I'll wear my violet silk tonight." The gown had puffed sleeves that were slashed so that her bare shoulders were revealed.

She was not surprised that Charles came into their bedchamber while she was dressing and signaled for Molly to leave. He cupped her exposed shoulders. "Will you wear the pearls for me tonight, sweetheart?"

"Of course. That's why I chose to wear this violet

silk. It was made for black pearls." She lifted the hem of her gown. "As were these stockings. Thank you for the present; I've never seen anything so pretty."

His voice was husky as he gazed at her legs. "You can thank me later." He brushed his lips against hers. "I must get dressed, though I'd far rather stay home."

Sarah moved across the room for safety. "We can always leave early," she tempted him.

At Leicester House, the reception rooms were crowded. Princess Caroline tended to hold court with her female friends, while the men gravitated toward the Prince of Wales. Most males preferred the gaming rooms to the ballroom.

Prince George greeted the couple as soon as they arrived. "Ah, just the man I wanted to see. Please excuse us, Lady March, I have business to discuss with your husband."

Anne went off in search of Albemarle. She was looking forward to dancing.

Sarah made her curtsy to Princess Caroline. "His Highness commandeered Charles the moment we arrived."

"Ah, the Prince of Wales heard about the horses your husband sold the king. You know how competitive George and his father are. He won't rest until he, too, owns some of those incomparable Thoroughbreds."

Charles is selling horses? Goodwood horses? Sarah was shocked. *He must be desperate for money!*

"I have some new musicians I'm trying out tonight," Princess Caroline declared.

Prince Frederick held out his arm to Sarah, and

everyone followed them to the ballroom. Anne and Albemarle were there before them. "I believe congratulations are in order. When may we celebrate the nuptials?"

Anne showed the Princess of Wales her ring. "We have decided on July 4. The Countess of March has generously invited us to hold the wedding at Caversham Park in Oxfordshire. It's far more convenient for everyone than Goodwood."

The musicians began to play and Frederick partnered Sarah in the first dance.

It wasn't long before the Dowager Duchess of Marlborough arrived with Lady Diana Spencer in tow, and her grandson, the Marquis of Blandford, trailing behind.

While Anne proceeded to make young Diana toad green with envy over her ring, Sarah asked Blandford to dance. Though he was eager to partner her, she found him less eager to answer questions about her husband.

"William, did you know that Charles was selling some of the Goodwood horses?"

"Mmm, I may have heard a vague reference to it."

"He must need money," she prompted him.

"Don't we all? Raising money for a project is akin to squeezing blood from a stone."

"Does this *project* have anything to do with paying off gambling debts?"

"My dear Lady March, Charles doesn't confide his *private affairs* to me. He plays his cards close to his chest—he wouldn't appreciate my discussing his business with his wife."

"Forgive me, William. I didn't mean to make you uncomfortable."

When the dance ended, Blandford left the ballroom,

and Sarah chatted with his grandmother about the up-coming wedding at Caversham Park.

"Lady Anne has made a good match with Albe-marle. He's a solid fellow with a noble title, but it's the man that matters, not the rank."

Sarah hid her amusement. *The rank will certainly matter when it comes to a match for Lady Diana.*

"Sarah, my dear, would you mind chaperoning Diana? I prefer the company of the big dogs in the gaming rooms. Can't do much business in the ball-room."

The moment the dowager duchess left, Sarah steered Diana toward Prince Frederick. His eyes lit up at the sight of the pretty young lady, and he asked her to dance. *A match made in heaven. Even the duchess can-not cavil at a royal prince.*

Promptly at eleven, Charles came to escort Sarah to the supper room. She was rather surprised to see that he had the Dowager Duchess of Marlborough on his arm.

"I've brought your godmother to join us. I've been bending her ear for the last hour and think she's in need of a drink."

On the way to the buffet, Sarah's suspicions mounted with every step. "I was under the impression you didn't indulge in gambling, Your Grace."

The old girl gave a bark of laughter. "There's frip-pery gambling, then there's *real* gambling! I prefer the latter . . . business, stocks, shares, trading. Neck or noth-ing is my motto. That sort of gamble takes far more guts than betting on cards."

Charles handed Sarah a flute of champagne, but he

secured Scotch whiskey for the duchess. Her Grace raised her glass, "Bottoms up!"

Sarah felt his hand stroke her bum and drew in a swift breath.

"I promised my wife I would take her home early. There are some things that even take precedence over business."

"Ha! Funny bloody business," the duchess chortled. "You are a devil, Charles Lennox."

"And then some," he said with a grin.

Chapter Eight

"I won't be a minute. Wait for me," Charles said when they arrived home. He went into the library and emerged a couple of moments later.

He took something to his desk. She was wildly curious about what it could be. Her thoughts evaporated, however, when Charles swept her into his arms and carried her upstairs.

Sarah blushed. "Molly! You shouldn't have waited up for me."

Charles winked at the maid. "Lady March won't be needing your services tonight."

He set Sarah's feet to the carpet, removed her cloak, and dropped a kiss on her bare shoulder. She took a deep breath. "Anne said Albemarle would bring her home. Everyone was so happy for her; it was a rewarding evening."

Charles dipped his head and whispered in her ear, "It isn't over yet." He lifted her arm and began to remove her evening glove. He dropped a kiss into her palm and reached for the other glove. This time his lips didn't stop at her palm. They kissed the inside of her wrist, then trailed up the inside of her bare arm, making her shiver.

When his lips touched her throat, she remembered the pearls and reached up to remove them.

"No, no, I'll do the undressing." He turned her about and unfastened her gown. When the violet silk pooled at her feet, she stepped out of it. He undid the ribbons of her petticoat and let it fall to the carpet; then he unfastened her corset strings and lifted it off. Charles turned her to face him before he reached up to remove the pins from her hair. It fell over his hands in silken splendor and it was his turn to shiver.

He unlooped the double row of pearls so that they fell in a single long loop between her naked breasts. "I want you to leave them on. Their black luster turns your flesh luminescent." He held her at arm's length as his gaze swept over her from head to toe.

When you look at me like that, I feel beautiful.

"I've been waiting all night to see you in your pretty stockings and garters. I want you to leave them on."

That's why you gave them to me. You want me to wear them to bed!

She tossed her hair over her shoulder and felt it whisper against her back. She knew she made an erotic picture with her golden curls cascading about her shoulders, the black pearls decorating her pale breasts, and the black stockings embroidered with violets.

Sarah knew with the age-old knowledge of Eve that tonight he would take her virginity. This was the time she had been waiting for. She savored the inevitability of the act. The climax was fast approaching. It would be followed by the denouement when he plunged into the abyss, and then she would take her revenge.

Sarah didn't get into bed; instead she walked across the chamber and poured herself a glass of wine.

His eyes never left her as he removed his clothes.

She came toward him slowly, swaying her hips. She dipped a finger into the wine and sucked it provocatively. Then she painted his nipples with the wine and licked them.

Charles groaned. "You are tempting as sin, my beauty." He took the wineglass from her and set it down. Then he lifted her against his heart and carried her to their bed.

He pulled the covers aside, laid her down gently, and worshipped her with his eyes. "You fill my senses, sweetheart."

She watched him slip into bed beside her and felt his tenderness as he gathered her into his arms. When the kissing began, her thoughts of revenge floated away as pleasure engulfed her. He began with quick kisses to her temples, her eyelids, her nose, and the corners of her mouth. Then his lips trailed down to brush against her throat, and she longed for his mouth to take possession of hers.

When his lips sought hers, they lost themselves for an entire hour in slow, melting kisses. The tip of his tongue tempted her to open her mouth and invite him inside. When he thrust in and out, imitating what his body was about to do, she moaned softly.

With his lips against her throat he murmured, "Your skin is so delicate and fair against my dark body, it makes me long to devour you." He brushed the golden tendrils from her forehead and threaded his fingers into her curls. "Your hair is so wondrous, it tempts me to touch it every time you come near me." His other hand cupped her breast, and his thumb caressed its pink tip.

Sarah loved the feel of his hands on her body. His touch thrilled her. *He has such beautiful hands. His fingers are long and slender like an artist's.* She sighed and arched against him. She felt his hard erection brush against her thigh, and her lashes fluttered up so she could watch his mounting desire turn his eyes dark with need.

Charles rose up and straddled her with his knees. He gazed down at the exquisite picture she made. The black pearls lay in the valley between her upthrust breasts. The bare flesh of her thighs above the black stockings and the honey-colored tendrils on her high mons made his senses reel.

He took her hand and brought it to his cock. He drew in a swift breath as her fingers encircled him. "Sarah, you are so precious to me. I'll try not to hurt you, my love."

Charles slid his shaft back and forth in the cleft between her legs so she could get used to the feel of him. Sarah dug her fingers into his shoulders and arched against him.

"Wrap your legs about my back."

She obeyed without question and felt his cock thrust inside her slowly and firmly.

She experienced a sharp pain that took her breath away. But as he held still inside her, the pain quickly subsided and was replaced by a fullness that made her feel like a real woman for the first time in her life.

He began to move in a tantalizing rhythm that sent her desire spiraling high through her belly and breasts, deep into her woman's center. Heat leaped between them, arousing a thousand pulsing pleasure points when he unleashed the fierce passion he had been holding in check for weeks.

She cried out his name, shattering the stillness of the night. At that moment, nothing in the entire world mattered to her but the feel of him inside her. When he felt the first flutter of her orgasm, he allowed his own release. They climaxed together, then lay entwined as their bodies softened with surfeit.

He took his weight from her and gazed down at her with adoration. "You consume me. I love you, Sarah."

He curved his long body about her back and tucked her head beneath his chin.

She lay in a warm haze feeling safe and protected. Above all she felt loved. Sleep beckoned, and unable to resist it, she succumbed.

Hours later, Sarah awoke and opened her eyes. Their bodies were no longer touching, and she lay absolutely still as she contemplated what she would do. She had gone over her plan many times and even rehearsed the cutting words she would say.

In the dark, a wave of guilt for what she was about to do washed over her. Charles had told her he loved her, and she wished he hadn't opened his heart to her. She firmly pushed away the gnawing self-reproach. *This is the moment you've been waiting for. The timing is perfect. You've thirsted for revenge. Have the courage of your convictions and settle the score!*

Sarah inched slowly to the edge of the bed and set her feet to the floor. Quietly, she moved to the adjoin-

ing bedchamber and closed the door. Her pulse raced
and her heart hammered as she lit the lamp. She removed the black pearls and laid them on the dressing
table beside the rubies. Then she peeled off the embroidered stockings. She poured water into the bowl to
wash, and then she dressed.

She glanced toward the adjoining door and the
chamber beyond. *Don't look back! Don't ever look
back.* She opened her wardrobe and began to fold her
clothes. Her thoughts strayed to the events of last night,
and she knew she would not be satisfied until she found
out what Charles had put in his desk.

Silently, she made her way to the library and lit the
lamp. Her heart was in her mouth as she slid open the
desk drawer and pulled out a handful of papers. She
saw two bills of sale for horses—one to the king and
the other to the Prince of Wales. She gasped at the
amount of money they had paid for the Thoroughbreds.

She picked up a piece of paper and saw it was a
bank draft in the amount of ten thousand pounds,
payable to Charles Lennox and signed by William van
Keppel.

*Christus! He is extracting payment from Albemarle
to marry Anne. William should be receiving money for
Anne's dowry, not paying money. How on earth did he
persuade Albemarle to hand over ten thousand
pounds?* She had never dreamed that Charles Lennox
could be so crass. It was tantamount to selling his sister.

Sarah picked up the last piece of paper, which was
another bank draft. She was shocked to her core to see
the signature. It was from Sarah Churchill, the Dowager
Duchess of Marlborough, in the amount of fifteen
thousand pounds.

Her anger flared. "That devil! How did he coerce my godmother to hand over her money?" *He has a dark attraction that females cannot resist. His smooth charm could lure the ducks from the pond.*

Sarah flung the papers back into the desk drawer and closed it. She looked up quickly as a shadow fell across the doorway.

"Are you looking for something, Lady March?" Henry Grey asked in a puzzled voice as he came into the library.

"Thank you, Mr. Grey. I found everything I was looking for."

"Is something amiss, Lady March?"

"Nothing . . . everything! We met once before, Mr. Grey."

Henry's brows drew together. "I'm sure I would have remembered, my lady."

"It was more than three years ago aboard the *Green Lion*. I am the idiot girl who barreled into Charles like a *bloody baboon*."

She watched his expression turn to horror as he recalled the incident aboard ship.

"I humbly beg your pardon, my lady."

"You have nothing to apologize for, Mr. Grey. You stopped the Earl of March from savaging me. I thank you for your gallantry."

Sarah swept past him and went back upstairs to her bedchamber. With each step her outrage mounted. If he wanted to sell his sister, it had nothing to do with her. But extracting money from her godmother was another matter entirely.

By the light from her window she saw that it was

dawn. When the adjoining bedroom door opened, she was waiting for him, ready for him.

Charles, clad in hastily donned breeches, stepped into the room. "Sarah, what's wrong? Did I hurt you?"

"Yes, you did."

His eyes filled with concern. "I'm so sorry. I tried to be gentle."

"I'm not talking about last night. I'm referring to the hurt you inflicted on me the day I was forced to marry you. You were a brute. You treated me with utter contempt. The words you threw at me were vile." Sarah raised her chin. "I vowed to even the score. The only reason I came to live with you at Richmond House was to seek revenge." She saw the concern in his eyes turn to pain.

He said with disbelief, "You used my love as a weapon against me."

The truth of his accusation goaded her to inflict more pain. "I'm glad the weapon I chose found its mark and wounded you."

His look became guarded as he masked the hurt he felt.

"I'm leaving. From now on we'll live apart. I won't stay under the same roof with a man without morals. Where money is concerned you are exactly like your father. You have sold Goodwood horses to pay off gambling debts."

She saw him clench his fists, and she tossed her head in angry defiance. "I don't really give a damn that you have sold your sister, because it is none of my business. But taking money from the Dowager Duchess of Marlborough *is* my business. To use the affection of my godmother in your manipulative schemes sickens me. If you have an ounce of integrity you will return her money immediately."

She saw his black brows draw together and his jaw harden.

"I'm going to Caversham Park to help Mother prepare for Anne's wedding. Once she is married, I will be living at the Cadogan town house."

A dreadful silence stretched between them.

"I shall put the carriage at your disposal." He turned, went into the adjoining bedchamber, and shut the door.

Sarah's knees turned to water and she sank down on the bed. She should have been triumphant that she had taken her revenge, but all she felt was a sinking sensation and her heart was heavy. He deserved every word, she thought, forbidding herself to dwell on the hurt she had seen in his eyes.

She stood up and squared her shoulders, then rang for Molly. When the young woman arrived, Sarah said, "We are leaving. Pack your things and get a footman to find my trunks. Better get yourself some breakfast; we are going to Caversham Park."

Molly noticed Sarah's pale face and stiff back. She refrained from questioning the young countess. It was plain as a pikestaff she'd had a row with her husband.

Downstairs Sarah penned a note to Anne explaining she was going home to Caversham to help her mother prepare for the wedding. She did not mention that she was leaving Charles permanently. Anne was her friend, and the last thing she wanted to do was upset the bride-to-be. She left the envelope sitting in Anne's place at the table.

* * *

"Sarah, we only left London yesterday. If we'd known you were coming to visit, you could have driven down with us." Margaret eyed the trunks and the large amount of luggage the servants had carried in. "You must be intending to stay for a while."

"Yes, I'm going to help plan the wedding festivities. There will be a lot of work involved preparing for the guests, to say nothing of the expense you will incur. This is extremely generous of you, Mother."

"Your husband is shouldering all the expenses. Charles insisted. He gave your father the money when we were in London."

Sarah was surprised. "Good. It's only fitting that he pay." She removed her cloak. "You remember Molly? I took her with me to Richmond House as my lady's maid."

Molly bobbed a curtsy. "Lady Cadogan."

"I thought she could have the room next to mine." Sarah beckoned a male servant. "Please have the luggage taken up to my old chamber." She had no idea how polished and confident she appeared to her mother and Caversham's servants.

"Here's Father." She dutifully kissed his cheek.

"The carriage horses are safely stowed in the stable. I've ordered the grooms to give them a good rubdown."

"Thank you. I'll just go up and change my shoes, and then I'll take a ramble through your glorious gardens. They will make a perfect setting for the wedding."

* * *

After dinner, her father invited her into his study for a drink and a talk. He handed her a glass of port. "I propose a toast to the lovely Countess of March."

"I'd rather you didn't call me that."

"Ah, do I detect a lingering resistance over the fact that you had an arranged marriage, Sarah?" He set his glass down. "I wanted a noble husband for you, my dear. When the opportunity presented itself to make you the Countess of March, and the future Duchess of Richmond, I would have been remiss as a dutiful father to pass up such a match for you. You've seen Goodwood, its treasures, and its thousand acres of property. Surely you cannot fault me for doing the right thing?"

Sarah stared down into her blood-red wine. Then she raised her lashes and met his gaze. "The match brought me a noble title and wealth, but it was unconscionable to marry me at thirteen. I was a child."

"But Charles was embarking on his Grand Tour, and you were sent back to London to your fancy finishing school. It was a marriage in name only."

"And will remain so."

Her father stared at her aghast.

Sarah set down her wine. "Good night, Father."

Why can't I sleep? Sarah had tossed and turned for hours. When she finally laid still, one disturbing thought after another chased each other. At last she had taken her long-planned revenge, and it should have given her a little satisfaction. But it hadn't. Not even a smidgen.

She told herself that it wasn't in her nature to be unkind, and that's what was troubling her. But it was more than that. Guilt was gnawing at her. *Why should I feel guilty? He deserved it!* But she knew that was only half true. The youthful brute she wed at The Hague deserved it, but not the man who returned to London after three years abroad. He had never said an unkind word to her.

Finally, she faced the truth about why her conscience was torturing her. *I purposely set about to deceive him. I deliberately used feminine wiles to lure him into losing his heart. Then I took my cruel revenge. It was more than unworthy of me, it was unconscionable.*

Sarah finally fell asleep, but the next night her troubling thoughts started the cycle of sleeplessness all over again. To add to her dilemma she realized that she missed Charles. She missed his company, missed his laughter, and missed his teasing. She felt forlorn in the empty bed. She missed his warmth and his tenderness. She admitted that Charles had banished her loneliness, which had now crept back with a vengeance. She realized there was nothing she could do about it. *I burned my bridges. I must suffer the consequences.*

Chapter Nine

"How the devil could I have been so naive?" Charles Lennox asked his reflection in the mirror. The man in the glass had no answers.

I am better off without her. All females are selfish jades that take pleasure in a man's pain. He didn't believe either of the thoughts he had just considered. *Sarah was so young and sweet, how could she possibly have been so deceitful and vindictive?*

Charles went down to breakfast. *Admit the truth. At eighteen I was a cruel and utterly selfish bastard. I deserved the things she said about me.* Sarah's words echoed in his thoughts: "I'm referring to the hurt you inflicted on me the day I was forced to marry you." *Didn't she realize that I was being forced to marry, just as she was?*

He scorned himself for the weak excuse. *Sarah was no more than a child. The hurt and humiliation we suffer as children are burns that never come out.*

Charles went into the library and opened his desk.

He took out the papers she had seen. He shook his head at the interpretation she had put on them.

Henry Grey spoke up. "Lady March came to the library at the crack of dawn."

Charles nodded. "Yes, I know."

"But did you know when we crossed to The Hague on the *Green Lion* that she was aboard? She is the young girl you soundly cursed for running into you."

"I don't even remember the incident."

"Lady Sarah did. She quoted your exact words."

"Remind me, Henry."

"You called her a *clumsy idiot girl*. When she apologized, you said, *Sorry be damned. You haven't the brains of a bloody baboon, barreling down the gangway like a loose cannon.*"

"No wonder she shrank in horror from me when I turned out to be the groom."

Charles took the bank draft from Sarah's godmother and put it in his pocket. "I have an errand to run. I should be back before Albemarle arrives. This partnership we've formed won't all be smooth sailing. It will likely take years before we achieve our goal. If William gets here before me, I'm sure Anne will be happy to entertain him."

On his way out, his sister hailed him, flourishing a note in her hand. "Charles, did you know that Sarah has gone to Caversham Park to help prepare for the wedding?"

"Yes, she informed me of her intentions."

"But I'm choosing the material for my wedding gown today. I wanted her advice."

"Well, she cannot be in two places at once. I'm sure

she is needed at Caversham for all the necessary wedding preparations." *She wants to make sure your wedding is happier than hers.*

"Even though Albemarle serves His Majesty, King George won't attend the wedding." Sarah and her mother were in Caversham's guest wing. They decided the bridal chamber would be on the third floor, and the other guests would be assigned bedchambers on the second.

"That is such a relief. King George travels with an entourage we could never comfortably accommodate."

"We will give the Prince and Princess of Wales the best bedchamber, and we can put the Duchess of Marlborough next to the royals."

"Do you think Her Grace will require a separate chamber for her granddaughter?"

"Lady Diana is very young. I think the duchess will want to keep an eye on her with all the bachelors who've been invited. We'll give the rose room to the mother of the bride. The Duke of Richmond is incapacitated. Anne's aunt Adelaide, the widowed Duchess of Shrewsbury, can have this adjoining chamber." Sarah marked her list.

"The bachelors can go in the smaller rooms on the east side. I know young Prince Frederick will be attending. Who are the others?" her mother asked.

"The Marquis of Blandford, of course. We can also expect Lord Hartington and his cousin, the Duke of Bedford." *Charles Lennox can stay with the bachelors. I don't know how I'll be able to face him.*

It took the rest of the day to rearrange furniture and

direct the maids to put fresh linen on all the beds that would be needed.

Sarah devoted the following day to planning the menu for the wedding banquet. Her days, busy with plans and preparations, went by quickly. Her nights, however, were interminable. When she was alone in her bedchamber, it seemed as if time stood still, and the lonely hours stretched before her endlessly.

Thoughts of Charles pervaded the darkness. She could still see the hurt in his eyes. Sarah regretted moving into Richmond House and living a lie. How much better it would have been to confront her husband with her grievances and have it all out in the open. Pretending to be attracted to him until she could take her revenge was wrong. *Trouble is, I was attracted to him—I wasn't pretending.*

Whenever she closed her eyes she could see his handsome, sun-bronzed face with its sculpted cheekbones. She visualized his burnished body and remembered how attractive his hands were. She lay in bed wishing his arms were around her.

Sarah finally admitted that what she felt for her husband was more than a physical attraction. She missed his laughter and his teasing. She missed the adoration in his warm brown eyes that made her feel special. She missed his companionship that had so effectively banished her loneliness.

What made it unbearable was the guilt she felt over her deception. *What's the use of having remorse unless I confess my sins and ask for forgiveness?*

* * *

"I refuse to take the money back. I have no intention of letting you and Albemarle take all the credit." The Duchess of Marlborough held up an imperious hand. "It's such a worthy cause—children are abandoned daily in London. It will take far more money than you've collected to establish a foundling hospital. Who else can help our cause?"

"King George, of course. We'll need a royal charter." Lennox smiled. "That's where Albemarle comes in. His persuasive powers will be worth their weight in gold."

"Your lovely wife must be impressed with your philanthropic endeavors. Give her my best regards, and I shall see you next at Caversham Park."

As Charles lay abed alone, night after night, sleep eluded him. *I cannot stop thinking about Sarah. No, the truth is that I don't want to stop thinking about her. I miss her. I want her beside me.* A dozen times a day, he thought he could hear the rustle of her gown or smell the scent of her perfume. *She is my wife. I can force her to return to me.* But Charles knew he would never do that. He was gravely at fault for what had transpired between them. *That first time we met, after I returned to London, I should have gone down on bended knee and begged her forgiveness for the brutally cruel things I said to her the day we were wed. Then we could have started with a clean slate.*

He threw the covers back and padded over to the adjoining door. He opened it and stepped into Sarah's room. He imagined he could feel her essence. His fingers brushed over the black pearls and touched the ruby earrings. *I tried to buy her love, but she couldn't be bribed.* He refused to put the jewels back in their lacquered chest. He was determined to leave them where she would find them if she returned. *She'll never return.*

The pain in his heart was unbearable.

Two days before the wedding, Charles made his way to the poverty-stricken St. Giles area. He often came here when he felt low in spirit. It never failed to make him appreciate how fortunate he was. He gazed up at the dilapidated tenements known as the Rookery. He walked the slum streets of White Chapel. He tossed coins to the dirty, ragged urchins who clustered about him begging. *My grandfather King Charles II wrote stories about walking these same streets, giving pennies to every child he saw. It is past time that something must be done. When Parliament opens, we must press for change.*

Charles promised himself that when he became the Duke of Richmond, and took his seat in the House of Lords, he would introduce bills and petitions to alleviate the conditions of those who lived out their lives in abject poverty. He would do it in memory of the grandfather he had never known.

When he arrived back at Richmond House, he was still feeling melancholy. He knew he would not feel restored until he had seen Sarah. He made up his mind in an instant. Charles saddled his horse and set out for Caversham Park.

* * *

"The only things left to do are the cake and the flowers, and we still have two days before the wedding." Sarah handed the list to her mother.

"I truly appreciate all your help, my dear. It's been lovely having you at home."

"It was my pleasure, Mother. The cake should be baked today and decorated tomorrow. And we should definitely consult Father about the flowers. He's the expert."

Sarah conferred with the head cook, and they decided on the number of tiers. Tomorrow they would put on the almond paste and the white icing.

When Sarah left the kitchen, an idea was beginning to form in her head. She didn't want the animosity between her and Charles to spoil Anne's wedding. *When a girl marries, it should be one of the happiest days of her life. I have time to go up to London and apologize to Charles for my deceit and vindictive behavior.*

Sarah went to the stables and asked the grooms to ready the carriage. Then she went upstairs to change into a traveling dress and pack an overnight bag.

An hour later she climbed into the coach, assuring herself she was doing the right thing. She settled back against the squabs as the horses picked up speed on Caversham's long driveway. A rider on horseback passed them, and it took a minute for Sarah to realize who it was.

"Stop the carriage!" she cried, and hammered on the panel behind the driver.

Charles saw the coach coming toward him as he galloped down the drive. As it passed him, he caught a glimpse of its female passenger and knew it was Sarah.

He turned his horse about, and when he saw that the carriage was slowing, he dismounted.

He reached out his hand and opened the door. "Sarah. I have to talk to you." He swung up into the carriage and sat down facing her. He saw how pale she was and noticed the mauve shadows beneath her lovely eyes. *My God, she knew I'd be coming for the wedding and tried to flee because she couldn't bear the sight of me.*

"With all my heart, I wish I could undo the terrible things I said to you that day in The Hague when we were married. I'm so sorry for the cruel words I used."

"Charles, you, too, were being forced to marry. I was too young to understand."

"When I returned to London and saw you for the first time, I was stunned by your beauty. When I learned you were my wife, I couldn't believe my good fortune. Instead of begging you to forgive the brutal words I had flung at you, and the unconscionable thing my father did, I arrogantly believed I could make you fall in love with me."

"Charles, I've been guilt ridden over the way I deceived you. I led you on purposely and plotted my revenge."

He reached out and took her hands. "Sarah, I don't want you to feel guilty. Look what it's doing to you. I can't bear to see the dark shadows beneath your eyes and know that I'm responsible for your unhappiness. The thought that you were fleeing from me fills me with despair."

"Charles, I wasn't fleeing from you. I was coming to London to see you."

"Really?" His brow cleared as a glimmer of hope began to dawn.

"I need you to forgive me for hurting you."

"Sarah, there's nothing to forgive. I love you. I don't want to live without you. Can we begin all over again?"

"Oh, Charles, that's exactly what I want, too."

He wanted to take her in his arms and crush her to him. *Don't jump on her, you fool. You'll spoil everything. Sarah is delicate. You must do things right this time.* He raised her hand to his lips and kissed it gently.

"I don't want to leave, but I have to go and get Anne. When I come back, we'll talk. There is so much I have to tell you, so much I want to share with you."

"Of course you have to go. The wedding is the day after tomorrow. It will be here before you know it. You take the carriage back to London, and I'll stable your horse." She smiled into his eyes. "Charles, I'm so glad you came."

"Wilt thou have this man to thy wedded husband? Wilt thou obey him, and serve him, love, honor, and keep him, in sickness and in health; and forsaking all other, keep thee only unto him, so long as ye both shall live?"

"I will," Anne answered solemnly.

Sarah was following every word of the marriage ceremony. *I must have said these vows and made all these same promises to Charles. I don't remember saying the words.*

She was acutely aware of her husband's compelling presence and guessed that he, too, was thinking of their own wedding.

"Who giveth this woman to be married to this man?"

Charles stepped forward. "I do." He placed his sister's hand in William's, then he stood beside Sarah while the bride and groom pledged their troth.

When the formal ceremony was over, and everyone was busy congratulating the newly wed couple, Charles clasped Sarah's hand and drew her away from the others. More than anything in the world they wanted to be alone.

They slipped from the house and ran across the wide lawn, past the formal gardens with their rectangles of blazing flowers and neat borders. With Sarah now leading the way, they skirted the fishpond with its ornamental fountain as well as the circular rose garden. They passed through a row of tall yews and didn't stop until they reached the wild flower garden, where a natural stream wound its way through the middle and tumbled over a small waterfall.

Breathless and laughing, they stretched out beneath a hawthorn tree, amid buttercups and Queen Anne's lace dancing on the summer breeze.

"The bride was beautiful."

Charles knelt before her. "To me, you were the bride."

"I followed the words of the ceremony closely."

"I never proposed to you . . . I'd like to do it now. Sarah, will you be my wife?"

She smiled into his dark eyes. "Yes, I will."

He reached into his pocket and pulled out a wide gold wedding band. He took hold of her hand and pledged his vows. "I, Charles, take thee Sarah, to my wedded wife, to have and to hold from this day forward, for better for worse, for richer for poorer, in sickness and in health, to love and to cherish, till death us do part, and thereto I plight thee my troth." He slid the ring onto her finger.

"Do you promise to keep me warm, and to make me laugh, and to keep me from ever being lonely again?"

"I do," he swore solemnly.

"Then you may kiss the bride."

Charles drew her into his arms and sealed the promises he'd made with a kiss. Then they lay together amid the wildflowers, whispering and sharing all their secrets, hopes, and dreams.

"So that's why you sold the horses. It wasn't to pay off gambling debts." She traced his cheekbone with her finger. "When we were at Goodwood, I opened your cabinet and looked at all the poignant drawings. In my heart, I knew you were the artist."

It was hours before they joined the other guests, and they were unmercifully teased about wanting to be alone and acting like newlyweds when they were a long-married couple.

They did their duty by mingling with family and friends and thanking them for coming to Caversham.

The Dowager Duchess of Marlborough took Sarah aside. "I am delighted that you invited both Prince Frederick and the Duke of Bedford. Either one would be a worthy match for Lady Diana. My granddaughter is a treasure in herself, besides what I shall give her."

"Diana is indeed an exceptional young lady," Sarah said diplomatically.

"And speaking of monetary matters, that impertinent devil you married tried to return the money I donated to build that infernal foundling hospital."

I've only just learned of his plans. "Ah, that was my suggestion, Your Grace. I didn't want him to take advantage of you."

The old dragon threw back her head and laughed. "As if any man could!"

With intimate glances and stolen touches, Sarah and Charles managed to endure the banquet, the toasts, the speeches, and the remaining wedding celebrations. Though they ached with longing, they managed to restrain themselves from leaving until the bride and groom went upstairs. Most of the guests were well aware of their impatience. The sexual sparks between Charles and Sarah heated the air.

While Anne and William were subjected to a traditional bedding, where everyone trooped into the bridal chamber making lewd suggestions and laughing at their own outrageous jokes, Charles and Sarah sought her bedchamber.

He carried her over the threshold and locked the door. For the next two hours Charles made tender love to his wife. After that, they threw all caution to the wind and indulged in wild, passionate lovemaking.

He gathered her against his heart and rolled with her until he was in the dominant position. "Sweetheart, I will devote the rest of my days to making you happy."

She reached up and entwined her arms about his neck. "I love you, Charles. Promise you will always love me as much as you do tonight?"

"No, Sarah. Tomorrow I will love you even more."

How to Seduce a Wife

KATE PEARCE

Chapter One

London, 1816

"That will be all, Parsons, thank you."

Nicholas March, the eighth Earl of Stortford, nodded at his valet and retied the sash of his brown silk dressing gown. He waited until Parsons had left the room and then strolled across to the internal door that connected his bedroom to the dressing area between him and his wife.

Light shone under Louisa's closed door, and he smiled. It wasn't that late. He'd even remembered to send word to his wife to ask her if it would be convenient for him to visit. He was punctilious like that, tried to respect Louisa in ways his father had never done with his mother. She would have no cause to complain about his boorish manners or his drunken outbursts. No fears that he would openly demean her in public.

His marriage was going to be a pattern card of respectability. Nicholas found himself sighing as he tapped on the door. It was harder than he had imagined to abandon his rakish bachelor ways and treat his wife as a lady should be treated: with respect, gentleness, and forbearance—especially in the marital bed. He knocked again. "My lady?"

There was no answer, and he frowned and tried the door handle. It opened easily and he stepped inside the room. The bed was empty, the tasteful silver and blue drapes he'd chosen for his new bride drawn back, the satin coverlet undisturbed. Nicholas looked around the large cozy space. His wife of almost one year sat curled up in a chair by the fireside, her bare feet tucked under her and her brown hair neatly braided for bed. A pair of spectacles balanced on the narrow bridge of her nose as she read intently from a leather-bound book.

She wasn't beautiful. Nicholas hadn't chosen her for her looks, but she had a lovely smile and warm brown eyes the color of toffee. He'd been attracted by her quiet demeanor, her obvious intelligence, and, to be perfectly frank, the size of her dowry. Her family was on the up, her father one of the new industrialists willing to pay to hoist his daughter even higher.

He'd met Louisa at one of his older sister's interminable parties, and she'd made no effort to capture his interest. That alone had guaranteed his. It hadn't taken him long to persuade her to marry him with both families' avid support.

She still hadn't noticed him. He cleared his throat. "My lady?"

She held up one finger as if he were a servant or a child interrupting her, and didn't look up. Nicholas moved closer until his shadow blocked the candlelight. With a martyred sigh, Louisa raised her gaze to his face. He swept her a bow.

"Am I interrupting?"

She took her spectacles off and regarded him seriously for a long moment. "Yes, you are." She gestured at the book she held. "Couldn't you see that I was reading?"

For a moment Nicholas stiffened. She'd known he was coming. Why wasn't she in bed waiting for him like a good wife should be? His ready sense of humor resurfaced, and he found himself smiling at his own conceit.

"I'm sorry, my dear. I thought you were expecting me."

She glanced at the clock and jumped. "Oh, my goodness! You did say you would be visiting my bed this evening, didn't you."

Nicholas's good humor faltered again. "You don't sound very pleased about that."

She bit her lip and slowly shut the book with a longing look. "It's just that this novel I'm reading is so exciting. The pirate king has taken the heroine on his ship and is threatening to ravish her if she doesn't reveal the secrets of her family's hidden treasure." She sighed and hugged the book to her bosom. "It was so diverting, I could hardly put it down."

"It sounds like the sort of book that should be put down the drain." He realized he sounded quite caustic. Good Lord, was he jealous of a book?

"It's a love story."

He raised an eyebrow. "Exactly. Who reads such unrealistic drivel?"

She raised her chin at him. "I do, and I enjoy such books *excessively*."

"So I can see." He simply looked at her. A flush rose on her cheeks.

"I'm sorry. I'll get into bed immediately."

He waited as Louisa rose to her feet and placed the book on the small table beside her chair. She walked across to the bed with all the enthusiasm of a child going off to receive a beating. Nicholas stared after her. Was he really so unwelcome?

"I can leave if you are tired."

She turned to look at him as she shrugged out of her dressing gown and summoned a wan smile. "No, that's all right. You are here now; you might as well get on with it."

He strolled toward her, aware of the thrust of her nipples beneath her simple white nightgown. "If it won't inconvenience you too greatly."

She climbed onto the bed, giving him a glimpse of long pale legs and the rounded curves of her buttocks. "I know my duty, my lord."

He sat on the edge of the bed until she was completely under the bedclothes. He blew out the candles around the bed and stripped off his dressing gown. Despite his reservations, his cock was erect and also ready to do *its* duty. With a sigh, he carefully folded back her nightgown and fitted himself between her thighs.

She didn't protest his presence, but she didn't seem to welcome him, either. With sudden resolve, he grabbed her hands and linked them behind his neck. She could at least hold him while he made love to her, make him feel like more than a beast ravishing an innocent.

Her cold fingers settled against his skin, and he nudged at the entrance to her sex with his cock. She wasn't wet for him. Did ladies ever get wet with desire? Was that why his father had strayed? He shoved that thought out of his head as he eased his aching cock inside her tight passage. Her fingernails dug into his flesh, and he tried to move more slowly. Was he hurting her? If he asked, he knew she would deny it.

With exquisite care he began to move, tried to keep his weight off her to minimize the effect of his thrusts and save her from his more aggressive instincts. He sensed her move her head to one side and opened his eyes. She was staring over at the fireplace where her book lay. He went still.

"Louisa, am I boring you?"

Her gaze flew back to his and he saw it there, saw the truth. "No, my lord, I . . ."

He thrust himself deep twice and came fast, the sensation almost as unsatisfying as his own hand. He stayed where he was, braced over her, and waited until she looked at him again.

"Perhaps I should apologize again for distracting you from your book. It is obviously far more important than I am."

He probably sounded petulant, but her inattention had wounded his manly pride. She bit down on her lip and tried to shake her head.

"I'm sorry, my lord."

With a groan, he eased out of her but he didn't leave the bed. "Why is the book more interesting than I am?" He gestured at the marble-covered tome. "Would you prefer the hero of your ridiculous novel to be here in your bed rather than your legal husband?"

She pushed down her nightgown and sat up, her brown eyes glinting with tears. "Perhaps I would. At least he seems to enjoy ravishing the heroine!"

Nicholas stared at her for a long moment. "You wish to be ravished?"

"I wish . . ." She sighed and looked down at her clenched hands. "I expected . . ."

"What?" He was determined to have this out now, to have perhaps, the first honest conversation of his married life. "You can tell me."

She hunched her shoulder at him. "My mother told me I was not to bother you with my feelings or thoughts. She said that men are not interested in such matters."

"*I* am interested."

"Are you sure?"

"Indeed. Otherwise why else would I still be sitting here asking why you prefer the hero of a gothic novel to a real live man in your bed?"

"My mother also said that men's feelings are often hurt if a woman criticizes them."

"That is true, but I am made of sterner stuff. I am quite willing to hear your thoughts on this matter." He found he was glaring at her, but she didn't shrink away. "We are bound together for life; don't you think that a little sincere communication between us might be a good thing?"

"I suppose so."

"Well?"

She peeked at him from under her long eyelashes. "Are you *sure* that you won't get angry?"

He sketched a cross over his chest. "I swear it. Now tell me what the problem is."

"I thought that marriage would be more . . . exciting."

"I do not excite you?"

"You are all that a gentleman should be. You are kind and pleasant and good natured, but . . ."

"But what?"

She studied him dubiously. "You *sound* as if you are getting annoyed. Perhaps I should stop."

He set his jaw and forced a smile. "No, please go on."

"I thought, I *hoped,* that when we were alone together we would become closer and more intimate."

"You wish me to spend more time with you?" She nodded. "I can do that. I assumed that like most ladies of my acquaintance you wouldn't want me around interfering with your social life."

"It's not just that." She wrapped her arms around her drawn-up knees and leaned back against the headboard, her long braid hung over her right shoulder. She smoothed the sheets with one hand, her slight northern accent more apparent than usual. "After the way you kissed me during our courtship I thought that being bedded by you would be wonderful."

For a second he struggled to find words. He was a renowned lover! Women fought over the right to share his bed or to be seen in his company. He opened his mouth and then shut it again, and finally forced out: "I beg your pardon?"

Louisa sighed. "I knew you wouldn't want to hear that. My mother was right. Men are definitely more fragile than women."

"What exactly were you expecting to happen in our marital bed, my lady?"

"I expected pleasure." She raised her head and met his heated gaze. "Was I wrong to expect that?"

"And how am I supposed to give you pleasure when all your attention is fixed on that damned book?"

"That is hardly fair. I only started reading the book

tonight. I hoped it would help ready me for your appearance."

"So that you could imagine the pirate hero in my place?"

"Perhaps."

He held her gaze, his own frosty. "Am I so inadequate as a lover, then, ma'am?"

She regarded him seriously. "I don't know. Are you?"

He got off the bed and retrieved his dressing gown, took his time putting it on and tying the sash. "Perhaps I was trying to be considerate, ma'am. Perhaps I assumed that as a young untried lady you would appreciate my *restraint*."

She swallowed hard and then lifted her chin at him. "If you are suggesting it is my fault, I accept that. I do not have the experience you do, that is true. I do not know how to please a man."

He stared at her and then bowed. "Good night, ma'am. I'll leave you to your pirate."

She nodded back at him, her back as straight as the queen's and her expression just as serene. "I knew you'd react like this. My mother was right."

He headed for the door. "And how nice for you that your mother is always right. It must be such a great comfort."

"No." He turned around and saw her hastily wiping away a tear "It isn't. Good night, my lord."

Nicholas placed his palm on the dressing room door and stared at the ornately carved panel. He was acting like a fool, running away like a cockerel that had lost a fight. Louisa was his wife. He owed it to both of them to try to resolve this issue. With a soft curse he turned back, only to see his wife resettle herself in bed with the damned book.

He wrenched open the door and allowed it to slam shut behind him. He hoped it made her jump and lose her place.

Louisa winced as the door shut with a definite bang. She should never have started that conversation. Apparently, her mother was right about men being fragile little flowers where matters of their sexual prowess were concerned. Nicholas was furious with her. But at least he'd shown her some emotion other than his usual smiling politeness. Although she'd been slightly afraid, she'd almost enjoyed the experience. She'd half-hoped that he would take her back into his arms and make love to her with all the dash and daring of the pirate hero.

But it was not to be. Louisa put her book down and pulled up the sheets. Between her thighs she was both sore and wet from Nicholas's five-minute possession of her body. She curled up into a ball. Before their marriage she'd heard so many erotic rumors about him that the prospect of being his wife had half-terrified her. She hadn't expected to be reduced to reading gothic romance novels simply to endure his regular weekly appearances in her bed.

There had to be something more . . . Louisa blinked away a few tears and stared up at the silver and blue canopy above her bed. Would he stay away from her now for good, or would he display the good sense she knew he had and think about what she'd said and how to resolve it? One never knew with a man, particularly a husband. They were peculiar creatures, but she'd hoped for so much more with Nicholas.

When she'd met him, he'd seemed like the embodiment of all her dreams and longings, and he'd liked her back. Or so she had thought until they were married and he treated her with all the warm politeness of a distant acquaintance. She knew he'd married her for her money, she wasn't that naive, but she'd also thought there had been something between them . . .

Maybe Nicholas was right and she was too inexperienced to know what she wanted after all.

With a determined sigh, Louisa closed her eyes. At least she'd told him what was wrong. How he reacted to her comments was now up to him. If he chose to ignore her pleas, what would he do next? Send her away to the countryside and set up a mistress in Town?

Louisa clutched at the sheets and whispered a prayer. Surely he wouldn't go that far. He had always treated her with the greatest of respect both in public and in private. She swallowed down a sudden urge to cry. Perhaps she was naive but she didn't want to be respected in bed. She wanted to be loved . . .

Chapter Two

With extreme trepidation, Louisa opened the door to the breakfast parlor. It was only eight in the morning, and she hoped to catch her husband before he went about his daily business. Not that she knew quite what he did all day, only that he was rarely home, leaving her to her own devices. The smell of coffee, sausages, and toast assailed her nostrils, and her stomach growled.

Louisa slapped a hand over her stomach and felt herself start to blush. At the table, the newspaper twitched to one side to reveal her husband's startled face. Nicholas rose to his feet and bowed. He was dressed in a brown coat, buckskin breeches, and top boots as if he intended to go riding. "Good morning, my dear."

"Good morning, my lord."

Before he could come around the table to aid her, she slipped into a chair opposite him and sat down with an audible thump. The solitary footman poured her some tea and provided her with her usual plate of toast and marmalade. She glanced at the back of the newspaper, but there was no further sign of Nicholas.

Louisa nibbled her toast and sipped her tea; the sounds loud in the quiet of the sunny breakfast room. Eventually, she sighed so hard that the pages of the *Times* buckled inward. A moment later, Nicholas's face appeared.

"Is there something you wish to discuss with me, my lady?"

Despite the fact that he was smiling, there was none of the genial warmth that normally filled his blue eyes when he spoke to her. She swallowed hard and only succeeded in choking on her toast. By the time she finished coughing, Nicholas had dismissed the footman and put down his paper.

"I wish to apologize, my lord."

He raised an eyebrow. "For what?"

She made a helpless gesture. "I should never have spoken to you so openly. My mother *insisted* that I should *never* disagree with you. Apparently men don't like their wives to think for themselves or have an opinion about *anything,* let alone the delicate topic of marital relations."

A smile flickered at the corner of his generous mouth. "Indeed."

She tried to look apologetic. "If we could just go back to the way things were? I promise I'll keep my immodest opinions to myself and simply agree with everything you say."

He frowned. "But I don't think I'd like that at all."

"Are you sure? Most men *seem* to like it, although in my opinion, if that is all they require in a wife, they might as well purchase a parrot."

A dimple appeared on Nicholas's cheek, and Louisa

clapped a hand over her mouth. "Oh, I'm so sorry and after I promised to keep quiet."

He regarded her seriously. "I can't see how we can go back to where we were, and, to be honest, would you want to? If I can counter your honesty with some of my own, I confess I haven't exactly looked forward to sharing your bed."

"Oh." Louisa folded her napkin and looked down at the toast crumbs scattered over the pristine white linen tablecloth. She jumped as Nicholas reached across the table and grasped her hand.

"Louisa, we can do better than this, don't you think?"

"I'm not sure, my lord. What exactly do you require me to do?"

"To start with, you can stop pretending you no longer have an opinion of your own. I'm quite sure you do." He hesitated. "I'm not that much of an ogre am I?"

She looked up at him then. "No, not at all, you have always treated me with respect and kindness and . . ."

He squeezed her hand. "And I always will, but, perhaps I have been at fault."

She blinked at him. Her father had never uttered those words to her mother, of that she was certain. "*You* have been at fault?"

His charming smile flittered across his face. "Don't sound so surprised. I've been thinking about what you said to me last night."

"Really?"

"Indeed." He released her and sat back, his other hand now curved around his coffee cup. "Mayhap I have neglected you after all."

Louisa went still. What had she roused with her impudent questioning? Her mother had always said her quick tongue would be her downfall.

"In truth, you have offered me an interesting challenge. How *should* a man seduce his own wife?"

"I have no idea, sir."

His gaze was full of sensual intent, and he patted her hand. "Perhaps I should start by reading that gothic novel you were so enamored of. Do you have it with you?"

Color heated her cheeks, and she snatched her hand back. "I scarcely think you would enjoy it, sir, or that I would really wish to be manhandled in such a rough and ungentlemanly way."

"Would you not? Yet you seemed quite enthused by the novel."

Louisa bit down on her lip. "I'm not sure what you mean, my lord."

He leaned forward, his elbow propped on the table, his chin resting in his hand. "Did the story make you feel . . . restless and excited?"

"It certainly increased the rate of my heartbeat, sir, and I confess that I felt a little strange and overheated after reading it."

"That's good."

"But what does that have to do with what passes between us in bed?"

His smile was slow and raised all her feminine suspicions. "Therein lies the problem."

"I do not understand you, sir."

He rose to his feet. "You will."

"You intend to make me feel those heated emotions for, for you?"

He bowed. "Why not? I'm certain I can inspire the same feelings in you."

Unaccustomed annoyance crowded her chest. "I do not wish to know about your previous conquests or experience, sir. And I doubt that you can inspire such insipid devotion in me."

"There's nothing insipid about it, my dear." He smiled again. "You'll just have to trust that I am man enough for the challenge, won't you?"

Louisa got to her feet, too. "What challenge?"

"How to seduce a wife." He bowed low. "I believe I'm quite looking forward to it."

"And what are the stakes, sir? What do you win?"

He went still and stared down at her. "A wife who doesn't have to read gothic novels to experience the pleasures of love? A willing bed partner? Surely, I cannot lose."

Before she could answer he exited the breakfast room, leaving her standing there clutching a hand to her chest. A sudden qualm assailed her. What if she proved incapable of being seduced? She prided herself on her calm good sense, not her ability to drive a man to his knees with lust. What if she didn't have the capability to enjoy passion?

She gazed after her husband and then sank back down into her seat. Her plans for a quiet morning at home were overset by the strength of the emotions Nicholas aroused in her. She had to talk to someone about this most delicate of matters, and who better than her husband's oh-so-sophisticated sister, April?

Louisa finished off her tea and rose to her feet. She needed help, and she wasn't afraid to ask for it. She paused at the bottom of the stairs as the clock struck the half hour. April *was* part of the family; Nicholas could hardly object to Louisa consulting her, could he? She grimaced as she mounted the stairs. Well, perhaps he could, but there was no alternative. She scarcely knew another soul in Town and she was not going to ask her mother about anything ever again.

Nicholas handed his hat and gloves to the doorman at his club and went inside. At such an early hour, there were very few gentlemen in the smoky oak-paneled rooms, so he took possession of the best seat by the roaring fire. Despite the cold, he'd enjoyed his ride. It had afforded him the opportunity to think about his wife and how best to initiate her into the joys of marital intercourse.

He found himself smiling as he pictured her face at the breakfast table that morning, her horror that her uninhibited discussion about his failings as a husband had inspired him to seduce her. He stared into the flames. But how to approach such a complex matter? How could he help her understand her sexuality without frightening her?

"Good morning, Lord Stortford."

Nicholas smiled up at one of his oldest friends. "Good morning, Captain Gray. Will you join me for a glass of brandy or something warmer?"

"Mulled wine would be welcome on a day like this." Captain Gray took the seat opposite Nicholas and rubbed his hands together. "I walked up from my lodgings, and it was far colder than I anticipated."

Nicholas beckoned to a waiter and gave him the

captain's order. "And that from a man who has sailed the seven seas, and survived, means it must be cold."

Captain Gray smiled. "Or I've become soft, chained to a desk since the war ended. That is another distinct possibility." He smoothed a hand over his windblown blond hair that was tied back in an old-fashioned queue. "What are you doing out and about so early?"

Nicholas shrugged. "I took my new horse out for a gallop."

"Despite the cold?" Captain Gray looked impressed. "You've never struck me as an early riser, but perhaps marriage has reformed you."

"In truth, thoughts of my wife did propel me out of my front door this morning before I'd really noticed the foulness of the weather."

"Don't tell me you've taken to battling over the breakfast table."

Nicholas sighed. "Not exactly."

Captain Gray lowered his voice. "I say, Nick, is everything all right?"

"Everything is fine, David, it's just that . . ."

"Marriage is harder than you thought it would be."

"That is certainly part of it." Nicholas frowned. "Although how you would know that, I have no notion."

"Just because I'm not married doesn't mean I haven't excellent powers of observation and decided opinions as to the wedded state."

"Really."

David shrugged. "And I'm quite willing to listen."

"I'm sure you are." Nicholas regarded David warily. "I'm not sure if I'm willing to indulge you."

"You don't have to." David crossed one booted foot

over the other and settled more comfortably into the chair. "But I am one of your oldest friends, and I promise I won't spread any gossip."

"I know that." Nicholas kept quiet as the waiter offered David a tall glass of steaming mulled wine and refilled Nicholas's coffee cup. "It's just that the situation is a little complicated."

David blew on the ruby-colored wine and then sipped it. The scent of cinnamon and cloves drifted across to Nicholas. "I like your wife. She seems intelligent and kind."

"She is."

"In fact, I was quite surprised you chose her."

Nicholas stiffened. "What did you expect me to choose? A flashy debutante with no money and a big chest?"

David chuckled. "Not at all. After your father's appalling example, I knew you'd be careful."

"My father was no example to me."

"Yet, there was a time when you emulated him."

"Until I grew old enough to know better and realize that I had no desire to turn into an elderly pox-ridden lothario."

There was a short silence as David seemed to reflect on Nicholas's outburst.

"What made you change your mind about him?"

Nicholas forced a smile. "When I saw how he treated my mother, and how he forced her to deal publicly with his mistresses and his bastards."

"Ah."

"What does that mean? And what does this have to do with your interest in my choice of a wife?"

David sat forward, his glass cradled in his hands.

"Because I now understand why you chose her. She doesn't come from an aristocratic family with no morals, and that makes her more attractive to you."

"That's true, but . . ."

"Which means that you hope she'll remain as faithful to you as you intend to remain to her."

"I've never told you that."

"But it's true, isn't it? You've been married for almost a year now, and I've heard no rumors of you frequenting any brothels, setting up a mistress, or enjoying yourself at Madame Helene's."

"Is there something wrong with a man wanting to keep his marriage vows?"

David's eyebrows rose. "Nothing at all. There's no need to sound so belligerent. It's actually quite refreshing."

"I don't intend to make a fool out of my wife. I intend to treat her with respect."

"And I salute you for that." David raised his glass and drank slowly. "But I'm sure such resolution brings its own problems."

"Why would you say that?"

"Nick, I've known you since Harrow; you like sex, you like it a lot."

"So?"

"So, going from your rakish ways to one woman and one woman alone must have provided you with some interesting challenges."

Nicholas sat back in his chair and studied his old friend. He had the perfect opportunity to ask for advice from one of the few men he'd ever trusted, but at what price? Only his pride and he wasn't that big a fool. "I find myself in a bit of a quandary."

"In what way?"

Nicholas glanced around the room and leaned closer to David. "My wife is quite innocent."

"I should imagine she is." David nodded as if Nicholas made perfect sense. "Does she find you a little 'overwhelming'?"

"She finds me boring enough that she'd rather read a gothic romance novel than entertain me in her bed."

David simply stared at him, a peculiar expression on his face. "Boring? You? One of the most sexually experienced men I've ever met?"

"Apparently, I fail to measure up to the exacting standards of the pirate hero from the gothic novel she is currently reading."

David started to laugh, his sea-blue eyes crinkling at the corners. "I don't believe it."

"It's the truth. I think my manly pride has been hurt."

"I should say it has." David studied him. "But what have you done, or not done, to make her feel like that?"

Nicholas shifted in his seat. "I've tried to treat her with respect and restraint, as I *assumed* one would treat the lady one has married."

"Ah."

Nicholas glowered at David. "Don't say 'ah' again. It's infuriating."

"You assume that married ladies wish to be set on a shelf like a porcelain figurine and treated delicately, the way your father should've treated your mother. Am I right?"

Nicholas managed a nod.

"Women are not meant to be divided into categories,

Nick. Wives can enjoy sex as well as mistresses." David sat back and placed his glass on the table beside him.

Nicholas shoved a hand through his hair. "I've already worked that out for myself. Now I just have to think of a way to fix it."

"Fix what?"

Nicholas looked at David with a quelling stare. "Never you mind. You've merely confirmed my own decisions."

"That's good to know." David nodded. "So you'll be taking her to Madame Helene's then."

Nicholas stood and glared down at his infuriating friend. "Of course I will."

David got up as well. "I'm sure you'll find plenty of pirate heroes there."

"Indeed." Nicholas kept his face as blank as possible as he considered David's outrageous suggestion. Madame Helene's House of Pleasure catered to the sexual fantasies of the rich. He'd frequented her premises during his wilder days and had come to consider Madame Helene a friend. He wasn't sure if his membership was still current. "Thanks for the advice, Captain Gray. Perhaps I'll see you at Madame's?"

David bowed. "I'll keep an eye out for you."

Nicholas nodded again and left, his thoughts in turmoil. David had proved as helpful as ever, and his suggestion of Madame Helene's was inspired. Now all Nicholas had to do was go and visit Madame and find out if she would let him return to her exclusive establishment in Mayfair—with his far too innocent yet sexually frustrated wife.

Chapter Three

"So there I was, darling, stranded in the middle of the ballroom with that obnoxious little toad, Lord Monkfish, on his knees in front of me searching for his false teeth!"

Louisa smiled obediently at Lady April Fotherskill and glanced at the ornate gold clock on the marble mantelpiece. She'd been at her sister-in-law's house for over an hour, and she still hadn't managed a complete sentence. April stopped smiling and stared at her.

"You seem a little distracted today, Louisa. Is there something wrong?"

Louisa took a deep breath. "Well, not exactly, wrong, but . . ."

"Is it my brother? Has he been behaving himself?" April's handkerchief fluttered in front of her prettily flushed oval face. "Nicholas promised me that he intended to behave perfectly toward you, not like Papa treated poor, dear Mama . . ."

"Nicholas always treats me with great respect, April. It's not that, it's just . . ."

"Are you breeding? Oh, my word, that would be exciting news! Or have you come to ask me if you are? I do have two children of my own."

In desperation, Louisa gripped her hands tightly together on her lap. "No, I'm not breeding, at least I don't think I am. I did want to ask you about something, though. Something quite personal."

April's blue eyes, which were just like Nicholas's, met Louisa's. Beneath her artless chatter, Louisa had discovered April was no fool and that her affection for her younger brother ran deep and true.

"Is something wrong with Nicholas?"

"No, he's in perfect health. Please don't worry." Louisa groaned. "For someone who prides herself on her intelligence, I'm not making much sense, am I?"

"Not really." April leaned forward to pat Louisa's knee. "Tell me what the problem is. I promise I won't interrupt this time."

Louisa cleared her throat. All at once her idea of confiding in April seemed ludicrous. She wasn't sure how to approach such a delicate subject without implicating her husband. She had wit enough to realize that Nicholas might not appreciate his older sister being told he was inadequate in bed.

She managed an uncertain smile. "I wondered whether you would mind me asking you something about married life."

"Not at all! We're like sisters, aren't we?" April rose to her feet and linked her arm through Louisa's. "Let's go through into my bedchamber where we can have a comfortable coze without fear of being interrupted."

After another anxious glance at the clock, Louisa allowed herself to be drawn away into April's fragrant boudoir. The lemon-and-silver-colored walls and bed coverings seemed a trifle bright to Louisa, and the amount of lace and ruffles that adorned every surface made her a little claustrophobic. She much preferred her own blue bedchamber, which Nicholas had decorated for her as a surprise on their marriage.

She studied April's sympathetic face. She'd grown so used to asking April for advice that she hadn't thought the matter through properly. How could she have imagined it possible to discuss such an intimate subject as her marital woes with her husband's sister? Now she'd have to think of something that didn't involve Nicholas at all.

But perhaps there was some more general information she could acquire . . .

"Well?" April inquired brightly as she sat next to Louisa on a small, yellow-striped chaise longue.

"It's just that, I haven't been married for very long and I wondered . . ." Louisa stopped talking and gazed at April, who made an encouraging gesture. "I wondered whether other women enjoy the more 'physical' side of marriage." She finished in a rush and felt her cheeks heat up.

"Oh, my dear, there is nothing to worry about," April said and patted her hand. "It is perfectly normal for you to enjoy that side of things, don't let anyone, particularly your mother, tell you any different. If you are lucky enough to have married a man like Nicholas, who had 'quite' a reputation as a young man, then why shouldn't you enjoy the benefit of his experience?"

"That's not quite . . ."

"I have to tell you, that despite his outward appearance, my Gilbert is a most satisfying companion between the sheets. That man knows passion and I'm a lucky woman because of it."

Louisa tried to picture the rather portly Lord Gilbert Fotherskill cavorting in bed and found herself wanting to giggle. April hugged her. "You see? There is nothing to worry about, just consider yourself lucky and pity other wives whose husbands don't know their way around a woman's body and couldn't care less anyway." She kissed Louisa's cheek. "And it is also normal if your husband wishes to make love with you more than once a night and actually spends the whole night in your bed."

"Really?" Louisa tried to imagine Nicholas sleeping with her all night long, and liked the idea, especially if he held her close.

The clock struck eleven and Louisa leaped to her feet. "I'm so sorry; I have to go, April. My mother is expecting me."

April made a face. "She is always expecting you."

Louisa forced a smile. "And I am always willing to indulge her. There aren't many people here in Town she is comfortable with."

"She is a bit of a fish out of water, isn't she?" April got up, too. "I'm sorry you have to leave, but I do understand. My mother commands all my attention when she comes up to London as well."

Louisa put on her bonnet. "I think she'd prefer to go back to Cheshire for good, but unfortunately, my father's business interests keep him here for the majority of the year. She is too unsure of herself to make friends easily, and is quite terrified of you and Nicholas."

"Terrified?"

"She sees you as 'Quality' and thus too far above

her to be spoken to, and nothing I say or do can change that." Louisa sighed. "Sometimes I'm sure she feels the same way about me, as if I'm a stranger to her, with my boarding school education and exacting standards."

"I apologize, Louisa," April murmured. "It was unkind of me to comment about your mother's need for you in any way. She has always been very polite to me."

"Thank you. And thank you for the tea and the advice." Louisa kissed April's cheek and pulled on her gloves. Her mother would worry if she was late, and that would make Louisa feel inadequate again. She wasn't the daughter her mother wanted at all, with her aristocratic husband and her enlightened views. That had been all her father's doing. He'd wanted the finest cachet that his money could buy his daughter—a title—and he reveled in it.

Louisa left April's town house and stepped into the carriage that Nicholas had bought especially for her use. Her mother hadn't seemed to care about her advancement, had, in fact, spent many hours telling Louisa not to get above herself and to be a meek and obedient wife. She stared out the window. And where had that got her? Into a situation where she'd had to confront her husband about his apparent lack of desire for her and take refuge in a work of fiction.

With a sigh, Louisa sat back and waited for the carriage to arrive in unfashionable Hans Town, where her mother still preferred to live. Despite her concerns, Louisa couldn't help wondering what Nicholas planned to do to seduce her. He'd proven most efficient in his courtship of her, and she guessed he would pursue this new challenge just as adroitly. Thinking of Nicholas was a far more pleasurable subject than her mother's scolding and might help her through yet another dreary afternoon.

Nicholas paused at the entrance to the grand scarlet and gold salon on the first floor of Madame Helene's House of Pleasure. A few guests were scattered around the vast space, but most of them appeared to be sleeping off the excesses of the previous night rather than engaging in amorous sexual activity.

One couple lay entwined in the large silk cushions beside the buffet. Both were naked, and the man was feeding his lover grapes and kissing her between each offering. Nicholas couldn't help but admire the woman's pert breasts and rounded arse. He wondered whether he would ever be able to satisfy Louisa until she was as languid and glowing as the woman he'd just passed, to fuck her into satiated exhaustion . . .

His cock swelled at the thought of it. He hadn't even seen her completely naked, hadn't explored her body with the thoroughness she deserved, hadn't satisfied her at *all*. He was truly an appalling husband.

He'd had no problem being admitted into the pleasure house, so he assumed his credit was still good, but making sure of that with the lady proprietor was important. By the far wall he spotted Madame Helene in conversation with her butler. She wore a plain blue muslin dress, and her blond hair was braided away from her face, a direct contrast to the thin silk gowns and floating ringlets she normally displayed in the evenings. In truth, she looked like the businesswoman she obviously was rather than the flirtatious madam he was used to.

At the age of seventeen, his father had brought him

to Madame's and insisted he experience everything the house had to offer. Luckily for him, Madame Helene had ignored his father's instructions, offered him excellent advice, and allowed him to find his own pleasures. In a strange way, he had come to consider her a friend.

"Madame?"

She turned and whisked a pair of spectacles from the end of her nose. "Good morning, Lord Stortford."

"If you have time, ma'am, I'd love to have a word."

Nicholas bowed as she handed a sheaf of notes over to her butler and then gave him her full attention. Her piercing blue eyes scanned him with quiet interest. "Of course. Would you like to come down to my office?"

He nodded his assent and followed her out of the salon. The naked couple on the silk pillows had finished eating and returned to lovemaking. The man moved over the woman with lazy ease, her heels locked together in the small of his back, her soft cries almost inaudible in the big room.

A wave of lust shuddered through Nicholas as he breathed in the scent of sex, perfume, and desire that always swirled around the pleasure house. He wanted this again. He needed it, and if the only way to achieve it was to find it with his wife, he was more than willing to try.

"Please sit down, my lord."

Madame Helene waved Nicholas to a chair in front of her desk and sat herself, her hands folded together over a large ledger. "Now, how can I help you?"

"I was wondering if my membership was still current for your establishment."

Madame Helene raised her eyebrows, and her smile

died. "If my staff let you in, you are still a member. But I will check for you if you wish."

She opened the large leather book in front of her and turned a few pages until she settled on one. "Ah, here you are. It seems you have another month left on this year's membership."

"Thank you, ma'am. I can only hope that will be sufficient."

"For what, my lord?"

At the bite in her words, Nicholas looked up from contemplating his boots. "Do you think I'm up to no good, ma'am?"

She raised her chin at him. Helene had never been afraid to speak her mind, and Nicholas suspected she was going to speak it right now. "That is none of my business, sir, but I would respectfully remind you that you have been married for less than a year."

"And you think I mean to resume my lascivious ways and abandon my wife? I wouldn't be the first man within your establishment to enjoy another woman. Why are you being so judgmental? It's not like you."

"That's not the point." Helene's eyes narrowed. "May I take this opportunity to inform you that a month is all you have? I don't intend to offer you another year of membership, but, despite my reservations, I will honor this current one."

He grinned at her. "You do think I'm up to no good."

"It would appear so, and I confess to some disappointment." Madame Helene took a deep breath. "I've known you for years, and, in truth, I thought better of you."

"That is exactly what I wanted to speak to you about. I'm allowed to bring a guest with me, aren't I?"

"You are, my lord." Her blue eyes were frosty now, her posture rigid.

He sat back and watched her for a long moment, then drew a leather bound book out of his pocket and placed it on her desk. "Then you won't object if I bring my wife. I believe you might be able to help us with something important."

By the time she reached home, Louisa had a terrible headache and a strange reluctance to do anything but crawl into her own bed and pull the bedclothes over her head. She'd braved her husband over the breakfast table, misled his sister into thinking she was filled with marital bliss, *and* managed to endure a lecture from her mother as to her shortcomings as a daughter and a wife.

She walked up the stairs, trailing the ribbons of her bonnet behind her, and went straight to her bedchamber. Polly, her maid, was adding coal to the fire and stood to welcome Louisa back.

"Good afternoon, my lady. Would you like some tea?"

Louisa shuddered as she took off her pelisse and tossed her bonnet onto the nearest chair. "I've had enough tea to drown in today. Could you bring me a glass of brandy instead?"

Polly curtsied and deftly removed the pelisse and bonnet from where Louisa had flung them. "I'll see to that now, my lady, and then I'll start your bath. Are you dining at home this evening?"

"I believe so." Louisa took the chair next to the fire, kicked off her slippers, and curled her cold stockinged feet up on the seat. When Polly returned with her glass of brandy, Louisa took a long sip and felt the spirits burn a fiery path down to her stomach. She shivered and placed the glass on the small table beside her chair. The crystal chinked against her spectacles, and she picked them up and placed them on her nose, her hand delving down the side of the chair for her book.

With a frown she tried the other side of the chair. "Polly, did you move my book?"

"No, my lady. Which one was that?" Polly stood framed in the door to Louisa's dressing room where she was preparing her bath. "If I'd seen it, I would've put it on the table by your chair."

"The pirate novel I was telling you about." Louisa climbed off the seat and upended the cushion, but there was no sign of the book. "I wonder where I put it?"

"Oh, I hope you find it, my lady. I can't wait to hear what happens to that dastardly pirate!"

"Me neither," murmured Louisa as a truly awful thought occurred to her. Had she merely misplaced it, or had Nicholas found it and decided to read it for himself? The idea made her simultaneously excited and scared. He would think her a feather-headed fool, just as her father did. A lowering thought when she'd tried so hard to convince Nicholas that she had a brain and was capable of discussing anything he wanted, anything at all.

"Your bath's ready, my lady." Polly's cheerful voice floated out from the dressing room.

"Thank you." Louisa got up and headed toward the steam-filled room. Polly helped her out of her damp clothes and then left, promising to be back in time to dress her for dinner.

Louisa lay back in the rose-scented bathwater and closed her eyes. Why had she ever said anything to Nicholas? If she'd just kept quiet, everything would still be the same and she wouldn't be feeling so vulnerable, her confidence in her abilities shaken yet again.

"Good evening, my dear."

Louisa opened her eyes and found Nicholas smiling down at her through the perfumed steam. Instinctively she crossed her hands over her breasts and drew her knees together. "Nicholas . . ."

He sat on the edge of the bath and tucked a strand of her curling wet hair behind her ear. He'd taken his coat, cravat, and waistcoat off and his shirt had fallen open at the throat. "I didn't mean to startle you."

"You didn't, I . . ." His hand lingered on her skin, traced a soapy path from her earlobe down to her throat. She swallowed convulsively. "Was there something you wanted?"

His gaze followed his fingers, slid to her shoulder and to the swell of her breasts below. She tensed as his fingertips disappeared below the water and followed the curve of her generous bosom.

"It occurred to me today that I've never seen you naked."

"Are you sure?"

"Oh, I'm quite sure." His whole hand vanished beneath the clouded water and he weighed her breast in his palm. "I'm sure I'd remember your breasts."

"My breasts?" Goodness, it was hard for her to even say the word. Her mother would be horrified. She hunched her shoulders forward. "I've probably tried to keep them hidden. My mother always said they were vulgar."

"Vulgar?" She watched in fascination as he leaned closer and kissed the upper part of her breast. "How absurd." He whispered the words against her skin, the faint brush of his unshaven jaw making her tremble. His thumb moved upward and stroked over her already tight nipple, and she jumped. He did it again and then brought her whole breast higher in the water and settled his mouth over her nipple.

"Oh!" Louisa gasped and grabbed frantically at the back of his head, her fingers tangling into his thick brown hair and clinging on. "Oh, my goodness."

She forgot to say anything else as he cupped her other breast in his hand and played with that nipple, too. When he transferred his mouth from one breast to the other, she moaned his name and hung on to him even tighter. Heat gathered low in her belly, and she pressed her thighs together to assuage the unaccustomed ache. She wanted more, she wanted something . . . but what exactly was it, and how on earth was she supposed to ask for it?

When he finally raised his head, his eyes were narrowed, his breathing as erratic as hers. He kissed her mouth then, his tongue delving deep, demanding a response, which she willingly offered him. The rattle of a coal scuttle made him pause and glance behind him. He kissed the top of her head.

"My valet will be looking for me. I have to go. I'll see you at dinner."

"Yes." That was all she could manage before he smiled and walked away from her, leaving her in a state of anticipation—for what? For more of his kisses? She touched her breasts and shuddered at her sensitive nipples. He'd kissed her there and made her feel beautiful. She got out of the bath and wrapped herself in a big drying cloth. Apparently her mother was wrong about something else as well. It seemed some men did like large breasts after all.

Chapter Four

Nicholas watched Louisa through the candelabra placed on the table between them. Her skin was flushed, her color high, and there was a dreamy look in her eyes that made him confident that his foray into the dressing room hadn't shocked her too badly after all. His cock swelled at the thought of her nipples in his mouth, how she'd gasped for him, how much he'd wanted to slide his mouth and fingers lower and taste her core. Were her nipples still hard from his mouth, and was she wet for him? He wanted to pull her onto his lap and find out.

"Did you have a good day, my lord?"

Her hesitant question made him blink, and he hastily refocused his attention on her face. "Yes, my dear, I had an excellent day. How about you?"

She made a face. "I saw my mother, of course, and your sister."

"And how were they? Both as charming as ever?"

She sighed. "Well your sister was charming. My mother was . . . her usual self."

"Perhaps you shouldn't visit her quite so frequently." He said it gently. The last thing he wanted was to find himself at odds with her over her blasted mother. "She depends on you rather too much I fear."

"You're right, but what am I to do?"

"Tell her you're busy."

"She's my mother, my lord."

He reached across the table and took her hand. "And I'm your husband, and I want you at home more. Tell your mother that. She won't argue."

Louisa's smile was hopeful. "She'd certainly understand if you started issuing commands to me like my father does—and she'd tell me to obey you."

"Exactly." He squeezed her fingers and stood up. "Now come to bed."

Louisa glanced over her shoulder at the lone footman stationed by the door. Her attitude to the servants still surprised him. Having grown up in large, sometimes well-staffed houses, he tended not to give his servants much thought. Louisa still struggled to forget that they were constantly surrounded by people and thus rarely alone.

He tugged at her hand. "Come on. It's our house, we can go to bed whenever we like, and I think it's time to begin your seduction, don't you? We've wasted quite enough of our marriage already."

He led her upstairs, and rather than bidding her his usual punctilious good night at her door, followed her in. She glanced back at him, her brown eyes wide, and a wary question in their depths. Nicholas nodded at Polly, who had risen from her seat by the fire and dropped her piece of mending.

"Good evening, Polly."

Polly curtsied and awkwardly scooped up the lace-edged petticoat that had fluttered to the floor. "Good evening, my lord. Shall I come back later, my lady?"

Nicholas answered her. "That won't be necessary. You can retire for the night."

He watched her leave and then turned back to his wife who was staring at him, one hand gripping the chair by her dressing table. What did she think he was going to do? Ravish her? Well he was, but not quite yet . . .

"Don't worry, I'll help you out of your gown." Nicholas smiled encouragingly at his silent wife. "I'm quite competent."

"I'm sure you are."

Her quiet words made him want to kick himself. Alluding to his expertise at coaxing other women out of their clothes was hardly going to endear him to his wife. "I *meant* that when I was younger I used to help April dress."

"You did?"

He shrugged. "Sometimes my father forgot to pay the bills, and we were left without many servants. We learned to make do for ourselves."

Louisa sat down on the small couch at the bottom of her bed; her expression arrested and fixed on his face. "I never thought of you as being without every comfort a man could dream of."

"Having a title doesn't necessarily mean a family has wealth. My father preferred to piss away his inheritance on gambling, horses, and women." He took the seat beside her. "As long as he could keep up appearances, he didn't care if we were penniless or as near to it as possible. It was a good thing that he died when he did, or else we would've really been in the suds."

"Which is one of the reasons why you agreed to marry me."

Nicholas held her gaze. "That's true. I'm glad we can speak openly of it. I would hate to think I had deceived you in any way."

"Oh, I was not deceived." Louisa stood up and walked across to her dressing table. She pretended to fiddle with the clasp of her bracelet. "Not at all. I knew exactly what you wanted from me."

She jumped as he appeared in the mirror behind her and took her hand. He leaned in close to finagle the bracelet clasp open. He lifted her hand to his mouth and kissed the inside of her wrist and then the center of her palm. "Is that one of the reasons why you don't ask me for anything?"

"I don't understand."

He kissed her throat and wrapped his arm around her waist, drawing her back against his chest and torso. She found herself looking at herself in the mirror, his dark head close to hers, his blue eyes intent. "You don't ask me to buy you things; you don't ask for jewelry, or lap dogs, or a larger dress allowance."

She frowned at his reflection. "I have everything I need."

His smile was full of sweetness. "I don't believe I've ever heard a woman say that before. I obviously married a saint."

"I'm not a saint, I was just brought up differently."

"And thank God for that." His teeth grazed her ear and settled over her earlobe, then slowly bit down. She shivered and realized she could feel the hard pulse of his arousal through the thin silk of her gown. "But what can I give you, if you want for nothing?"

"Your company?" she whispered. "Your interest?"

His mouth left her ear, and he kissed his way down her neck to her shoulder. He trailed his index finger along the edge of her bodice. "Oh, you have my interest. In truth, at dinner I wondered whether your nipples were still hard for me." Louisa gasped as his fingertip delved beneath the silk of her bodice and past the stiff barrier of her corset. "Ah yes, they still are."

Before she could reply, he turned her away from the mirror and sat her on the couch. He came down beside her, trapping her into the corner between his hands and his body. "I wanted to touch you, to have you sit on my lap and let me fondle you."

"In the dining room?"

"Yes, in front of the servants. Luckily, I restrained myself and decided to bring you up here instead."

Louisa struggled with the desire to simply lie back and let him touch her, but unfortunately, her passion for honesty wouldn't allow it. "Why are you being like this, with me?"

"Don't you like it?"

"That's not the point."

He regarded her seriously for a long moment. "Because a very good friend of mine pointed out to me today that you aren't just my wife, but a woman."

"I've always been a woman."

"I know that, but . . ." he hesitated. "I fear I labeled you as 'wife.' "

"I have no idea what you are talking about, and I'm not sure if I appreciate you discussing me with someone else." Even as she spoke she was guiltily aware that she'd spoken to April about Nicholas as well, but at least she'd *tried* to be discreet.

"I can assure you that my friend will not gossip about us." He took her hand. "Will you please forgive me, and let me carry on kissing you? We have a lot of lost time to make up."

Louisa looked doubtfully at him. "I suppose that will be all right, but . . ." His mouth descended over hers, and she forgot what she had been about to say as he took his time kissing her. She learned how to breathe through her nose to prolong the intimate contact, how to use her tongue against his to drive him wild. He was almost on top of her now, one leg drawn over hers, the hardness of his cock pressed against her hip. Strange things were happening low in her belly, and her breasts ached for his touch.

He drew back and stared down at her. "While I sat there imagining you on my lap during dinner, I also imagined tasting more than your breasts. Will you let me remove your gown?"

Louisa barely managed a nod as he sat up and maneuvered her around so that her back faced him. She closed her eyes and let the dress slide from her shoulders, heard the soft hiss of the silk, the sudden catch of his breath.

"Stand up a moment and step out of the gown." She obeyed him and waited as he tossed the swathe of blue silk over the nearest chair. A sudden chill swept through her, but it wasn't just from the cold. "Would you object if I removed my coat and waistcoat?"

This time she shook her head and watched him strip off his outer garments. It reminded her of the earlier moment in their shared dressing room when he'd bent over her in the bath. Her nipples tightened even more and she had an absurd desire to touch herself there, to soothe that promise of heat and the ache of desire.

He knelt at her feet and guided her back down onto the couch. He was so much taller that even when she was sitting his face was almost level with hers. She studied his thick brown hair and narrowed blue eyes, the hint of desire that both softened and hardened his face, as if a stranger lurked behind the amiable visage she saw every day. A harder, more brutal man, and a man who took what he wanted when he wanted it. He reminded her of someone . . .

He touched her knee, his hand heavy and hot over the thin muslin of her shift and stockings. "May I remove your corset? It will be in the way."

Louisa wanted to ask him of what, but she turned sideways on the seat to allow him access to the spiral binding of her corset. His fingers moved deftly against her back, and she was soon able to breathe again. She looked warily down at him as he placed his hands on her waist and settled her back against the couch.

"As I was saying, at dinner I was contemplating all the places I had yet to touch or taste you." He leaned against her knees and kissed her breast through the sheer muslin.

Louisa managed to clear her throat. "I believe you have already touched and tasted me there." She couldn't believe how prim she sounded. He must think her a complete fool. He looked up at her, and she saw nothing to indicate he thought her stupid. In truth, he was looking at her as if he might possibly devour her. It was quite exhilarating.

"I'm just reacquainting myself with my newest territory before moving on." He sucked on her nipple until Louisa found her fingernails digging into her palms. "I have to make sure that I am welcome and well remembered."

While he touched her, he also moved against her, exerting gentle pressure on her knees until she had no choice but to open them and allow his upper body to press against her in a most intimate fashion. He continued to suckle at her nipples, his fingers testing and touching everything his mouth was not. Her hand stole into his hair, and she held on as he sucked on her, the rhythm lending itself to the sway of her body, and to the motion of her hips as she rubbed herself against his stomach.

She moaned as one of his hands slid around her hips and he spread his fingers over her bottom, moaned even more when he drew away from her, leaving her wet shift clinging to her hard tight nipples and to the junction of her thighs. He looked down at her and smiled, cupped her between the legs in the palm of his hand. "That's better."

He took her mouth, his tongue plunging inside. The heel of his hand pressed in the same pattern of advance and retreat on her sex. Heat throbbed and flowered beneath the hard edge of his hand, making her forget about anything but the need for him to continue, for him never to stop, for him to keep her on that brink of pleasure that had suddenly become more necessary to her than breathing, or dignity, or civility.

Nicholas made a growling sound in his throat and stripped the muslin away from her sex, needing the contact of her bare skin against his hand. He groaned as his fingers dipped into her swollen wetness, swirled around her tight hot bud, and dipped inside her. She was moving with him, her fingernails digging into his shoulders, into his scalp. He didn't care; he wanted to make her come for him more than anything he had ever wanted before.

God, but he needed to taste all that hot wetness as well. He swallowed at the thought and knew he had to have her before she shattered in his arms. It took all his strength to wrench away from her kisses, to not kiss her breasts, and to settle his head between her thighs. She smelled divine, so wet and wanton that he forgot she was his wife, forgot everything but the urge to lick and suckle and bite her into complete submission.

He drove his tongue deep twice and then withdrew, swirled around her swollen lips, the hard bud of her clit. He licked her and sampled her until he could no longer see or taste anything but her, until even the pain as she tugged at his hair was dimmed by the spectacle of her pushing herself in his face, until he was drowning in her and not caring at all.

"Nicholas." She sounded as desperate as he felt, her voice high. "Please . . ."

He managed to slide three fingers inside her, used his mouth and his thumb on her clit and took her over into pleasure, felt the waves of it throb and ebb around his embedded fingers, wanted to shove his cock into her to experience it more deeply. God, his cock . . . he was going to come in his pantaloons if he didn't get some relief soon. He wanted her mouth, her sex, his shaft between her breasts covering her in his seed . . .

Nicolas slowly opened his eyes and sat back. Louisa was just staring down at him, her legs still open, her nipples still hard. His cock protested as he slowly eased away from her.

"Are you all right?" she asked breathlessly. Nicholas could only stare back at his disheveled wife and yearn. "Nicholas?"

"I'm fine."

Louisa scrambled to sit up and pull down her shift as Nicholas remained crouched in front of her, a peculiarly desperate expression on his face. Was he disgusted by her? Had she somehow behaved inappropriately? She hadn't even realized women were capable of doing "that," let alone that it would prove so liberating.

His smile was strained, and one of his hands rested over his groin. Louisa couldn't help but stare at the thick bulge of his cock and the wetness that marred the front of his pantaloons. She might have achieved that glorious state of release, but had Nicholas? And if not, how on earth was she supposed to ask him what to do next?

"Are you sure you are all right?"

He grimaced as he managed to get to his feet, still protecting his groin as if he were fielding close to the wicket in a game of cricket. "I'll be fine."

He sank down next to her and fumbled with the buttons of his pantaloons. "I apologize if this might shock you, but I need to . . ."

She couldn't help but stare as he shoved down his pantaloons and smallclothes to reveal his swollen cock.

Had she ever seen it before, like this, erect and in the candlelight? If so, she had probably shut her eyes, but now she was intrigued. His shaft was thick with a swollen purplish crown that was wet. She leaned toward him as she smelled the salty tang of his seed. That at least was familiar.

Nicholas wrapped his hand around the base of his shaft and sighed. "Don't look if you don't want to, I'm not trying to shock you, I just need . . ." He started to move his hand, the motion jerky and abrupt, violent almost. She moved closer. He studied her through narrowed eyes. "Either help me or move back; at this point I care not."

He sounded quite desperate, as desperate as she had felt just before he'd made her world fly apart. She added her fingers to his, flinched at the heat of his flesh, the hardness beneath the softness, the way his skin moved over the whole. He groaned and guided her into a fast rhythm, his hips joining into the thrust and pull of their fingers, his mouth tightening, his eyes closing.

With a hoarse cry, he grabbed her other hand and placed it palm down over the top of his shaft. Louisa held still as she felt the hot wetness of his seed cover and overflow her fingers. It took several moments before Nicholas collapsed back onto the seat and covered his eyes. He was breathing hard as if he'd been in a race.

Experimentally, she moved her hands, felt his now diminished shaft twitch beneath her questing fingers, and the thickness of his seed drip through her fingers.

"Take this." He gave her his handkerchief and she

carefully wiped her fingers and then patted helpfully at his groin where the black curls were now as wet as her own. As she worked, his shaft jerked against her hand and she paused to observe it.

Nicholas gave a short laugh. "He wants more, I think, so don't tempt him with your clever hands."

"More? Didn't we just . . ." Louisa didn't know quite where to look, at his expanding shaft or into his eyes, both seemed equally dangerous.

"I've always been quick to recover."

Which was probably why he'd been so popular with the ladies of the *ton*. Louisa handed him back his hand-kerchief and wrapped her arms around her raised knees. Is that what he'd resorted to doing after visiting her bed? Used his own hands to pleasure himself while she slept on in blissful ignorance of the pleasure she might've been having?

He sighed. "What's wrong, Louisa? Have I shocked you immeasurably?"

She managed to smile. "No, it was all . . . quite fascinating. I didn't know . . ." She stopped speaking and simply gazed into his eyes. Who had been hurt most? Her for being so ignorant, or him for depriving them both of such pleasure? She wasn't sure, didn't even want to think about all their wasted opportunities at that point. One thing she did know was that she was never going back, that she would embrace her newfound knowledge and not be ashamed.

"I'm glad I gave you pleasure," she whispered.

He surprised her by lifting her into his arms and walking her across to her bed. He pulled back the covers and deposited her in the middle. For one wild second he hesitated, and she hoped he'd get in with her, but he drew back and rebuttoned his pantaloons. "Thank you for allowing me to share your joy."

Louisa clutched at the covers and suddenly felt awkward. What exactly did you say to a man who had made you lose all sense of propriety and scream his name, even if he was your husband? "I wouldn't have known it existed without you."

His smile was warm as he patted her knee. "Better than a book?"

She swallowed hard. She'd forgotten that she was a challenge, that he had something to prove, and that he was determined to seduce her. "Messier."

He chuckled and kissed her mouth. "Thank goodness. If you can still joke with me—I didn't shock you too badly. Go to sleep and I'll see you in the morning. I believe we have a ball to attend at my sister's tomorrow evening."

His ability to return to making casual conversation after he'd simply shattered her world was breathtaking— but then the experience hadn't exactly been new to him, had it? She struggled to keep smiling. "Indeed we do. Good night."

He blew her a kiss as he walked away, his coat and waistcoat slung over his arm. She managed to keep the smile on her face until he gently shut the door, before she sank down into the pillows and pulled the covers over her head. Her body was still tingling from the attentions of his hands and mouth, her nipples hard. Her hand drifted down to her sex, and she found she was still wet, still wanting. She imagined a naked Nicholas leaning over her as he slid his thick length deep inside her . . . Whatever he thought of her, she knew it would happen again, and that it would always be different, because her body finally understood what it had been created for—to accept a man. Perhaps her mother had been right about that after all . . .

With a sigh, Louisa curled onto her side and stared into the darkness. Nicholas was probably already asleep without a care in the world, one step closer to achieving his aim of proving himself better than any fictional pirate could ever be. Hadn't he known that anyway, and if not, why? Had she been so concerned about not asking him for everything, of not bothering him that she'd neglected to ask if there was any possibility that he might come to love her?

Chapter Five

Louisa smiled nervously at Nicholas as she sat opposite him in the carriage on the way to the ball. He was dressed in a black coat, gray waistcoat, and white pantaloons. His cravat sported a black onyx pin that caught the feeble light inside the comfortable carriage. He appeared relaxed, one arm braced on the back of the seat, his feet touching hers.

"You look very nice, my dear."

She glanced down at the deep rose of her low bodice and instinctively sucked in her stomach. "Do you think so? April assured me that this color was not only fashionable but that it suited me as well."

He studied her for a long while, almost as if he hadn't ever really looked at her before. It was quite disconcerting, especially as he had recently lavished his attention on parts of her that no other human being has viewed since she was a small child. "April was right. The color is perfect on you." He winked. "It's strange that someone who has such appalling taste in decorating has such immaculate style, don't you think?"

Louisa couldn't help but smile back at him. "April has been very kind to me."

"I should imagine she's simply glad I've finally settled down and stopped creating gossip for the *ton*."

"Were you really that bad?"

His smile died. "When I was younger, yes. I blush to remember some of my more foolish exploits, but luckily I grew up and became far more discriminating in my choices."

Louisa eyed him dubiously. She didn't quite have the nerve to ask him either about his conquests or about his current arrangements. Her mother insisted he would still keep a mistress for Louisa's sake and that she should be grateful he refrained from exposing her to the more bestial side of his nature.

The thought of him turning to another woman brought a strange tightness to her chest. Was that what he'd been trying to tell her before? That a wife was not required to behave like a woman who enjoyed sex? Could it be possible that he agreed with her mother? But no, he had touched her far more intimately last night, and she'd welcomed the intimacy, not recoiled from it.

"I think we're here," Nicholas announced, and reached for his hat and gloves. "Do you have a shawl, my dear? It is perishing cold out there."

He helped her out of the carriage, and she started to climb the steps. She grabbed on to his arm as someone pushed past her and ended up with her face against his chest. The scent of bay rum and warm male enveloped her, and she simply breathed him in. She wondered how it might feel to kiss his naked chest, to lick a path from his small flat nipples to his muscled belly and then perhaps even lower.

"Are you all right, my lady?"

She gasped and looked up into his eyes. His gaze intensified and he drew her hastily up the stairs and into the cavernous crowded hall beyond. Inside, the chatter of voices bouncing off the walls and chandeliers created a roar fit for a county fair.

"Whatever were you thinking about?" His amused question made her blush as he nodded to his sister's butler and maneuvered her through the crowds and toward the back of the house where it was quieter and less stifling. Her back hit a wall and he loomed over her. "Would you like to tell me?"

She stared at his cravat. "You would think me . . . forward."

He leaned into her, one of his hands planted on the wall by the side of her face. "I would think you honest enough to answer your husband from whom, surely, nothing should be withheld?"

She licked her lips. "I was wondering how your skin would taste if I kissed it."

He went still. "Which particular part of my skin?"

She forced herself to look into his eyes. "Your chest, your belly, your . . ." Oh, my goodness, she couldn't say it, she just couldn't.

"My?" he prompted. "My knee?"

"Not quite."

He edged even closer until his mouth hovered a tantalizing half inch away from hers. "What then?" he whispered, "My cock? I'd like you to kiss that, take it into your pretty little mouth, and suck me dry."

His tongue traced a leisurely path along the seam of her lips and then plunged into her mouth. Louisa couldn't have moved if her life had depended on it. Could a woman do that? *Would* a woman want to do that? After all, he had done a similar thing to her, licked and sucked her into complete shivering abandon.

He stopped kissing her but didn't move away. In the confines of the dark corridor, with his body covering hers, she felt quite brave. "Would a man like that?"

A visible shudder ran through him. "This man would. Perhaps you might think on it."

"Perhaps I will."

He straightened and took her hand, placed it firmly over the tented front of his pantaloons. "Now we will have to wait until I'm decent to be seen again."

She sighed. "I don't suppose we could just go home, not when it is your sister's ball. She would never forgive us if we didn't turn up."

Unconsciously, she petted his shaft until his fingers closed around her wrist. "Madam, if you keep that up, I'll be coming into your hand and disgracing myself."

She looked around the deserted hallway and realized that they were near Lord Fotherskill's secretary's office. "But what if I wanted to try what you suggested?"

"Do you think I'm going to stop you?" He grabbed her by the shoulders and hurried her into the secretary's office, locking the door behind them.

She sank to her knees and looked up at him. "Not if it brings you as much pleasure as you brought me."

"You're sure?" he asked, even as he fumbled with the buttons of his placket. For once he sounded even less certain than she did. Somehow that helped her become bolder. "Otherwise I can . . ."

She took over the task and revealed his thick thrusting shaft. From this angle it looked rather fearsome and far too large to fit into her mouth.

"It's all right. Just take as much as you want, I don't expect . . ." he broke off with a groan at her first tentative lick over the crown. He was already wet and she tasted him carefully: the merest hint of salt, almost like thick tears. She rested one hand on his thigh, wrapped the other around the base of his shaft, and opened her mouth.

"Ah . . ." He exhaled as she sucked him slowly into her mouth until the whole of the crown disappeared. She discovered that if she moved both her mouth and her hand back and forth over his flesh he seemed to adore it. He cradled the back of her head in his hand, urging her onward with every slow sucking motion.

She also found that even as she sucked him she could use the very tip of her tongue to lick at the top of his cock, feel the wet slit, the rough texture of the under skin, and the smoothness of the whole. He groaned her name and started to angle his hips toward her mouth as if trying to push himself deeper. She gripped him tightly and restricted his motion, which seemed to excite him further.

"God, Louisa . . . I . . ."

He made one last convulsive movement, and her mouth was suddenly full of his seed. She had to swallow fast to avoid choking. She waited until he released his grip on the back of her head and sat back. Nicholas looked like a man who had just experienced bliss, and she was suddenly proud of herself. It seemed that lovemaking was not all about a man's needs and desires after all.

She waited while Nicholas tucked his cock back into his pantaloons and rebuttoned the placket. He held out his hands and brought her to her feet in one easy motion.

"That was very kind of you, my lady."

"Kind? Did I not do it correctly?"

He patted his groin. "Well everything is still attached, so I assume you did."

"Would it hurt if I bit you there?"

He winced. "I should think so, although I've heard that in certain situations it can be quite alluring."

She frowned and he grinned at her, his expressive face alive with warmth and appreciation. Just seeing him like this made her want to offer to kiss him again. It felt as if she was being admitted into his affections, as if he was finally opening up to her.

He kissed her forehead. "We should go. April will be wondering where we are."

"Of course." Louisa patted her hair and opened the door. There was no one in the dark hallway, so they walked back to the main hall and ascended the stairs to the ballroom. April stood at the entrance to the ballroom, flanked by her portly smiling husband. Her expression lightened when she saw Nicholas and Louisa approaching and she rushed toward them.

"Oh, where have you been? I'd quite given you up! My dear Gilbert was wishing me at the devil having to stand here for so long." Since her admonishment was delivered with a smile and a hug, Louisa didn't take her too seriously. "You look lovely, Louisa, I told you that color would suit you, didn't I?"

"Indeed you did. I . . ."

April poked Nicholas in the chest with her fan. "Doesn't she look well? Have you even noticed she has a new gown on yet? You probably haven't." She rolled her eyes in Louisa's direction. "Men are positively dreadful at offering a compliment, even when one has spent hours at one's toilette."

Nicholas took Louisa's hand and kissed it. "I have not only noticed the gown, but I've complimented Louisa on it already, so you can stop your twittering, sis."

April gave an exaggerated sigh, linked her arm through Louisa's, and led her toward the ballroom. "We'll ignore him, my dear, and perhaps he'll go away and make himself useful in the card room or something."

Louisa turned her head to look back at Nicholas, but his attention had been claimed by a fragile-looking beauty who clutched his arm and gazed up at him adoringly. Not that Nicholas seemed to mind, his smile was as wide and welcoming as the one he had just given her.

April pinched her elbow. "Louisa, it is not proper to look back at your husband in that slavish manner. People will think you are hanging on his sleeve! Come and circulate with me. I'm sure Nicholas will find you later."

Louisa sighed and obediently followed her sister-in-law into the crowded ballroom. They were immediately engulfed by well-wishers who wanted to compliment April on the ball. Louisa could no longer see Nicholas at all. Had he even entered the ballroom? April was forever lecturing her about how best to ignore her husband in society settings. It seemed that was the fashionable thing to do. What amused Louisa was how much her mother would've approved of April's instructions. Mama was always telling Louisa not to expect too much of her husband's valuable time and attention.

Louisa sat next to April in the ballroom and suffered through the next half hour listening to April collect all the latest gossip and criticize everyone else's gowns. It all seemed so silly to her, and not what she'd expected of society at all—or of marriage. She'd imagined days with Nicholas at her side and evenings filled with quiet conversation, and the promise of the intimacies of the marriage bed.

"Oh, look!" April whispered. "There's that horrid Lady Basingstone. She's always had her eye on Nicholas. I wonder why he's dancing with her?" She nudged Louisa. "Now that Nicholas is married himself, she probably thinks he's fair game."

"Is that so?"

"Oh, you know what I mean. Once a woman has given her husband an heir or two, most men turn a blind eye to her having a little affair of her own." April's smile was tinged with sadness. "And truthfully, my dear, don't you think that a wife deserves a little fun after the inconveniences and humiliations of one's husband having a mistress?"

"I don't know, April. It's not something Nicholas and I have discussed."

"Of course you haven't, my dear. You and Nicholas are newlyweds. I'm sure the thought hasn't entered your mind." April's laughter sounded forced, and the glance she threw toward Nicholas was distinctly worried. "But you must know, my love, that if he *did* ever stray, Nicholas would always treat you with the greatest of respect."

"Why do you say that?"

April squeezed her hand tightly. "I heard a silly rumor this evening that Nicholas had been seen in . . . well, in a place that he should not have been near. I'm sure it meant nothing. It was probably just a mistake, although the person who told me did know Nicholas quite well, but . . . anyway, I thought you should be on your guard. And, don't think I won't be speaking to him about this, because I will!"

Louisa set her teeth as her husband swept past them with yet another woman in his arms. He seemed to be enjoying himself immensely, and yet, less than an hour ago she'd allowed him to persuade her to . . . she stood up abruptly. "I'm going to fetch myself a glass of ratafia. Would you like something, April?"

"Oh, no, dear. I'll be fine. You run along."

Louisa stayed in the quiet supper room until she felt marginally more in control of her emotions. Perhaps this was why most society marriages never developed into anything more than mild liking and mutual respect. Did Nicholas have a mistress, and how on earth could she find out without publicly embarrassing herself?

Jealousy was a horrible thing, and she suspected she was in the throes of it. Her fingers curled around her glass. Every time one of those glamorous women looked at Nicholas, she had a strange desire to launch herself at them and pull their hair out. She bit her lip. What a lowering thought. Perhaps she really did lack class.

"I wondered where you'd gone."

She looked up into Nicholas's amused blue eyes and manufactured a smile. "Were you looking for me?"

"Of course I was. I was hoping you'd dance with me."

Louisa put down her glass with a thump. "You don't have to, you know."

He glanced down at her. "And what exactly does that mean?"

She allowed him to take her hand but didn't move. "Just that April says we have no obligation to be seen together at all. In fact, spending time with one's spouse at a ball is considered quite gothic."

"Well, I've never agreed with April about anything, and that just sounds absurd."

"But she's right, isn't she? It isn't fashionable for us to be seen together." She swallowed hard, tasted him on her tongue. "I fear my ridiculous attempt to gain your attention is fruitless and bound for disappointment."

His smile disappeared. "Is that so?" He placed her hand on his sleeve. "Come and dance with me."

She was so surprised that she followed him back into the ballroom where a waltz was just beginning. She shivered as he slid his arm around her waist and held her far closer than was considered appropriate. To complete her confusion, he bent his head so that his mouth brushed her ear.

"Have you forgotten that you set me a challenge?"

"I didn't set you a challenge, you just decided to, oh." She gasped as his teeth grazed her skin.

"Have you also forgotten that not an hour ago you had your lips around my cock?"

Heat burned on Louisa's cheeks, but she continued dancing; Nicholas was holding her so tightly she could hardly breathe, let alone fall.

"I liked that, Louisa, I liked coming into your mouth, the way you swallowed my seed and took all of me without protest." He twirled her around a corner so fast that the other dancers and spectators seemed like a blur. "And as soon as I get you alone I intend to slide my tongue inside you and have you scream and dig your nails into my skin. Will you like that?"

She looked into his eyes. "I'm not sure."

"You will, because I'm going to do it until you've come so many times that you're begging for my cock, begging to be fucked as hard and as often as I want. That's what makes this evening exciting to me, the fact that even if I don't stand next to you all night, I know I'll have you all to myself soon, and that I can do what the devil I want with you."

"Oh." Louisa concentrated on her steps as her body heated and yearned toward Nicholas.

"Because you're wet for me now, aren't you? You're thinking about what I'm going to do to you, how you're going to feel, how you'll arch your back and rub yourself against me."

"Yes." As Nicholas whispered his erotic litany into her ear, Louisa could barely function. Despite everything, she wanted to rip his clothes off, wanted to bite him, pull his hair, and ravage his mouth until he cried out, too. "I want that."

The music paused and he drew her off the dance floor. "Do you understand now why I'm quite happy to watch you go off and sit with your friends and dance with other men?"

"I believe so, but . . ."

"But, what?"

She managed an unsteady breath. "But you must

know that I would never . . . share myself with another person."

"Are you suggesting I might?"

She met his gaze, her heart beating uncomfortably loud in her chest. "I don't know."

He released her hand. He looked as if she had slapped him. "I suppose I should thank you for your honesty, but at the moment I feel more like putting you over my knee. Go and sit with April. I'll come and find you when I'm ready to go home."

He bowed stiffly and walked away from her, leaving her prey to the watchful eyes of the other dancers, who, sensing trouble, closed in on her, false sympathy filling their faces. With all the dignity she could muster, Louisa made her way back to April's side and sat down. Her pleasure in the evening ruined by her lack of sophistication and stupid desire for honesty. No man liked to be confronted by unpleasant truths in the middle of a ballroom. Even she knew that.

Nicholas headed for the card room, his expression so forbidding that several of the other guests moved quickly out of his path. What the devil was the matter with his wife? It seemed that every time he advanced the smallest step in her affections, she immediately took three steps back. What kind of man did she think he was?

He stopped walking. The kind of man she was used to seeing in a society marriage, the kind his father had been. Damnation, she was right to be skeptical. Even he wouldn't have believed himself capable of fidelity before he'd met and married her.

"Nick?" He looked up into the amused blue gaze of Captain David Gray. "Is everything all right?"

He attempted a shrug. "I'll never understand women."

"Then why try?" David offered him a glass of brandy. "Women do tend to complicate the simplest of matters with all that unnecessary emotion, don't they?"

"Sarcasm doesn't become you." Nicholas cast David a blistering look as they settled into two upright chairs against the wall and pretended to watch the card players. "Perhaps I should be more specific. I'll never understand my wife, and unfortunately, due to the potentially long-standing nature of our relationship, I have to bloody try."

"That's true." David contemplated the scene in front of them. "She is quite young and inexperienced, Nick."

"I know that."

"And, perhaps if I might be so bold as to mention it, your sister isn't."

"What do my problems with Louisa have to do with my sister?"

David looked at him. "Because it's obvious that April is your wife's closest friend in Town. Perhaps the advice your wife is receiving is a little too sophisticated and worldly for her."

Nicholas let out his breath. "I haven't considered that. I was just pleased that they deal so well together."

"I'm sure that was important to you. You're very fond of April, aren't you?"

"We survived my father together. We protected each other." Nicholas sighed and took a long drink of his brandy. "April is eight years older than me. That makes her fourteen years older than Louisa."

"Between April and a socially unacceptable mother,

your wife's perception of her place in society and your affections might be a little confused."

Nicholas smiled. "She won't be confused after to-morrow night. I'll make damned sure that she understands exactly what I'd like from her."

"And how do you intend to do that?"

Nicholas clinked his glass against David's. "I'm taking her to Madame Helene's for a spot of adventuring."

Chapter Six

"We are going out, again?"

Louisa looked up at Nicholas who had appeared in her bedchamber just after her solitary dinner. She hadn't seen him all day, had imagined him languishing in the arms of his mistress while complaining bitterly about his terribly unsophisticated wife.

"Indeed we are." Nicholas inclined his head an inch and pointed to the box he had deposited on the bed. "And I'd like you to wear these clothes. Ask Polly to help you put them on. I'll see you downstairs in half an hour."

Louisa bit her lip. He didn't exactly sound delighted to be asking for her company, but at least he wasn't ignoring her. She sighed and walked over to the bed, lifted the lid of the dress box. "Whatever does he want me to wear? It looks like something from my mother's wardrobe."

She took out the old-fashioned gold satin overgown and held it up against her. Beneath the dress lay a brown lace underskirt, a single petticoat, a thin shift, a plain set of stays, and a matching brown bodice.

"Ooh, my lady. Whatever is this? Are you going to a masquerade ball?" Polly breathed close to Louisa's ear. "It looks like the dress in that portrait in the hall the earl's grandmother is wearing."

"It does, doesn't it?" Louisa allowed Polly to help her out of her thin high-waisted muslin dress and remove all her clothing but her stockings and garters. She shivered and drew closer to the heat of the fire. "I'm sure there should be more petticoats and some kind of frame or bustle to hold the skirt out."

Polly dropped the new shift over Louisa's head. It was made of such fine lawn that it barely made a difference to her comfort or her modesty. "That's true, my lady. Do you want me to go and find some more petticoats? Maybe the modiste forgot to put them in."

Conscious that Nicholas had told her to wear only what was in the box, Louisa shook her head. "No, thank you, Polly. I'm sure I'll be fine. I wouldn't want all those layers anyway. I don't know how our ancestors managed with all those heavy petticoats on."

"Neither do I, my lady." Polly laced Louisa into the long stays, tied the petticoat, and then pinned the bodice to it. Lastly Louisa stepped into the underskirt and pinned that to the bodice. "At least the gown has long sleeves and some lovely gold lace on it. That should keep you warm enough."

Louisa shrugged into the overdress and waited while Polly settled it around her shoulders and drew it closed at her waist with two small hooks. She looked in the mirror and saw how well the brown underskirt contrasted with the gold and how the stays pushed her bosom up to overflow the bodice of the gown. She flattened her hands over her chest, but there was no place for her breasts to go other than outward.

"Do you think it is . . . quite decent?"

Polly giggled. "I'm sure his lordship will think so. Now let me fix your hair and find you a nice warm cloak and you'll look perfect, my lady."

A quarter of an hour later, Louisa scooped up the gold mask that Polly had discovered in the bottom of the dress box, gathered her cloak around her, and descended into the hall. Nicholas stood waiting for her; his long, flowing cloak concealed his clothing. He wore riding boots rather than his usual shoes.

He held out his hand. "Are you ready, my lady?"

"Yes, my lord."

His smile was quite wicked as he escorted her through the door and into the carriage. "I'm glad to hear it. I hope this evening lives up to your expectations."

"My expectations?" She studied him as he took the seat opposite her. "I wasn't aware that I had any."

"Of me, or of marriage?"

"That is hardly fair, sir." She looked away and gathered her skirts more closely around her.

"True when the only confidantes you have on the subject are your mother and my sister." He crossed his booted feet at the ankle. "And I should imagine their views on the subject of marriage don't always agree."

"That is true, my lord." She tried to smile. "I have received a great deal of advice from them both, and all of it conflicting."

"Did it ever occur to you to ask me?"

She finally looked at him. "Why would I do that?"

His smile was full of warmth. "Because, surely I am the person most involved with your future happiness and well-being."

She licked her lips, aware that with Nicholas in such a confiding mood she had nothing to lose and perhaps much to gain. "I did ask you."

He leaned back and studied her, his eyes narrow. "I suppose you did, in your own unique way, and I hope you will be pleased with my efforts to accommodate you."

Louisa was about to ask for clarification when the carriage stopped moving and the door was opened to let the steps down.

"Put your mask on, Louisa," Nicholas commanded.

By the time she was helped out of the carriage and up the wide steps of a large mansion, she was too intrigued to ask anything at all. Nicholas led her into a large marbled hall where a footman stood stationed at the bottom of the stairs.

"Good evening, my lord, ma'am, and welcome. May I take your cloaks?"

"Good evening. You may take the lady's cloak."

Louisa shivered when Nicholas untied the ribbons of her cloak and handed it to the footman. Nicholas remained staring down at her, his gaze fixed on the swell of her bosom. She resisted the temptation to cover herself. He'd chosen the gown for her; he must have known the effect such tight lacing and the old-fashioned stays would have.

"You look very nice. Very . . . ravishable."

"Thank you." He took her hand and kissed the palm. "Where exactly are we?"

He led her toward the curving staircase. "We're at the pleasure house, I thought you might enjoy it."

Her fingers clenched on his sleeve. "A bawdy house?"

"No, a house of sexual pleasure for the rich."

Louisa dug in her heels and stopped moving. "Isn't that the same thing?"

"Not at all. There are no prostitutes here, only willing members of the upper classes who like a bit of variety in their sexual pleasures."

"Oh." At the gentle pressure of his fingers on her elbow, Louisa resumed walking, her mind in a whirl. Nicholas's calm explanation about such a forbidden subject unnerved her. It was all very well to pretend that such sexual excess existed in her *mind,* but to actually find out they were available in real life? That was both deliciously decadent and surprisingly tempting.

At the top of the stairway a large portrait of a beautiful blond woman dominated the landing.

"Who is that?"

"That's Madame Helene, the remarkable woman who founded the pleasure house."

"She is very beautiful." Louisa wondered if she sounded as wistful as she felt.

"She is not only beautiful, but intelligent as well."

"You've been here before, then?"

"In my past, yes."

"And why did you bring me here?"

He drew her close and tipped up her chin with his fingertip. "To allow your fantasies to come to life, why else?"

He kissed her hard, his tongue moving possessively into her mouth, his arm wrapped around her waist holding her close. When he drew back, she couldn't help but look around to see if anyone had noticed their passionate embrace.

He nuzzled her ear. "My dear, this is a place to *indulge* your fantasies. No one will mind if I kiss you as much as I want to, or if you kiss me back."

There was a challenge in his voice that fired her blood. "Then perhaps you might show me around."

He looked down at her for a long moment. "If, at any time, you wish to leave, just tell me and we'll go."

"Having gone to all the trouble of bringing me here, you suddenly assume I won't like it?"

"Not that you won't like it, more that you will be shocked."

She gathered her courage. "Mayhap it is time for me to be shocked."

He kissed her fingers. "Then come with me, and don't remove your mask."

Nicholas led Louisa into the main salon on the first floor. He had no intention of taking her to the two floors above, where the more unusual and perverse sexual activities took place. He was certain the erotic antics being played out in the salon and the various viewing rooms attached to it would be enough to entertain Louisa—at least for tonight.

To the left of the double doors, two women and a man were sprawled naked on a couch. The man was busy suckling at one of the women's breasts while he enthusiastically fucked the other woman. Nicholas felt

Louisa stiffen and experienced a corresponding response in his cock. He bent his head and kissed
Louisa's throat, admired the way her breasts plumped
up over the tight bodice.

"What is it, my dear?"

She turned to whisper in his ear. "That man is with
two women."

Nicholas stopped to admire the tableau. "So he is."

Louisa shivered. "Everyone can see them."

"Yes." He took her hand and moved her farther into
the room, where a set of chairs were laid out in a circle.
In the center of the circle, two men were carefully undressing a woman. Her eyes were closed, but a small
smile played over her mouth as the men attended to
her. "Would you like to watch?"

Louisa didn't reply, but he maneuvered her into a
chair anyway and placed his arm around her shoulders.
He waited until one of the men began to unlace the
woman's corset before dropping his fingers down to toy
with the edge of Louisa's bodice. When the man kissed
the woman's breasts, he slid his fingers lower and
found Louisa's nipple. He squeezed and teased it into a
tight bud while she moved restlessly against him.

When the second man latched on to the woman's
other breast Louisa sighed, and Nicholas covered her
mouth with his and continued to fondle her nipple. He
was hard now and quite willing to pull up her skirts
and have her. But he had much more to show her, so
much more for her to enjoy with him. And that was
what it was all about, wasn't it? Not a quick poke, but a
lifetime of erotic experiences to share with one woman—
this woman.

He helped Louisa to her feet and took her over toward the buffet table, which was situated at the other end of the long room. He offered her a drink, and she shook her head, her gaze now avidly flitting around the room, her cheeks flushed, her teeth constantly biting into her lower lip. He wanted his teeth there, his mouth possessing hers, his cock between those rosy lips.

He tried to sound nonchalant. "Well, what do you think?"

She looked up at him, her brown eyes wide. "It is like something out of a dream."

"You have dreams like this?"

She blushed. "Sometimes. Doesn't everyone?"

"Indeed. You've dreamed of me, I hope."

"Of course, my lord."

"And what exactly do I do to you in these dreams?"

She met his gaze. "Everything."

His cock jerked at the shy invitation in her eyes. "Trust me. I intend to offer you more than you have ever dreamed of."

Louisa caught her breath as Nicholas kissed her again. She wasn't brave enough to tear at his clothing as many of the other patrons of the pleasure house were doing to their men. She yearned to feel his skin against hers, to see if she could reach the sexual heights he had shown her such an intriguing glimpse of.

"Come on."

She allowed Nicholas to take her hand and lead her out of the large red and gold salon and into a quieter hallway lined with white painted doors.

"Where are we now?" she whispered as he continued to walk down the long line of closed doors. Each door had a small plaque. She tried to read some of them, but found that only added to her confusion. What on earth did ANCIENT ROME or A MEDIEVAL FANTASY mean? It was almost as if they were titles of books or paintings.

Nicholas stopped and held her close. "Do you trust me?"

She studied his expression. "Yes, of course."

His smile was tender. "Good. Then close your eyes, count to five hundred, and then open the door and come in." He kissed her hard on the mouth. "Don't worry, I'll find you."

"But . . ." He kissed her again and then walked away, leaving her facing one of the doors. The handwritten sign on the door simply read LOUISA. With a sigh, she closed her eyes and began to count. She'd said she trusted him and had agreed to come to this oddly exciting place, so what else could she do but obey his surprising request? Her body was already quivering with a strange mixture of anticipation and arousal.

When she finished counting, she took a deep breath and opened the door. Darkness met her gaze, and she stepped forward onto a wooden-planked floor until she could see the faint outline of a lantern. Around her were several large stacked barrels, a torn sail, and what looked like a mast and rigging. For some strange reason she could smell the sea, and a small breeze lifted her skirts.

She had almost reached the pool of light surrounding the lantern, when a body crashed into hers and she instinctively yelped. A large hand covered her mouth, and she was pinned to a man's chest.

"I've got her, sir!" Instinctively, Louisa kicked out at

the man's shins and he laughed. "She's a feisty one, Captain. Be careful she don't rip your balls off with her teeth!"

Hearty laughter met the man's ribald remarks, and Louisa fought even harder. Whatever was going on, she had obviously blundered into the wrong room. Where was Nicholas and who on earth was manhandling her? Whoever he was, he smelled like a wet kipper. Two other men appeared with lanterns in their hands, and she gaped at them. They were dressed as sailors, one with an eyepatch, the other with a thick beard and a cutlass clasped in his hand.

She kicked out even harder. "Let me go!"

"Not until the captain gets here, my lady. He doesn't like stowaways, even pretty ones like you."

Louisa's thoughts swirled, slowed, and settled on a most peculiar notion. This scene was almost identical to the one at the beginning of her favorite gothic novel. The very one that had gone missing from her room. She took a deep breath and hoped she was right.

"Unhand me, sirs. You don't know who you are dealing with. I'm Lady Clarissa Devine, daughter of the Duke of Clifftopville. He will have your heads for this!"

Crude laughter and jeers greeted her retort, and for a moment she wondered if she'd gotten it completely wrong. Then another figure joined the three men, and her throat dried up completely. It was definitely the pirate captain, his billowing white sleeves edged with lace, the neck of his shirt open to display a hint of dark hair and his muscled chest. A long blue sash was tied around his waist, tight black breeches, and top boots completed his attire. Louisa hardly dared look at his face as he swaggered toward her.

"What have we here, Dawkins?"

"A lady, Captain, well she says she's a lady, but no real lady would be hiding aboard a pirate ship."

"I was not hiding, sir. I fully intended to confront this, this brigand."

A rakish smile displaying excellent teeth greeted Louisa's challenge, and the pirate captain moved even closer. He forced her chin up and stared down at her, his blue eyes stern.

"Aye she is a beautiful wench, and indeed a true lady. I'd recognize Lady Clarissa anywhere." He nodded at the crewmen. "You may leave us now. I'll take care of her." His eyes narrowed. "I'll teach her a lesson or two about creeping aboard my property."

" 'Tis hardly your property, sir, when you stole this ship from my father!" Louisa retorted.

"I stole nothing. Your father is the thief. He stole not only my ships but my birthright from me."

"You lie!" Louisa opened her eyes wide and threw herself away from him as the other sailors disappeared, leaving her alone in the semi-darkness with the pirate captain.

His hand snaked out and grabbed her shoulder, bringing her hard against his chest. "It matters not. You are mine now, and I would claim my prize."

Louisa closed her eyes as he kissed her possessively. His hand roved over her buttocks, bringing her up against the thick bulge in his tight buckskin breeches. She gasped as he threw her over his shoulder and marched purposefully toward the narrow cot in the corner. She landed on her back and he was on her immediately, his hands busy with her laces, stripping her out of her over gown and her bodice to reveal her old-fashioned stays and shift.

He reared over her, his gaze hungry, and produced a knife. Louisa couldn't help but moan as he cut through the tight lacing of her stays and tossed them to the floor. His mouth descended over her breast, and he caught her nipple and sucked hard. She writhed against him as his fingers tangled in her hair and then lower to tease and taunt her other breast. He shoved one leather-clad knee between her legs, opening her even wider to him.

The silk of her stockings felt too thin against the heat and hardness of his thigh. He moved up, and his knee met her mound and pressed against her most tender flesh. She could do nothing but hold on to any part of him he allowed. Soon her hips moved in rhythm to his urgent suckling, heat built between her legs, and she moaned his name. "Please."

He brought his head up and stared down at her. "What do you want, my little minx?"

In the book, this part of the scene had never been very explicit, so Louisa had to find her own words. "You, I want you."

He arched an eyebrow and whispered, "Aren't you supposed to make one last desperate bid for escape?"

"Oh, yes!" She shoved at his chest and managed to roll off the bed. "I'd rather drown than become your plaything, sir!"

"You'll not escape me." He caught her easily and brought her face down over his lap, pulled up her shift to expose her bare bottom.

Louisa stared down at the floorboards and realized she couldn't move. "You aren't really going to . . ." She gasped as his hand connected with her buttock, and then did it again. She began to grow unpleasantly warm as he alternated his smacks between her cheeks.

Suddenly, his hand slipped lower and slid between the heated wet folds of her sex, teasing and enticing, penetrating and then withdrawing. His palm settled over her most sensitive bud, and he buried two fingers inside her. She shrieked as his other hand descended on her heated buttocks, felt the twin pressure of the pain and the pleasure his hands could bring to her, felt it until they blended together into a blaze of desire that consumed her.

With a harsh sound of need, he brought her upright and down onto his thick waiting cock. Her scream was buried in his mouth as his hands took control of her hips. He soon had her moving up and down his shaft, bringing her closer and closer to a fiery explosion that threatened to shatter them both.

She climaxed and heard him groan, his fingers like iron bands on her hips keeping her down onto his still hard flesh. With a roar he stood up and, still holding her, returned to the narrow cot where he laid her down and continued to pound into her. His strokes shorter, yet more powerful, his mouth fused with hers as he came deep inside her.

She came again wrapping her arms and legs around him, biting his shoulder simply because she could, and because she wanted him to experience the wildness of the feelings he aroused in her.

* * *

Nicholas levered himself away from Louisa and stared down at her ruined shift. With a smile, he drew his dagger and slit it from top to bottom. Her breasts were flushed, her nipples hard and tight. Between her legs his cock still nestled, trapped in her luscious folds. Even as he enjoyed their joined flesh, his cock demanded more and began to fill out. He withdrew and crawled up the bed until he straddled her breasts. He wrapped his fist around the base of his shaft and touched the tip to her mouth.

"Make me hard again, wench. You know how to do it." She didn't argue and he liked that, liked that she had fallen so happily into the character of the heroine and allowed him to flaunt himself as the pirate captain. The lurid dialogue from the book might be ridiculous, but it had created a curious sensation in his loins and on his lady. Perhaps he should consider it a fine work of literature after all.

He leaned forward and eased the thick crown of his cock between Louisa's lips. He was already half-erect and it wouldn't take much to have him wanting her again. And he intended to fuck her to the best of his ability. She should never forget this night, or the many nights that were to come. Never forget that he was all the man she needed—with a little help from her obviously fully fleshed- out fantasies.

"My lady . . ." He moved his hips into the rhythm of her sucking, let the pleasure build slowly before he withdrew his cock from her mouth. "Turn around and place your hands on the wall." She got onto her knees and turned away from him. He paused, one hand stroking his shaft, to admire the sleek curve of her arse, her back, and the wetness already sliding down between her thighs. His seed, his woman. His to do anything he wanted to with—if she was agreeable.

Nicholas knelt behind her and rubbed his aching cock against the crease of her buttocks. He reached around to cup her breasts, stroked his thumbs over her nipples.

"You are beautiful, my captive. I'm going to enjoy taking you like this, from behind, where I can play with your breasts and your pretty little sex, where you can only open yourself to me and beg me never to stop, to stay inside you forever."

"Yes."

He'd long forgotten the script he'd so carefully learned. Louisa needed to know that sex was not all pretty words, that it could be graphic and crude and messy. He needed to know that she could accept him as he was, his wet, hard cock demanding entrance as often as he could persuade her to accept him.

On that thought, he slid inside her, enjoyed the way her muscles clamped down on his shaft, the heated wet glide of her flesh against his hardness, the kick of her heartbeat. She could be enough for him: he sensed it, perhaps had known it from the very first. If only he'd allowed himself to see it.

Louisa came again, and again he kept moving. She was moaning his name constantly now, the pleasure so intense and her body so sensitive that she'd forgotten how many times she'd taken him inside her. He'd demanded everything she'd had to give, taken her to heights of pleasure that she'd never dreamed of, shown her quite comprehensively that even dressed as a pirate he put all fictional pirate heroes in the shade.

With a deep satisfied groan, Nicholas collapsed over her, his breathing as erratic as her own, his heartbeat slowing and finally returning to normal.

"Nicholas?"

"Hmm . . . ?"

"Whenever I dreamed about the pirate captain, he always had your face. I always hoped . . ."

He rolled off her and lay beside her, his blue gaze fixed on hers. "Hoped what?"

"That you'd be my hero. In bed or out of it."

His mouth curved in his generous smile. "I'm glad to have been of service, my lady." He brushed the corner of her mouth with his fingertip. "And I'm also glad that you told me about that blasted book."

She wanted to blush but had neither the energy nor the necessary shame left to try. "There is another book that I love almost as well as this one."

He came up on one elbow and looked down at her. "There's another one?"

She smiled into his eyes, finally confident that if he was willing to go this far to please her, he would be willing to continue entertaining her deepest fantasies. "Well, there is this knight who returns from the Crusade . . ."

He placed his finger over her lips. "Perhaps you could tell Madame Helene about it. I'm sure she'd love to help you."

Louisa sat up, wincing as her body protested. "You asked Madame Helene to help you organize all this?"

Nicholas shrugged. "That is her business, to provide opportunities for her guests to enjoy their most erotic fantasies."

"Did you come here earlier this week, then?"

"I did."

Louisa smiled at him. "That explains why April was so concerned about me the other day. She must have heard the rumors that you were out on the prowl again."

His brows drew together as he glared down at her. "And you assumed I would do that?"

"I was told that every man eventually takes a mistress, and that I should be grateful you intended to spare me the worst of your bestial nature."

"April never said that load of ridiculous drivel, did she?"

"No, that was my mother. April just assured me that it was not my fault, and that when I had provided you with an heir or two, I should take a lover of my own."

Louisa gasped as Nicholas brought her back down onto the bed and loomed over her. "You will not take a lover."

"If you will not take a mistress."

"I have no intention of taking a mistress. I saw what havoc and humiliation that caused my mother and sister. I have no desire to do that to my own wife!"

His biting words no longer scared her. She wrapped a hand around his neck and kissed his nose. "I'm glad to hear it."

He kissed her and his voice sounded gruff. "Then you believe me?"

A warm sensation coalesced in the region of her

heart. "Why would I not? You've stooped to reading and acting out a gothic novel in a sexual pleasure house just to show me how happy you intend to keep me in bed. What else could a man do to show that he cares?"

"What indeed?" He moved away from her and handed her the remnants of her shift. "You might want to cover yourself before you move away from the bed."

She studied the ruined garment. "Why is that?"

He grinned as he stood up stark-naked and bowed toward the other end of the room. "Did I forget to mention that these rooms are sometimes opened to the other guests? I wonder if they enjoyed it as much as we did?"

Louisa stared at him open mouthed. Was he telling her the truth? She grabbed the sheet from the bed and hastily wrapped it around her. Nicholas offered her his hand to help her crawl off the bed, and Louisa buried her face in Nicholas's chest.

Nicholas started to chuckle. "It's all right, my love. There's no one there. I'd hardly do that to you on our first night here. Mayhap another time?"

She thumped him hard on the chest, and he laughed even more and hugged her tightly. She wasn't quite sure what she was going to do to get back at him yet, but she was certain that with Madame Helene's help, she'd find a way. Nicholas led her through another door where a maid helped her dress in a different set of clothing that Nicholas had brought for her.

She met him in the hallway, her mask firmly in place, her smile bright. He looked down at her, his head on one side. "You have forgiven me, then?"

"For tonight." She tucked her hand into the crook of his arm. "The pleasure you brought me far outweighed the embarrassment."

"I'm glad to hear that." He hesitated. "I would never do that to you; publicly humiliate you with another woman."

She smiled into his eyes. "I know. And I doubt I will ever want another man in the way I want you." She stood on tiptoe to kiss his mouth. "I love you, Nicholas. I know that is a terribly unfashionable thing to say to one's husband, but I do love you. I loved you from the first moment I saw you arguing with April at her birthday party."

He touched her cheek. "Even though she is infuriating, I love her, too." His smile was beautiful. "And, although I cannot claim to have fallen in love with you over the tea cups at April's, I do love you."

"Then we are lucky, aren't we?"

"Lucky?"

"To be married and thus free to be as unfashionably devoted to each other as we wish."

"We can start a new fashion," Nicholas said. "We'll become as popular as my sister for our devotion to each other." His gaze darkened. "Would you like to go home? I'd like to see you naked in my bed, and love to sleep beside you."

Louisa bit her lip. "As long as we can come back here one night."

He grinned. "I'll ask Madame Helene if she'll renew my membership. If you are included, I'm sure she'd be more than happy to oblige."

"And you'll ask her about my medieval knight?"

He pretended to groan, but she knew he was intrigued by the idea. Louisa smiled at her husband, the man not only of her reality, but of her dreams. And what possibly could be better than that?

Not Quite a
Courtesan

Maggie Robinson

Chapter One

Darius Shaw had been in many vermin-infested hovels before, most recently a berth of *The Star of the East,* docked right outside this filthy ale house. But his current surroundings quite took his breath away. He devoutly wished they would rob him of his sense of smell, too, and at the same time improve his hearing, for his brother Cyrus made no sense at all.

"Tell me again. Slower this time. You eloped with Sophia?"

"Sophronia actually, but as that's such a mouthful everyone calls her Sophy. Met her in Bath. She's a taking little thing with pots and pots of money. An orphan in the nominal care of a sickly aunt but guarded by her dragon-cousin. The woman wouldn't let her out of her sight, but you know us Shaws. Creative, we are. I managed. And then I had a stroke of luck. The aunt died and I seized my chance."

Darius rolled his eyes. "You eloped with a grieving child?"

Cyrus shrugged, unapologetic. "The aunt had been ill for years. Everybody knew it. Kept Sophy away from society, which was all the better for me, 'cause she don't know a thing about the Shaws. Well," he reflected, "she does now. When she opened Carmela's letter, all hell broke loose! Threw me out, she did. Wouldn't listen to a word I said, even when I told her I loved her." Cyrus rubbed a healing bruise under his eye rather furtively. Darius pictured a vase, good-quality but altogether unexceptional, being tossed in Cyrus's direction and hitting its mark. He liked Sophy already.

"Do you?"

"Do I what?"

"Love her, Cyrus," Darius said, losing patience.

Cyrus waved a hand in the direction of the tavern wench. "Whatever love is. She's really very sweet. I could love her if I set my mind to it."

Darius hoped his brother would not share these unsatisfactory sentiments with his new bride, or he'd never get back into her good graces and bank account. "So you've been staying on Jane Street—*Courtesan Court*—with Carmela. *That* should placate your wife." Darius's sarcasm was evident. His brother had inherited the Shaw looks and the Shaw charm, but none of the Shaw brains as far as he could tell.

"Where else was I to go? Haven't a sou. Carmela's a nice old bird. I can see why Uncle Algy popped off in her arms."

A great deal had happened since Darius left England; one event was that he and his brother were now the owners of a fully furnished love nest on Jane Street thanks to their dead uncle Algernon. The house was one of a dozen in that exclusive enclave that held the crème de la crème of mistresses—"Courtesan Court" as it was known to the *ton*. Unfortunately, the house also came with Carmela de Castro, who was not interested in vacating the premises until she got a proper congé after the indignity she suffered lying under their uncle's seventy-odd-year-old inert body for several uncomfortable minutes until her servants heeded her shrieks and pulled him off. While Carmela had kept her girlish figure, Uncle Algy had liked his dinner and his port a touch too much.

Neither Cyrus nor Darius had much ready cash. All of Darius's dubious riches were tied up in the tower of boxes that were piled outside on the wharf. The brothers couldn't very well sell the property "as is," with a rather mature Carmela in residence.

"So you see, you have to talk to her. I'm not getting anywhere."

"Talk to Sophy or Carmela?"

Cyrus snorted. "Carmela, of course. I can handle Sophy. Once I get close enough."

"And how do you propose I sweet-talk a sixty-year-old whore?"

"She's *not* an ordinary whore. She's still a looker, you know. And she knows more about the classics than I do."

That would not be difficult. *Anyone* was smarter than Cyrus. "I haven't any money left—it took all I had to come home," Darius said.

"Give her a trinket or two from your collection. You must have something in all that muck she'd like."

Darius hoped that what he brought back to his homeland was not muck. He had a good eye, and, unlike his brother, had paid close attention in his classics class. He also had buyers lined up to own very unique pieces of history if he could just find the time to unpack the crates. But he'd have to deal with his brother's domestic difficulties first.

"I'll see what I can do." He rose, thinking of anything he had handy in his portmanteau. The thought of rummaging through all the boxes on the pier was rather daunting for a variety of reasons. Besides, most of the valuables within were already promised to his clientele. They would not think kindly if he gave away their precious artifacts to a prostitute past her prime.

Cyrus brightened. "I knew I could count on you! I've been following the papers, hanging about the docks looking for *The Star of the East* every day for a week. I want to go home, Darius. You can move into Jane Street yourself once you get rid of Carmela. Although you might want to keep her on. She makes a delicious *flan*."

If Carmela were two decades younger, Darius might have reached an accommodation with her, for she had been one of the most sought-after mistresses in her day. He hadn't had sex in a very long while, but he was not about to embark on an affair with a woman old enough to be his mother, even if she could cook.

Gentlemen didn't *live* on Jane Street. They merely visited when the urge took them. But Cyrus's scheme had some advantages—Darius wasn't about to move in with his brother and spoil his honeymoon for the second time, and he couldn't afford a decent hotel. On Jane Street he'd have a place to store his boxes and inventory them, too, sparing him the expense of renting a warehouse. He could conduct his sales right at this discreet private address, which, considering the type of *objets* he dealt in, was rather fitting. Darius hated to admit it, but for once Cyrus might have a worthwhile idea.

"Keep away from the house for a few hours."

"Where am I to go?" Cyrus asked. "Carmela expects me back. We play bezique every afternoon."

No doubt the courtesan won every hand, too. "Take a walk. Stay here and finish your pint."

Cyrus squinted at the foul mud-brown liquid. "All right. I'll keep an eye on your boxes."

"No need of that. Malcolm's on it. Just tell him to bring them around to Jane Street."

"You're so sure you can convince Carmela?"

"I," said Darius Shaw, "am Darius Shaw." He had faced caliphs. Consuls. Reputed cannibals. He was sure one courtesan of a certain age would pose no trouble.

Prudence Thorne lifted her veil and examined the painting on the parlor wall. It was positively indecent, yet compelling just the same. She angled her head like a curious wren inspecting a worm, imagining the logistics of such a position. Certainly Prudence had never had occasion to find herself tangled up just so. If Carmela de Castro had remained, Pru might have asked her about its feasibility, but Senora de Castro was on her way back to Seville—or, more likely, Tunbridge Wells—with Sophy's second-best jewel case and a fistful of pounds.

Pru had been unable to dissuade her cousin from flinging her bits and bobs at the courtesan, who had seemed quite pleased with her payoff. Senora de Castro had left almost immediately with her elderly maid and her elderly manservant, asking Pru to explain to Mr. Shaw when he came home that he was no longer responsible for her and her ancient entourage, and could he possibly pack up her books and send them to her when she was settled?

Sophy had not flung her bits and bobs personally. Through a storm of tears and entreaties, she had begged Pru to do the flinging for her, and Pru, ever a loyal cousin, had girded her loins, donned her veil, and done so. And now she was responsible for the disposition of a courtesan's library, whatever horror it might hold.

Part of Pru's motivation in coming to Jane Street had been to reunite her young cousin with her worthless husband. Despite the difference in their ages, Pru cared for Sophy, even if she was silly and romantic. She had virtually raised the girl alone because Pru's widowed mother had been an invalid for years and couldn't even be bothered to raise her own daughter. It was Pru who arranged for Sophy's schooling—not that much had sunk in—Pru who met with Sophy's trustees, Pru who should have been chaperoning Sophy with more vigilance. She blamed herself for Sophy's runaway marriage. If Cyrus Shaw did not appreciate the prize he had in his innocent eighteen-year-old wife and preferred to while his time away on this indecent street, she was about to tell him where his duty lay.

But Pru would be lying if she denied a certain titillation in visiting the most wicked address in all of London. She was not here solely to give Cyrus Shaw a deserved dressing-down. One didn't reach Pru's advanced years without some knowledge of the world, but she had seized this opportunity to further her education. How many times would she be offered the chance to meet with a real, honest-to-goodness fallen woman?

Carmela had been a surprise. She was beautiful, of course, although quite a lot older than Pru would have thought. But there was no accounting for men's tastes. Blackguards and bastards, the lot of them. The only thing dependable about them was their undependability.

Pru did not relish the encounter with the errant bridegroom. She had seen the handsome Mr. Shaw at a distance several times in Bath and had not recognized him for the vile seducer that he was. He was astonishingly good-looking and had not given her a moment's attention. But Sophy, poor lamb, with all her golden curls and wide blue eyes, had not been so fortunate. While Pru saw to her ailing mother's comfort, he had secretly courted the girl until stars danced in her eyes and all rational thought deserted her head. Shaw had stolen Sophy away on the eve of her aunt's funeral, the scoundrel. But he was married to Sophy now and had responsibilities to *her*, not to a middle-aged mistress with a phony Spanish accent and suspiciously black hair.

Pru started at the ring of the doorbell. If it was Cyrus Shaw, surely he had a key to let himself in to satisfy his wicked ways. Her fingertips drummed against the painting's gilt frame. When the ringing did not cease, Pru pulled her veil down and went to the door, half afraid to imagine who would be calling upon the scandalous Senora de Castro in the daylight.

The man on the step was tall. Dark. Too handsome. "You!" she said. "I am glad you are here. We have business to discuss."

"We certainly do, madam, and I will not be put off like some other members of my family. But the discussion is not for outdoors where all the world can hear us." He brushed by her, and Pru became acutely aware she was the only one in the house. But being alone with her cousin's husband could not compromise her, could it? They stood for a minute in the front hall glowering at each other, although the man did not get the full benefit of her glower, veiled as she was. Pru retreated into the parlor, and Mr. Shaw followed.

He took up far too much room, looking out of place amidst the pink and purple stripes and patterns. To her horror, he picked up the reticule she had left on the sofa. The fortune hunter! But instead of shaking out the few coins she had, he slipped a velvet bag into it.

"This will have to satisfy you. It's rare and valuable and old. Just like you."

"I beg your pardon!" Pru said, stung. She was but nine-and-twenty. Old*ish*, but not yet dead.

"I mean no disrespect. But you must admit you're past the pinnacle of your profession."

Her profession? Good Lord, did this man take her to be one of the courtesans of Courtesan Court? "Well it is you who is old and addled, if you cannot even recognize your own mistress," Pru said with asperity. She tore the veil from her face. "And may I remind you that you have a young wife, who, God willing, will long outlive you and outlast the ignominy of being married to you! Only God knows why, but she wants you back. You may have a pretty face, but your character leaves a great deal to be desired, sir! If you do anything—anything at all to ever hurt or discomfort her again—leave the top to the toothpowder tin off, aim carelessly into the chamberpot, snore in your sleep—you will answer to me!"

To Pru's dismay, the man smiled slowly at her. He had shockingly white teeth—his toothpowder had been used to good effect—and an elegant crease on his left cheek, too sophisticated to be called a mere dimple. For twenty-three or so seconds she could see why Sophy had been smitten.

"I take it you are not Carmela de Castro."

Pru felt the blood rush to her cheeks. "Of course I am not!" She took a step backward. "And you are not my cousin Sophy's husband, are you?"

"I'm sure she is a charming girl, but I would not change places with my brother for all the sand in Egypt. I've just come back from there, by the way. Just in time to shovel Cyrus out of his usual mess, although it's my uncle Algernon's mess to begin with. Where is Carmela?"

"She's gone. I paid her off."

"Brave girl! Cyrus was completely under her thumb. And not," he said hastily, "the way you and your cousin seem to think. My brother is an imbecile, but he fancies himself in love with your cousin. More or less." Mr. Shaw ran a long brown finger under his collar. Now that Pru thought about it, his resemblance to his brother, while significant, was not absolute. This Mr. Shaw was darkly tanned and somehow more *tumbled* than the man she'd glimpsed across the Pump Room all those weeks ago. His hair was disreputably long and his clothing somewhat worn. Mr. Cyrus Shaw had looked like a fashion plate come to life.

Pru was not going to be taken in by a Shaw like Sophy was. "Explain."

"My uncle Algernon died here a few weeks ago." His face suddenly took on a mournful look. "And I understand your mother has recently passed on as well. My condolences."

"Your deviant brother eloped with my cousin the night before the funeral."

"Again, I am sorry. I have had little influence on Cyrus his whole life, I'm afraid. He's a bit ramshackle, but we should not be held accountable for the foibles of our relatives. We don't get to choose them, do we?"

Pru supposed she would not have chosen her drug-addled mother if there had been a mother store. She might have picked up Sophy in a shop, but had had many causes to return her for a refund over the years. "Go on."

"My uncle Algernon had a long-standing arrangement with Senora de Castro. When he died so suddenly, she was grief stricken and appealed to my brother for assistance."

"She wanted money."

"Exactly. And I do feel rather badly that you beat me to the punch. But now that she's gone, please explain to your cousin that she was mistaken in ever thinking Cyrus's affections were engaged in any way. He, like the two of us, was only doing his family duty, trying to tie up our uncle's loose ends, as it were."

"He has been *living* on Jane Street," Pru reminded him. "How can we know he remained faithful residing in such a hotbed of sin?"

"I intend to reside here myself for the time being. I assure you, some of us Shaws have self-control."

Pru sniffed. The man before her did not look as if he denied himself much of anything, or had anything denied him. He was far too virile for his own good. Whereas she, garbed in black mourning from head to toe and rather beige underneath it all, could pass for an Anglican nun.

Even if she wasn't a virgin.

A sharp rap at the door put an end to their discussion. Mr. Shaw excused himself, and before Pru could put her veil back down, a crew of brawny men toted crates into the parlor, filling the space even more effectively than Mr. Shaw had.

"What's all this?" Pru asked in spite of herself. She knew she should just pick up her reticule and go home.

One of the workmen stared at her before he put an enormous wooden box down quite near her foot. He whistled. "A living, breathin' Jane. Not what I expected, but not bad. Congratulations, guv'nor. Most of the men in London would like to be in your boots. And in your bed." He had the unmitigated audacity to *wink* at Pru.

A Jane! That's what the women of Jane Street were nicknamed. He thought she was—

"You are mistaken." Mr. Shaw's voice had shifted from smooth to sharp edged. "This lady is not a courtesan. You will apologize at once."

The man stared at her even harder, then shook his head. "There's no shame to it. We all have to make a livin', don't we, love. But if you'll take my advice, you'll get rid of that black dress. It don't do a thing for you, and you don't want a man like Darius Shaw to lose interest now, do you?"

"Malcolm! If you do not shut your gob this instant I will do what Sheikh Mahmoud's men did to you in Alexandria. Without hesitation."

Malcolm paled. "No need of that, guv. Sorry, miss. But we're on Jane Street. When his nibs's brother said we were to deliver the treasure here, I just supposed—"

"That's enough, Malcolm. Pay these men and go down to the kitchen. I am starving. Would you like to join me for lunch, Miss— Why, I just realized I don't even know your name."

"Prudence Thorne." But she was not going to tell the man her middle name was *Jane.*

Chapter Two

Prudence Thorne. She looked full of caution at the moment and seemed a bit prickly as well. It was a fitting name for her. Cyrus had described her as a dragon, but only if the dragon's scales were nondescript. Miss Thorne was of average height, but he still had to bend his neck to look at her. Her hair, what he could see of it beneath the brim of her black hat, was either dark blond or light brown depending on one's perception. She had blue eyes and an unremarkable figure. Darius was not quite sure why he invited her for lunch, except that he had seen her spark of interest when Malcolm mentioned the word "treasure."

It might be amusing to show off some of his prizes to an innocent. Darius was aware that his devil had the upper hand, for surely Miss Thorne was about to suffer enough with Cyrus for a cousin-in-law. But the woman looked in need of a little fun.

"L-lunch?" she stuttered.

"Yes. You are acquainted with the term? Food. Usually lighter fare. I have no idea what Malcolm will find in the larder, but I hear there might be *flan*. A Spanish dessert, you know."

The nostrils on Miss Thorne's neat little nose flared. "Carmela de Castro is no more Spanish than I am."

Darius raised a brow. "Really? My uncle Algernon always claimed she was. He even studied the language a little so they could converse more congenially. But perhaps they didn't do much talking after all."

Miss Thorne's full, pink lip curled. "Disgusting."

"Now, now. Uncle Algy was not married, you know. It was nobody's business but his where he spent his time and money. I never met Carmela, but she and my uncle were together for twenty years. I gather their relationship was rather sweet and cozy. Algernon was made to feel quite at home here."

Miss Thorne gazed about the room. "Those paintings are an abomination."

"There's no accounting for taste. I have a friend who collects such pictures. I'll have to see if he'll take these off my hands. For the right price."

"Speaking of which, I suppose your brother thinks he can run through Sophy's money. Well, he can't. Not until she's twenty-one." Miss Thorne looked pleasantly grim.

Cyrus wouldn't like the sound of that. "I thought a woman's money belonged to her husband upon marriage."

"Sophy's trustees are conservative men, and she married without their permission. The terms of her inheritance state she cannot come into all her funds—which are considerable—unless they approve of her marriage or until her twenty-first birthday. I'm afraid I've seen to it that they are not especially impressed with Cyrus at the moment. So he will have to settle for living on her quarterly allowance."

"I see. And how much is that?"

Miss Thorne named a reassuringly high figure, which would keep Cyrus away from him and out of debtor's prison, God willing. "I think even my brother can be expected to be satisfied by that amount." He felt just cheeky enough to ask, "Are you an heiress as well, Miss Thorne?"

She had a very pretty blush. He'd once seen a pale pink rose just that color in Damascus. "I am. Our fathers were both partners in a very successful shipping company. It was sold, of course, upon their deaths. They drowned at sea when Sophy was a baby. Her mother died in childbed. So I have been in charge of Sophy almost all her life and more than half of mine. I'll not stand by and watch your brother make her unhappy."

She had reverted to her belligerence, but Darius supposed it was warranted. "How is it you never married? I should think fortune hunters like my brother would have been after you in droves."

Her blue eyes went flat. "They were. And I did."

"I beg your pardon?"

"I married, Mr. Shaw. When I was not much older than Sophy. I am a widow. And glad of it."

Well now. It was *Mrs.* Thorne, and not grieving for her lost love. "I gather I should not offer more condolences."

Mrs. Thorne shook her head. "My husband died

soon after we were married. He was killed falling from his mistress's bedroom window. And it was not the fall that killed him but the gunshot wound. Her husband came home unexpectedly."

Her face was impassive. Each unembellished sentence was delivered with wooden precision. How many times had she felt it necessary to tell this story? "It was the talk of the *ton* for years. I wonder that you did not hear of it."

Darius took a closer look at her. If she was as bloodless and buttoned up with her husband, no wonder the poor devil looked elsewhere for comfort.

"I've been in and out of the country, traveling for quite some time. It feels odd to be home."

"I daresay. Were you in the army?"

"No, Mrs. Thorne. I am a treasure hunter for my sins, and the war put quite a crimp in my business. I've been in the East acquiring antiquarian collectibles and forgeries to sell to my unsuspecting countrymen for an exorbitant profit."

There. The flash of curiosity dashed across her face again. But also distaste. A woman like Mrs. Thorne might have better respected him if he'd died in battle. But Shaws had their own peculiar honor.

"You are in trade."

Darius stuck his gloveless hands out. "Yes. As you see, my hands are stained with filthy lucre. But not enough of it."

Her lips quirked. "I have no objection to men making an *honest* living. As I told you, my father had a shipping business. What is in all these boxes?"

"I will show you after lunch. Do say you'll join me."

She hesitated. "Sophy will be anxious to learn what has transpired here."

"I'll send Malcolm with a message. Or maybe Cyrus himself if he turns up. You have not met him yet?"

Mrs. Thorne shook her head. "I stayed in Bath seeing to my mother's affairs. It was too late for me to do anything about Sophy once she eloped. But when I got her letter, I came to Town right away." She paused. "I could press her to get an annulment."

"On what grounds?"

"A person cannot enter a legal contract until the age of twenty-one."

"Your cousin would be ruined. You might as well declare her insane."

"She is. She married your brother, did she not?"

Cyrus might not dip the sharpest quill in the inkwell, but there was no true harm in him. He just needed money, and at least had the wit to find a hen-witted girl with plenty of it. "My brother is not the devil you think he is. Stay to lunch and I shall charm you with tales of our boyhood so your opinion may change."

Mrs. Thorne sighed deeply. "Very well. One must eat, I suppose."

Darius thanked the gods. It was imperative the starchy Mrs. Thorne not interfere with her cousin's marriage any further. Darius did not want to be saddled with Cyrus any longer than he had to be. The care and feeding of his brother had been an expense over the years, causing him to do any number of unsavory things.

But lunch with Mrs. Thorne was not one of them. At the moment she looked like a tasty, if tart, morsel. He had indeed been without a woman too long if this virtuous little shrew was so appealing.

Whyever had she babbled on about Charles Thorne? It was most unlike Pru to ever speak of her late and un-lamented husband. They'd only been married seven weeks, after all. She could not even remember what he looked like.

She did recall that he'd been assiduous in his atten-tions, chasing her all around Bath just as Cyrus Shaw had chased Sophy. But once he'd caught her, he'd be-trayed her without two thoughts.

Because of Charles, she should have been so much more careful with Sophy. But it was not as though she never spoke to her cousin about the perfidy of men. The girl had received lecture after lecture even before she left her pinafores and pigtails behind. And where had Pru's words got her? A visit to infamous Jane Street and lunch with an attractive, no-doubt-disreputable man, while her cousin was still stuck in her marital bonds with a bounder.

The walls of the dining room were even worse than the walls of the parlor. Life-size life studies hung on every side. Breasts, buttocks, rapturous smiles—Pru had no choice but to focus on her food and eat as quickly as she could without choking to death. Mr. Shaw seemed untroubled by the scenery, tucking into the slapdash lunch that his man had assembled with gusto. Between bites he did everything in his power to assure her that his brother Cyrus was worthy of Sophy, but Pru remained unconvinced.

Her reluctance must have been obvious, for at last he pushed himself away from the table. "Mrs. Thorne, I have proof that my brother wants to be a better man. He has refused all his life to take part in the family business."

"And that makes him responsible? One who is idle and lives off the work of others?"

"Hear me out. The Shaws are not precisely respectable, I am sorry to say. My father founded an importing company and attempted to train both his sons to take it over when he passed. Cyrus would have nothing to do with it, and rightfully so. His sensibilities are far too refined, too delicate."

"Good Lord. What is it that you import? Opium? White slaves?"

"Nothing quite so egregious, but some in the *ton* might find the items equally repugnant. Come. Allow me to open one of the crates and you can see for yourself."

Pru felt herself pale. What horror could be inside the box. A shrunken head? A voodoo doll? She spent a great deal of time reading about the fantastical finds of great explorers and naturalists. She'd really had very little else to do as she sat by her mother's bedside. But to actually lay eyes on such things—she was by turns curious and terrified.

And continued to feel both emotions as she watched Mr. Shaw remove his jacket and roll up the sleeves of his linen shirt. His browned arms were sprinkled with fine dark hair. Charles had been fair, looked rather golden in the firelight. Pru shut her eyes at the unwelcome image. She did *not* remember what he looked like. She *didn't*.

Mr. Shaw rummaged through a leather satchel and unearthed a crowbar. With a few quick flicks of his wrist, the lid of the box popped open. Straw spilled out onto the rug, and Mr. Shaw sneezed quite violently.

"Damn. I mean drat. Pardon my language, Mrs. Thorne, but I seem to have an aversion to straw." He pinched the bridge of his nose in an unsuccessful attempt to quell the second, even more alarming, sneeze. He fished a handkerchief out of his pocket. His eyes looked watery and red already.

Pru counted the number of crates. "How on earth will you be able to unpack all these boxes?"

"My man Malcolm will help. He's a useful fellow, although he doesn't have a gentle touch. He's dropped more than his fair share of valuables." He stuck an arm into the straw and pulled out a bronze chalice. "This is as good a place as any to instruct you on the Shaws' wicked business. Step a little closer, Mrs. Thorne."

"I will not, you silly man. Bring it out into the hallway where you will not be subjected to the packing material any longer than you need be."

"Why, Mrs. Thorne, I'm flattered. Are you concerned about my health?"

"I don't wish to be sneezed on. What are you waiting for?"

Mr. Shaw grinned. "How did your cousin dare defy you? You frighten me to death."

"Nonsense," Pru grumbled, not letting herself be swayed by the twinkle in his eyes. Very fine eyes—

moss green with bits of gold. They navigated through the stack of boxes to the black-and-white-tiled hallway. The chalice gleamed in the shaft of sun from the front door's sidelights.

"Very detailed work, isn't it?" Pru began, but then she saw *all* the details. "Good heavens."

"I believe it's meant to be hell, actually. See the little cloven hooves? Shaw Antiquities specializes in sensual, some might even say pornographic, artwork and artifacts. We are the go-to people for those collectors who fancy something a bit different from the run-of-the-mill Staffordshire dog. I've traveled the globe to fulfill the wishes of my clients, always on the lookout for the rare and randy."

"I—I see," Pru said faintly. She certainly did. And despite her innate objections, her eyes remained open and in wonder at the cavalcade of sex acts depicted on the chalice. She squeaked. "*That* is possible?"

"Everything is anatomically correct and within the purview of a normally limber and morally ambiguous man," Mr. Shaw said, his twinkle now blinding.

Pru knew she was blushing, could feel the heat blossom from her breasts to her hairline. She wiped a bit of damp from her brow, inadvertently loosening the corkscrew curl she had pomaded down. She had just the one curl on her temple in her mass of straight, boring hair, a twirling little worm that got caught in her eyelashes. She blinked it back and aimed for a look of indifference.

"I really must be going, Mr. Shaw. I suppose I should thank you for showing me part of your collection, but I would be lying if I told you I felt any gratitude at all. This is—you are—I don't know what I shall tell Sophy about the family she's married into."

"You may tell her that Cyrus has no hand in the family business. And assure yourself that after I dispose of this lot, Shaw Antiquities will shutter its doors for good. I'll have enough to invest in something more respectable, and I'm tired of traveling. It's time I settled down. Like my brother."

Somehow Pru could not see this man at the center of domestic tranquility, surrounded by dogs and children. Instead, a vision came of him robed, riding an Arabian stallion, flashing a scimitar. And in the next second, she was beside him, veiled and warm from the desert sun. There would be sugared dates and roasted lamb at the oasis, and long lovemaking in a silken tent beneath a brilliant moon. They would whisper hours into the night, the gentle breeze beyond rattling the palm leaves.

"Mrs. Thorne, I say, are you all right? You look flushed. I would be happy to escort you home."

Mr. Shaw had brought her back to reality. How long had she been standing in the hallway with these inappropriate thoughts? She focused on the tile at her feet.

"That won't be necessary. As you know, Jane Street is conveniently close to the best addresses. I shall walk."

"I know you did not bring a maid or footman with you."

"How could I? It would have been even more scandalous to involve one of the servants in this scheme. Poor Sophy. Even if your brother is innocent of having an affair, I cannot think he will make her a good husband."

"Give him a chance, Mrs. Thorne. We Shaws are full of surprises."

Pru snorted. She fetched her gloves and reticule from the parlor sofa, and pinned her veiled hat to her chignon. "Good day, Mr. Shaw."

"I hope we meet again soon."

Pru was glad he could not see her face. Mr. Shaw was not a man she trusted herself to meet again.

Chapter Three

Sophy had inherited her father's well-appointed town house, and it was there she brought her new husband for the one week they lived as man and wife before Carmela's letter disrupted their connubial bliss. In the ensuing weeks, Sophy had attempted to make the place her home, rearranging outdated furniture and trying to order the skeleton crew of servants about between bouts of hysteria. Pru knew Sophy's domestic skills were lacking, so she was not at all surprised to find the front door ajar and the butler nowhere to be found.

Pru would have to see to it that the staff knew their proper place—for almost two decades they'd had Number 8 Rex Place to themselves without a mistress's interference. Sophy was young, but Pru was confident she could help her cousin get the upper hand over both the servants and her husband given enough time. Then Pru, duty done, would go back to Bath and her boring life.

But it might not be so boring now. Pru hated to

admit it, but with her demanding mother gone, she might have opportunities she did not have before. Even if she was in mourning, she could still indulge herself, attending lectures and concerts. She might even travel once Sophy was settled—perhaps to some of the exotic places that Darius Shaw had been to. She, of course, would not bring back such shocking souvenirs.

She crossed the threshold and removed her hat before the hall mirror. All the veiling in the world had not kept her safe from Darius Shaw. But she would never see him again unless they were in church, standing as godparents over the baptismal font with the newest little Shaw. Pru shuddered at the thought.

And then she heard Sophy's bloodcurdling scream. Pru dropped her hat to the floor, grabbed a brass candlestick from the hall credenza, and rushed into the parlor.

For the second time today, she was unwillingly exposed to an image she would have to scrub out of her mind with very strong mind soap. Pru could only presume that the bare arse of the gentleman rutting over Sophy was her husband Cyrus. Neither one of them were aware that she was standing there armed as they bounced on the divan, engaging in conjugal relations with unbridled enthusiasm in an extremely inconvenient place. Pru could not imagine sitting on the worn blue brocade cushion ever again. Perhaps she could persuade Sophy to re-cover it when they redecorated the house.

She crept out of the parlor, returned the candlestick to its rightful place, gathered up her hat and reticule, and climbed the stairs as quietly as she could, not that Sophy and Cyrus were apt to hear a thing. The house was absolutely silent save for Sophy's incessant screeching and Cyrus's manly grunts. Pru locked herself in her room, but the door was not quite thick enough to muffle the noise completely.

Good Lord. Pru devotedly hoped Sophy had given all the servants the afternoon off, else she would never get control of them. Pru had left her own maid in Bath when she received Sophy's summons. Barlow had a spring cold, and the trip would only have exacerbated her misery. So now Pru found herself alone—and more than likely unwanted—in the house with the newly-weds.

She had been a newlywed once. She had never, however, made noisy love on a parlor couch in the daytime where anyone at all might have come upon her. Charles had come to her bedroom quietly in the dark wearing a respectable nightshirt. He had pulled up her respectable nightgown and put his *thing* in, sometimes even forgetting to kiss her. Pru wondered if he bothered to kiss Lady Merrifield before her husband shot him. It seemed a shame to go to one's Maker—or more likely the devil—kissless.

Pru touched her own lips with her still-gloved hands. She would bet a crate of valuable indecent statues that Darius Shaw could kiss a woman senseless. He had a fine mouth—full lips that quirked in mischief. Heavy lids fringed with dark lashes. Capable brown hands, a little nicked from his adventures unearthing such dreadful objects. Shaggy dark hair that just begged for brushing back. A tall, rangy body—

Good Lord, again. Pru had been infected by lust. For ten years she had not permitted herself to think of sexual congress and all that it entailed. But after a few hours on Jane Street and a few seconds on Rex Place, she was ruined.

She tossed her reticule on the bed, and then remembered that Darius Shaw had stuffed something into it. Drat *and* damn. Whatever it was, she could send it back to Jane Street with a footman, if any of Sophy's came back. Curious, she tugged open the drawstring of her fringed little bag and pulled out the velvet pouch. Whatever was inside had not been heavy enough for Pru to notice that she'd inadvertently filched it away from Mr. Shaw.

When she shook the bag open, she gasped. An old gold ring studded with an oval of small rubies and a larger diamond at the apex fell into her hand. The design was oddly flowerlike, with a hole at the center where the flesh of one's finger would show. The rows of ruby petals curved around the opening and the diamond—a good-sized stone—was at the top, peeking out from a layer of red. Pru stared at it as it sparkled in a shaft of sun. She had never seen anything like it. An urgent need to strip off her gloves and slip the ring on her finger overtook her, so she did. The ring covered her knuckle completely, save for the circle of skin that was visible. Her finger grew warm, and she stroked the unusual setting, checking for loose stones.

She should return it immediately. Definitely. But Mr. Shaw had been prepared to give it away to Carmela de Castro, so perhaps he wouldn't miss it. Wanting to examine it in natural light, Pru walked to the window that faced the little garden in the back of the house and wiggled her finger. The ring's dazzle was most satisfactory. She was so blinded by it she almost missed the shadow of movement below. Reluctantly breaking her stare, she looked down. Somehow Sophy and Cyrus had managed to leave the sofa and were now writhing naked in the spring-green grass for all the neighbors to see. Pru looked up and saw the quick swish of lace curtains from the house opposite.

Double drat and damn. Sophy's reputation was ruined, even if Cyrus was her legal husband. One didn't engage in an al fresco affair with one's *husband*. It simply wasn't done. And just blocks from Hyde Park. She shoved the window open.

"Sophronia Prescott! Stop that this instant!" she hissed. She kept her voice as low as possible, although the couple's acrobatic activity had already attracted attention.

To Pru's relief, the writhing stopped. Cyrus Shaw cricked his neck up and frowned at her. "Mind your own business, Mrs. Thorne," he said loud enough to be heard at Speaker's Corner. "And it's Sophronia *Shaw* now."

"How dare you befoul my cousin outdoors like you are a common laborer and she a common streetwalker? Sophy is a *lady*. We are in Mayfair, for heaven's sake." Pru spoke a little louder, out of temper. Cyrus Shaw's smugness was enough to make anyone scream.

Sophy piped up, pink cheeked and sounding not one whit sorry. "It was my idea, Pru. To be under God's sky, to declare our love before nature—"

"Rubbish. Bad enough you used the parlor sofa. You have a perfectly good bedroom, Sophy. And may I remind you we have neighbors."

"I declare my love before them, too," Sophy said stubbornly. "You wouldn't understand, Pru. A woman

like you—you're old! You have no romantic soul. But
now that I know Cyrus was never unfaithful, my love
for him has no boundaries. We shall never be subject to
foolish conventions. We want to be free—free to love
and laugh, to flout silly rules. Kiss me again, Cyrus."
And with a parting sneer at Pru, he did.

Pru slammed the window shut. This was worse than
she thought. Unconscionable. She could not remain
here while Sophy threw away every bit of good sense
Pru had tried to drum into her and behaved with such a
shocking lack of decorum with a gazetted fortune
hunter. She would go back to Bath at once.

Ungrateful brat. Stupid girl. Empty-headed twit. Pru
let vent every epithet she'd held back in the raising of
Sophronia Eugenia Maria Prescott. She, Prudence Jane
Thorne, née Prescott, had given up the best years of her
life to nurse her peevish mother and nursemaid petulant Sophy. Neither one of them had ever appreciated
her. And her one attempt to escape her responsibilities
had ended in ignominy when she married a fortune
hunter of her own.

As she stuffed bits of clothing in her valise, Pru considered herself lucky that she had not brought much
with her on her flying trip to save Sophy. Hah. The
child did not want to be saved, but copulate in the grass
like a cat in heat. Well, Pru washed her hands of her.
Let her husband run through her monthly allowance,
then run through her inheritance if they were still married in three years. Pru would not stand by and watch it
happen. She was going back to Bath.

A woman like you. Old. No romantic soul. Sophy's
insulting words rattled around Pru's head. It was true
she was practical. She'd had to be. Her one step on a

romantic path had resulted in a grievous stumble. But now with her mother dead and Sophy married, she supposed she might do anything she liked.

The ring caught on one of Pru's sensible cotton stockings. She really should return it before she left London. It was indeed rare and valuable. *And old, like her,* a nasty little voice in her head said. An air of ancient mystery was steeped in its stones. She gave a tug, but the ring remained in place.

How embarrassing. Mr. Shaw would know she had tried it on. But perhaps he had something in his tool bag that would remove it. She was not going to stay on Rex Place one minute longer to look for a dab of butter.

Twenty minutes later, with her crewelwork valise in hand, Pru rapped on Mr. Shaw's blue Jane Street door. He opened it himself, tears streaming down his face.

"Good heavens! Whatever is the matter?"

Darius Shaw waved his hand and shook his head. "Can't talk," he rasped. "Throat's closed."

"Have you been at those boxes again, you foolish man? Where is Malcolm?"

"Errand."

"Then you should have waited for him to come back! It is clear you cannot unpack everything by yourself. Why, you might even perish! I can almost hear a death rattle in your chest right now!" It was true. Mr. Shaw wheezed and sniffled, sounding much like her mother's snappish bulldog Jack. The dog had sounded like it was dying for years, but much to Pru's annoyance, it clung to life until smelly old age. Pru liked dogs in general; however, Jack was just one more disagreeable thing she'd had to take care of over the course of her life.

Mr. Shaw took an unsteady step toward the parlor, but Pru held him back. "Do not go in there! Come, I'll take you down to the kitchen and make you a cup of tea. You might also stand over the steam to clear your head. Really, I don't know what you were thinking. Straw! Surely you could have found sawdust or cotton batting when you know you cannot abide the stuff. If you don't live long enough to enjoy your profits, what good is it to hurry? Patience is a virtue." She pushed him down the hall.

"Need the money."

"I agree, money is very useful," Pru said. "But it won't help you when you're dead." When they reached the bottom of the kitchen stairs, she fished a clean handkerchief from her reticule. "Here. Dry your eyes."

The kitchen was square, white, and pleasantly clean. Pru set about opening all the windows and propping the tradesman's door open. The sooner Mr. Shaw got some fresh air and the irritants out of his system, the better.

Obedient, Mr. Shaw fell into a chair and mopped his face. He stared at her with vampire-red eyes as she pumped water into a kettle and put it on the boil. "Thank you," he croaked.

"Think nothing of it. It's what I do, take care of people. Not that it's been worth my while. My cousin Sophy, for example. Hopeless." She slammed the sugar bowl down on the table. "Why, do you know what I found her doing when I got back to Rex Place? I couldn't possibly tell you. It's too shocking."

"Sex." Mr. Shaw coughed.

"Yes. Exactly. I cannot stay there. I am going home."

She filled a teapot with tea leaves and waited for the kettle to whistle.

"Why are you here?"

Pru felt her face flush. "Two reasons. I hoped you could talk some sense into your brother. He cannot go cementing his relationship on furniture and back lawns forever. Sophy will not be able to go about in society if people think she's a hoyden. She may not be of the peerage, but Prescott Shipping was a well-respected business. Her mother was the daughter of a baronet. She could have a place in society, despite your brother's background."

"Doubt it. Shaws are beyond the pale."

"Sophy told me your maternal grandfather was Baron Allgood."

"Yes, but the Shaws are all bad." Mr. Shaw laughed at his own joke, which had the unfortunate effect of making him gasp for breath for a full minute. When he recovered, he added, "My mother made an imprudent match, much like Sophy. My grandfather didn't acknowledge us, but his brother Algernon did, bless him. It is he who left us this house. Which I must sell as soon as possible. Time really is of the essence. I have clients waiting for their treasures as well. The sooner I go through all the crates, the sooner my future and fortune are assured."

Pru passed him a cup of tea. He had just delivered a rather long speech, wheezing less already. She watched his throat ripple as he took a long swallow of tea and forced herself to look away.

"And the second reason?"

Pru still had her gloves on, but she preferred to show

him rather than tell him. Either way, it was all rather mortifying. Pulling off the black kid, she held out her left hand.

To her surprise, Mr. Shaw grinned. "Can't get it off?"

She shook her head. "I have not really tried much. I needed to get away from Rex Place before I witnessed anything else of an unsavory nature. Is there butter in your larder? I shouldn't like to smear it with cooking grease."

Mr. Shaw shrugged. "Malcolm went to the shops. If there isn't, I'll send him out again when he gets back. I can't believe a woman like you put the ring on to begin with."

There it was again. *A woman like you.* Did no one think she might like a bit of fun and frivolity? Proper fun and frivolity, of course. She lifted her chin. "It's very pretty. Tempting. Any woman would have done the same as I."

Mr. Shaw looked as if he were about to have another coughing fit. "By God. Do you not know what it is?"

Pru looked down at the strange flower. "Rubies. Diamonds."

His eyes lit with amusement. "It is a woman's nether lips, Mrs. Shaw. The diamond is the center of all her pleasure."

"What?" Pru looked at her finger in horror.

"It is Indian work. Fifteenth century. Made for a maharajah for his favorite mistress. There are a pendant and earbobs to match, although there is some dispute as to where the earrings were actually to go. The dealer I acquired the set from seemed to think—" He broke off suddenly, as if aware that Pru's finger was on fire. "Don't worry. If we can't get it off, people might not notice."

"Not notice?" Now that Pru knew what the horrible ring was, she could not help but see the truth. The tiny gold curling hairs that she thought was simple filigree. The bright red folds of rubies. The sparkling erect diamond, poking out. The hole—Pru felt her face flame. "Where are the knives kept?"

"Now, now. You might cut your finger off."

"If I have to, I'll cut off my hand."

"Entirely unnecessary. I'm sure we'll manage to remove the ring somehow. In the meantime, I've got an idea."

Pru couldn't think for the buzzing in her head. She wore a concubine's ring. Had the maharajah also sported one—a golden penis that fit into the hole? Trembling from head to toe, she sat down on the kitchen bench before she fell.

"I wonder if you wouldn't mind helping me here for a day or two. It's obvious I cannot tackle the boxes myself—you were right. I had a great deal of trouble drawing breath toward the end. If you hadn't arrived when you did, I might very well be dead. So," he said with an earnest smile after he blew his nose—sounding like the maharajah's trumpeting elephant, Pru thought sourly— "you've saved my life. But I really need to dispose of everything as quickly as possible. Would you mind staying and supervising the unpacking? Malcolm is so ham-handed, and to tell you the truth, he does not read very well. I have a manifest that must be checked and objects labeled for distribution. I'm afraid even if I sat out in the hallway, I would be most unwell. This attack was the worst it's ever been."

Pru looked at him as if he'd sprouted two heads. "You want me to work on *Jane Street?*"

"Not in the usual sort of way," Mr. Shaw said with a quick smile. "Our relationship would be entirely businesslike. It might be convenient, however, if you did move in. That way we could get through everything so much faster. And I'm sure you have no wish to trip over my brother and your cousin enjoying their honeymoon. Outside on the lawn, you said? I do hope they didn't pick up any *Trombicula autumnalis.*" At Pru's blank look, he clarified. "Chiggers, you know. Devilish little things. They get under your skin—"

"Mr. Shaw," Pru said with as much frost as she could muster, "I am on my way back to Bath, and I most certainly will not delay my departure to assist you with your—your so-called *treasures.* I don't care how much they're worth or how desperate you are to sell them. I cannot handle such vulgar things."

"Yet you wear such a vulgar thing on your finger. If you agree to help me, I shall not make a fuss about you returning it."

"I don't want it!" Pru cried.

"And I really don't want you to keep it. I was a fool to break the set up. The parure will fetch much more intact. But it was the first thing I could lay my hands on with ease in order to bribe Carmela." He pitched his head backward and let loose a terrifying sneeze. "Pardon me. Despite the tea and the cross-ventilation, it seems I'm not over my indisposition. The inside of my throat is rather itchy as well. Is there any honey?"

"How would I know?" Pru snapped.

"Well, you seem so capable in this strange kitchen. You seem capable anywhere, Mrs. Thorne. I cannot help but think that a woman like you is the answer to all my prayers."

A woman like you. And in a much better context. He thought she was capable. Well, so she was. And really, what was her hurry to get back to Bath? There was nothing there for her, not even Jack the bulldog. He'd been dead for years.

Pru bit a lip. Mr. Shaw's salacious collection would certainly expand her knowledge, for despite her widowhood, she was now aware that something had been missing between her and Charles in the short seven weeks they'd been married. She had never once made any noise approximating Sophy's delirious delight in her husband's prowess. And if she stayed on Jane Street, the most wicked of streets in all London, she might observe things she'd never see in Bath. What harm could befall her? No one would ever know she was here. She was nine-and-twenty and she had yet to begin to live her own life. Surely it was time to do so.

"Very well, Mr. Shaw. I shall stay and help you. Once the boxes are unpacked and the items cataloged, I will leave." She waggled a finger at him. "And you are to tell no one about our arrangement. Not your brother. Not my cousin. Let Sophy think I've gone home. If she decides she needs me again, I will not be found. That will teach her a lesson."

Mr. Shaw rose from his chair and clasped her hand to his wheezing chest. "Bless you, Mrs. Thorne. May I call you Prudence? If we are to work closely together, that seems far friendlier than your married name."

Pru looked up into Mr. Shaw's moss-green eyes and forgot for just a moment what her name was. "Pru," she said, extricating her hand. "My friends"—not that she'd had time to have many—"call me Pru."

"Please call me Darius. I expect we'll get along just fine, Pru. Let's plot out how we are to accomplish the unpacking."

He pulled a pencil and pad out of his waistcoat pocket and began making a list of how she was to handle the objects. He told her to wear gloves when she touched them, which was fortunate—she would not be able to see the wicked ring winking on her finger.

Chapter Four

Darius truly had not expected Mrs. Thorne—Pru—to agree to his proposition. If he'd not been seated, he might have fallen down in shock when she said yes. And he was still shocked by the dispassionate and professional way she had dealt with his erotic artifacts since yesterday. Even though she did not resemble any sort of voluptuary in her hideous black mourning gown and scraped-back hair, she had not exhibited one shred of emotion as she brought him one sensual thing after the next.

The three of them were making rapid headway uncrating Darius's valuables. It had been decided he would remain in his bedroom with the windows thrown wide open in case a stray bit of hay wafted its way up the steps. Below, Malcolm and Pru were busy prying off lids and disposing of the damned straw as speedily as possible. Everything had to be carefully brushed clean and checked against the manifest before Pru brought it upstairs to be tagged for its new owner.

She arrived a bit breathless every time, an enchanting taffy curl escaping from her coiffeur and a glistening of dew over her full upper lip. She would no doubt be much more comfortable if she unbuttoned her bodice, or better yet, threw her ugly dress away entirely. She seemed unused to the exercise—she had not spent the decade since her marriage spinning about in ballrooms but sitting at her mother's bedside. Darius was quite happy at the thought of her sitting at his, although he was not actually in bed.

Malcolm, the devil, had decided his gimpy leg was acting up, thus thrusting Pru into Darius's masculine lair like clockwork. Darius looked around. Amend that. The bedroom and its adjacent sitting room were pink and frilly, hardly masculine at all. By rights, Pru should have taken it, but perhaps the large mirror over the bed and the indecent pictures on the walls had deterred her. She had ensconced herself in one of the Spartan attic bedrooms.

Darius was grateful for the suite of rooms, for every flat surface was now covered with statuary, jewelry, and gilt-edged books. More indecent pictures were propped up against the walls. It had been amusing to see Pru wrestle with an especially deviant angel as she carried his portrait up the stairs. Darius had decreed that anything else that large should be left downstairs to spare poor Pru any further strain.

But she did not complain despite her glowing perspiration. And he had not sneezed in twenty-four hours.

He heard her footfall in the hallway and put his pen aside on the flimsy papier-mâché courtesan's escritoire. He'd been writing to his clients to arrange the transfer of items he'd been commissioned to find. Extras that had caught his attention in his travels would be auctioned off at an exclusive invitation-only event right here on Jane Street in two days' time. There was no better address to attract the connoisseur of the prurient and the profane.

Pru entered, blowing a wisp of hair from her damp forehead. Her white-gloved hands clutched a chased silver bowl studded with jewels and exposed bodies. She set it down on the dresser and sank into a rose-pink chair. "That's the last of the lot from Jerusalem, according to Malcolm. One would think such things would be forbidden in the Holy Land."

Darius grinned. "That's what's made them so sought-after. I was fortunate to buy the entire contents of an old reprobate's estate. His family was eager to be rid of it all. Any luck?"

Pru rubbed her finger, shaking her head. The enormous ruby ring had split the seam of the cotton work glove, but it had not fallen from her finger. Butter, goose grease, hair pomade, ice and heat and perspiration—even gravy from last night's roast—had had no effect on the thing. Darius had given up hope of ever being able to sell it. Pru, however, was hard at work right this minute trying to wiggle it off with the corner of her apron.

"Let me catch my breath before I go downstairs again. We still have a few more hours of natural light. What made your father ever get into such a business?" she asked, her golden brows knit over her task.

"I think it all started with a collection of naughty snuffboxes and what-not he inherited from *his* father. The old man had a good eye for unusual art, and it wasn't hard for my father to convince his cronies they needed everything he owned, and then acquired. He developed a certain reputation, and ladies and gentlemen of the *ton* have been relying on Shaw Antiquities for decades ever since."

"Ladies. Gentlemen." Pru sniffed.

"All this may not be to your taste, but I assure you we have supplied amusement to the finest homes in the country."

"What do people *do* with such—such—" Pru waved her hand at the panoply of objects.

"You'd be surprised." Darius rose from the desk and picked up a carved ivory box. It was dreadful to tease her, but he couldn't resist. "You see the scene depicted here?"

Pru's cheeks matched the chair she sat on. "Yes."

"Well, the object within serves a lady just as well if her gentleman is not at home to perform as pictured." He popped the latch and took out a large ivory dildo.

"Oh!"

"Would you like to examine it more closely?"

"Certainly not!"

"It should be somewhat familiar. You did say you were married."

"For a mercifully short time, and I never—put that thing away at once!"

Could it be that the virtuous widow had never examined a man's organ, whether made of flesh or ivory? Darius examined *her*. Her blue eyes were bright and her modest chest rose and fell. In indignation, exhaustion, or interest?

"How is it that you've agreed to help me if you are so averse to my collection?"

"I'm not precisely averse. It makes no difference at all to me how you earn your bread. I just didn't want your illness on my conscience," she said primly.

Darius raised a dark brow. "Or perhaps you were curious. Just a little."

Pru looked ready to bite his head off. Then her eyes slid to a corner of the pink room. "And what if I was? *Just a little.*"

"If you are curious, Pru, that's healthy. You are an attractive woman. It seems a shame that you should let one bad experience color your relationship with all men."

She tugged off the torn glove and tried to spin the ring around her finger. It remained stubbornly pinching in place, and her finger was turning an alarming shade of pink. He put the dildo back in its casket and leaned down, covering her nervous hands with his. "Have you never experienced pleasure, Pru?"

"Of course I have." Her tone did not convince him, and her downturned eyes would not meet his. Her lashes were tipped with gold—if she'd been a courtesan she would probably resort to blackening them, but Darius thought the gilt suited her. Her now blushing cheeks and rosy lips needed no artifice. The more time he spent in her presence, the more he realized that his initial impression of her was incorrect. He had thought her somewhat plain, but she was not. Her beauty was subtle and not aided by the deadening black clothes she was forced to wear for propriety's sake. He wondered what she'd look like out of them.

She was slight. Pale where the blushes did not stain her skin—too pale, as if she hadn't been outdoors to see sunlight in an age. He could see the blue of her veins in the wrists he held, just detect the erratic pulse at her throat. The neckline of her mourning gown was far too high and swathed with a black fichu, but he pictured small breasts, perfect in their way. He told himself his own idle curiosity might have a benefit to her. Who was better than he to awaken her slender body to its purpose? "If I can assist you in any way to find your pleasure, Pru, you have only to ask."

She looked at him now, her blue eyes wide. "Wh-what do you mean?"

"I think you know." He stroked the ring with his thumb, smoothing over the jeweled ridges. What would she do if he touched her in such a way? Darius decided he would try to find out as soon as possible.

If she would let him.

So far, she sat still. As still as and now much paler than the ivory object he'd recently shown her. She didn't try to free her hands. Taking that as a sign of permission, he peeled off the remaining glove and circled her palm with deliberate design. It was odd how one's palm was so sensitive to the slightest pressure. Darius had even stimulated himself as he practiced his seduction techniques on his own rough paws.

Pru shifted in her chair just a fraction, letting him know his practice had paid off and his touch was not unwelcome. He swirled and swooped lightly on the wavy lines of her small white hand, then pressed his lips to its center. She tasted a bit salty and smelled of rose soap. He moved to the blue of her wrist, his nose getting poked by the starch of the lace trim at her sleeve. He raised his eyes to hers. They were a darker blue, her pupils large as if he had drugged her. Well, he *was* drugging her—with a taste of long-deferred sin.

Surely she deserved some? Her husband had failed her in spectacular fashion.

She blinked twice and cleared her throat. "I only agreed to help you out of charity. I can see I was wrong to ignore the impropriety of our working together."

He switched to her other hand, licking a line from her cuff to her ring finger. "Propriety is vastly overrated, Pru." He turned her palm, then suckled the diamond in his mouth. Pru gave a strangled cry and snatched her hand away. She wiped the ring with the abandoned cotton glove in her lap.

"It's easy for you to say that. You are a man. You don't suffer the consequences of indiscretion. You'll just go off somewhere and buy more wicked things."

"I've told you I'm done with all this. I hope to buy a small property. Farm. Perhaps raise sheep." Darius realized his dream was rather prosaic, but there it was—he was determined to be the first boring Shaw in generations. His rackety father had not been the first to fall from the straight and narrow path.

"Sheep!" Her scorn was palpable.

"Yes. White, wooly animals. Although sometimes they're black. It's time to turn the family history around. Even Cyrus has tried to escape by marrying your cousin. I expect in forty years or so, no one will remember how we amassed our fortunes."

"How on earth can you live in the country? You'll die during haying season."

"I'll let my tenants do the hard work." He hadn't quite thought that far ahead. Surely as a landowner he would not be expected to fork hay into a wagon. Besides, the sheep would eat the grass right down to its roots.

"I believe I'm finished for the day," Pru said, rigid in her chair, her hands wound tightly in her lap to prevent any further assault. "And finished, period. It is too late for me to make arrangements to leave this afternoon, but I will go home tomorrow."

Damn. He'd moved too fast. Perhaps that bit with the diamond between his teeth was too much. But he knew a river of heat lay buried somewhere beneath all that black rectitude—he'd seen her face light up for a moment, watched her lids drop, heard a quickened breath. It was a shame to leave her as is. Untouched. Unloved.

But he had never taken a woman against her will. He'd never needed to. He was a Shaw, after all. He'd made a pledge to himself months ago that he would be more particular in the future after he got into a spot of trouble in Egypt, so it had been a long while since he'd shared a bed with anyone but the fleas aboard *The Star of the East*. No doubt he could find some congenial woman right here on Jane Street if he went around to a neighbor who had an idle moment. The Janes spent most of their time waiting for their gentlemen, and he might be able to take advantage of their boredom.

However, a practiced courtesan held no allure for him at present. It would be far more satisfactory to unleash Mrs. Prudence Thorne's latent passion.

"What can I say to persuade you to stay another day?" There were still crates to unpack before the auction. It would be crowded enough in the downstairs reception room with half of London's lascivious lords in it.

"Absolutely nothing. And tell Malcolm I will take dinner in my room."

So, she would try to avoid him this evening. "I'm

afraid he'll never manage the stairs with his bad leg, Pru. But I would be delighted to deliver it."

"Oh, bother!" she muttered. "Very well, I'll dine below in the kitchen. At least I won't have to look at those dreadful paintings." She sprang out of the chair, her back ramrod straight. "I shall read until then." She picked up one of his books, flipped it open, then dropped it back onto the table as if her hands were scorched.

"I believe Carmela has some conventional reading material in her sitting room." Darius loped through the open double doors and went to the floor-to-ceiling bookcase that stood between the windows that looked out onto Jane Street. His late uncle's mistress was, as Cyrus had said, well read. He perused the shelves, searching for something suitable for Pru's refined—dull—taste. "You'd better pick something yourself," he called to her.

She joined him in the sitting room, keeping as much distance between them as she could. Her pretty blushes were a thing of the past—she was now as icy as she had been when she first verbally assaulted him when she thought he was Cyrus. His brother had better behave—even though Pru was disappointed in her cousin at the moment, Darius thought she would soon go back to trying to manage her.

Pru squinted at the shelves. "She wants you to send them."

"Who wants me to send what?"

"Carmela. The books. She told me before she left. She'll be sending you an address." She pulled one book off the shelf, then put it back. "Pliny the Elder. In Latin. Who would have thought it."

Leaving her to decide on her book selection and marvel at Carmela's unsuspected intellectualism, he stepped to a window and gave a low whistle. "Well, look at that."

Pru didn't budge. "What is it?"

"An honest-to-goodness courtesan, Mrs. Thorne, out for an afternoon stroll. Someone to satisfy your curiosity. From the amount of boxes her maid is carrying, her protector must be a generous soul." Darius saw her hesitate, but then she moved to the other window and stared down into the short street.

"She is not what I expected, either," Pru said, her nose nearly pressed on the windowpane. They had discussed Carmela over dinner last night, and Pru had been shocked at Carmela's true age. Darius hoped when he was in his sixties—nay, seventies—he would still be functioning between the sheets to some degree.

"Well, courtesans come in all shapes and sizes."

"I wonder if her red hair is natural."

"There's only one way to find out, unless the lady has dyed that area, too. Or shaved it off."

Pru immediately divined his meaning and scowled. "You are every bit as bad as I first thought! You, Mr. Shaw, are not quite a gentleman!"

"And you, Mrs. Thorne, are not quite a courtesan, more's the pity. Unbend. Your expression is enough to wither the hardiest male."

"I have no interest in males, hardy or otherwise." She grabbed a book from the shelf and flounced out of the room.

Perhaps it was just as well she was leaving. Prudence Thorne seemed to require quite a lot of effort. He and Malcolm could manage the rest of the boxes downstairs. He'd wrap his face in handkerchiefs like a bandit and hold his breath. Within a few days, he would be plump in the pocket and on his way to owning a flock of sheep.

He returned to the bedroom and picked up the carved ivory box. Odd. It seemed too light. When he opened it, nothing greeted him but the blood-red velvet lining.

"I'll be damned." Prudence Thorne planned to unbend, possibly this very night. If he was very quiet, he might creep upstairs and catch her in the act of gratifying herself. He could hardly wait. It was too bad she preferred an inanimate object when Darius himself was so conveniently at hand.

Now she had stolen two items from him—the ring and the carefully carved ivory penis. Did she intend to replace it before she hied off to Bath? He relished asking her that question. Tonight. Around midnight.

Chapter Five

What had possessed her? The ivory *thing* in her apron pocket clunked against her thigh as she tore up the stairs to her room. Pru had taken advantage of Darius's absence when he went to find her a book to peek inside the box to get an unobstructed look at the object. Before she knew it, she had palmed it and stuffed it into her apron pocket. She'd only meant to glance at it, not to take it. The atmosphere on Jane Street was unhealthy indeed if it caused her, Prudence Jane Prescott Thorne, to throw her scruples out the window and become a thief.

The evil ring burned her finger, too. Pru had no idea what she looked like down there, but she did not think she was made of rubies and diamonds. She did have a small hand mirror in her valise. Perhaps she could—

What *was* she thinking? She mentally slapped herself and entered the stark, stuffy little chamber at the top of the stairs. The rooms on the top floor were meant for servants and storage. Malcolm slept in a room in the basement off the kitchen, so she had the entire space to herself. She divested herself of her capacious apron, folding it and what it held in a plain wooden trunk at the foot of the iron bed. She would try to return the *thing* before she left. If she could not, Darius might not miss it. It and its container were meant for the auction, and the box alone was wicked enough to satisfy the most discriminating lecher.

Pru was beginning to think she had been hypnotized by Darius Shaw yesterday. Somehow he'd gotten her to agree to help him—actually cohabitate with him, even if they slept on separate floors. She must have been so unsettled by Sophy that her judgment was impaired. Pru hoped it was not a permanent condition—she'd had no trouble distinguishing right from wrong for almost three decades. But now she was infected by her idiot cousin, her cousin's lascivious husband, and his rule-breaking, tempting, wretchedly handsome brother. Even the swaying hips of the red-haired stranger on the street had been provocative.

Pru tossed herself on the bed and tried to read the book she'd snatched from the shelf. It was completely devoid of illustrations, nothing like the volume in Darius's bedroom that depicted—well, she wasn't even sure what she'd seen when she'd opened it. Surely there had been too many arms and legs for just two people. *My word.* If more than two people could couple, was it still called coupling? Tripling? Heaven forefend, *quadrupling*?

Pru closed the book, her mind too disordered to make sense of the prosaic prose within. Rising from the bed, she opened the narrow window that faced the little walled garden below. From this vantage point, she could see into most of the six gardens on her side of the street. But thank goodness the courtesans seemed to have more sense than Sophy and Cyrus—there was no cavorting on the grass as far as she could tell.

In the seven weeks she'd been married, Charles had come to her less than seven times. Of course, he had needed no regular manly release with her—Lady Merrifield had been providing succor and who knew what else before and after their marriage. The woman had written a tear-stained letter to Pru after Lord Merrifield fled the country, more upset that she would forever live in disgrace than apologetic for stealing Pru's husband away.

No, Charles had not been stolen—Pru had never had him to begin with. To him, she had simply been a naive, nineteen-year-old heiress with insufficient chaperonage. Once she was married, her mother and little cousin made the same demands on her as ever, and there had been very little time for Charles, who had moved into their Laura Place home. Pru knew nothing about being a wife, and Charles had not seemed inclined to teach her. Why should he, when he had a longtime mistress to see to that side of his life? Pru just supplied the meals and clothing and roof over his curly golden head.

Drat and damn. Pru had not thought of Charles in ages. Now he popped up in her head like a jack-in-the-box, breezy, blond and just beyond reach.

He had not loved her at all.

To be fair, she had not really loved him, either. Pru knew now she had been too young and foolish to truly love anyone. But he had excited her, made her feel something besides duty and responsibility. She might have come to love him eventually, given time. Just as well the time had been cut short, for then she'd be suffering from a broken heart. She'd be one of those dreary widows who sighed and looked ethereally wounded at all social events.

Not that she'd had much of a social life this past decade. Lady Merrifield wasn't the only one who'd been mortified. It had been easy to bury herself next to her mother's bedside, plumping pillows and doling out laudanum to escape the whispers. Raising scapegrace Sophy had been a diversion as well. But now Pru's carefully constructed barriers were breaking.

But not breaking hard enough to engage in an affair with Darius Shaw. She might be curious, but she was not cracked.

Several hours later, after an uncomfortable dinner in Malcolm's domain, Pru was back in the attic. She had borne his disapproval as he muttered over the soup pot, castigating her for refusing to join his master upstairs in the dining room. Pru had stood fast and eaten as quickly as she could.

Malcolm was a fair cook—he seemed to be a jack-of-all-trades who had served Darius Shaw in various capacities for many years. If she had been interested in discovering more of their adventures, she might have used the opportunity tonight to ask the man questions, but the only time she opened her lips was to spoon soup in and take a bite of bread. Pru refused the roast chicken on principle—if Malcolm thought his forbidding expression was conducive to digestion, he was sadly mistaken.

So she found herself upstairs before the sun had finished setting over the chimney pots, still hungry but too proud to indulge herself. The evening was balmy— the spring days were getting longer, and Bath had been in full bloom when she left. But she didn't plan to spend the rest of her life on Laura Place. It was her hope to sell the town house and find a suitable small manor house in the country. There was no reason for her to stint on her comforts—she had plenty of money and a keen desire to live as *she* liked in the future. Darius Shaw might want sheep, but Pru wanted a garden to putter about in. Flowers. Fresh air. Grass that would not be flattened by writhing bodies.

Pru could not get her cousin's misadventure out of her mind. Of course, she had seen nothing but sexual acts and body parts in real life and art since yesterday. It was no wonder she felt a peculiar ache in her nether region.

She had not really expected to feel anything there ever again. There was no denying that in the less than seven times Charles Thorne had come to her, she had felt *something* of an indescribable nature. Although it had been dark and she had been as still as any lady was meant to be, there had been a tug. A tingle. A *frisson* of desire that had danced like a bright, quickly extinguished flame. Charles had not seemed to notice, but then his attention had never been truly focused on her person, just her fortune.

Pru stood over the trunk. Malcolm had told her Darius had plans to meet one of his clients tonight, so she had the house to herself. She had all the time in the world to examine the ivory object. The daylight was waning, but she had candles.

She opened the lid of the trunk and slipped her hand

into the pocket of the folded apron. The dildo was cool to the touch, and not entirely smooth. Pru fished it out of its hiding place and brought it to her little window. The carver had given the dildo lifelike details—there were raised veins running the length of it, folds at its head, and tiny curling hairs on the sac at its base.

Pru measured it with an approximate inch between her thumb and forefinger. It seemed altogether too large for comfort. She could not recall Charles being this size, but then, she could not really recall Charles at all. Did size matter? She rather thought it might.

Between her bouts of tears, Sophy had intimated that Cyrus had brought her to heights of unparalleled ecstasy in their marriage bed. Pru had wanted to close her ears and hum, but now she wondered—was Cyrus's brother as well endowed as he? Of course, Sophy was a silly, innocent girl with no basis for comparison—she'd been completely bamboozled by a handsome face and pretty words. And, Pru had to admit, her cousin was bored in Bath living with an ailing aunt and all of Pru's rules. No wonder Sophy had been easily tempted by that snake—she was a fresh juicy apple ripe for the picking.

Pru ran a finger around the ridge of what was meant to be foreskin. She'd read an anatomy book or two to make sense of the prognostications of her mother's ever-changing roster of doctors. She'd read a great deal on other subjects as well, but had never encountered such books as Darius Shaw dealt in. Imagine having such a collection on one's library shelf. Of course, one wouldn't have to read them, just look at the pictures.

Darius had said that this *thing* might be used when

one's husband was away. Well, Charles was most certainly away.

Pru struggled out of her black bombazine dress, grateful that her maid Barlow was not here to see the flush on her cheek. She didn't light a candle—best just to go to bed early in the gray light. She had a long day ahead of her tomorrow. Her valise was already packed—she really had not unpacked it save to hang up her two black gowns—and she shook out the white night rail buried at the bottom of the bag.

Her evening routine was always the same, and tonight was no different. She washed her hands and face in the tepid water that she'd brought up herself, braided her hair, and lay on her back in the middle of the narrow bed. Pru tried to focus on her nighttime prayers, but found her mind wandering to the ivory object that had inexplicably wound up under the covers with her.

And then, with a quick plea for forgiveness, she pulled up her nightgown.

It was no use. She could not insert the object into her dry—no doubt shriveled—passage. She'd been a fool to think she could do any better than poor Charles. Swallowing back a sob, she shut her eyes and willed herself to sleep.

Malcolm had left strategically burning candles for him, a wicked waste as Darius could see quite well in the dark. His servant had not waited up, even though Darius had had an early, and profitable, night. He had met a gentleman in his private club and discreetly passed a rather lumpy fertility statue to the fellow, who was on his third wife—literally—in hopes of adding a son to the six daughters he already had. For his part, Darius was almost glad he wasn't a peer, for how absurd were the laws of primogeniture? There must be a great many older sisters throughout Britain who wanted to club their baby brothers with fertility statues or anything else they could get their hands on. Presuming that men were wiser than women to manage the family fortunes was a foolish presumption indeed.

Look at his brother Cyrus, certainly all male but distinctly lacking in wisdom. Copulating with his own wife in the back garden was simply not done.

Darius took an experimental breath in the downstairs parlor. The space seemed to be free of straw, although there were still a number of boxes left to unpack. He supposed to be on the safe side he'd better flee to his room. He had a mediocre bottle of brandy secreted away in a cupboard, and that bottle was calling his name.

Unwinding the preposterous length of his cravat, he mounted the stairs. He'd much rather be garbed in the loose clothing men of the East wore, but to move about London society one had to adapt. Trouble was, movement was practically impossible in the jacket Malcolm had procured for him this afternoon. It had not been tailored to fit, and Darius had felt restrained and uncomfortable all evening. But everyone else in the room looked similarly mummified, shirt points cutting into cheeks and throats strangled by yards of linen.

Darius was at the top of the stairs when he heard the chink of hard surface to hard surface. The door to his room was ajar, and someone was in it. Light spilled out into the hallway, which would be conveniently handy in revealing the trespasser. A thief come to steal his hard-won treasures? Or a curious widow trying to return one? He slipped a knife from his sleeve and flattened himself outside his door.

Her scent betrayed her, soap and roses. He tackled her anyway as she came out of his room. She stilled instantly at the knife at her throat.

Darius knew he was cruel to do this to her, but he'd ever had an aversion to people poking about his things. Cyrus had learned his lesson early on after trying to steal Darius's original collection and still bore the scar on his forehead, the only thing marring his pretty-boy beauty. There had been valuable leather string, some pieces of rose quartz, a desiccated frog, three brass buttons, and a Neolithic arrowhead in Darius's bedside table when he was eight years old, and the arrowhead had still been viciously sharp even after centuries.

There had been quite a lot of blood, but seven-year-old Cyrus had deserved his punishment. Darius himself had taken a beating afterward from his father, which prevented him from sitting down for a week, but at least he didn't have to wear a plaster on his bottom. Cyrus had looked silly with his bandage drooping over his eye until the stitches were removed.

Darius was slightly ashamed now of his youthful ferocity, but only slightly. Cyrus had done much worse in the intervening years for which he remained untouched, no matter how hard Darius's fists clenched.

"Please let me go," she said in a tone far too calm. It was as if she found herself in a man's arms at knifepoint on a regular basis. Prudence Thorne never ceased to surprise him.

She was fitted up against him, her back to his front,

her nightgown too thin to blunt her womanly curves. Now that she was liberated from her black dress, Darius discovered her figure wasn't quite so unexceptional. Her rounded arse awakened his cock instantly. He'd always been fond of a woman's derriere, and until this evening, Prudence Thorne's had been concealed by miles of black fabric. As far as he could tell, her bottom was soft, lush, and eminently desirable.

He released her with reluctance. "What are you doing in my room?"

Her cheeks were stained crimson, and she refused to meet his eyes. "I—I was looking for another book."

Darius stared pointedly at her empty hands.

"I couldn't find one."

"There must be hundreds of books on Carmela's shelves. She was very well read."

Pru lifted her chin. "I'm sure she did any number of things well."

Darius quirked a grin. "So Uncle Algy said. He was a regular correspondent. I always looked forward to his letters when I picked up his missives at my *post restante.*"

Pru rubbed at her neck with a delicate finger. The blade had come nowhere near it, but at the moment Darius wanted to replace her finger with his own. He would trace a line beneath the starchy ruffles at her throat to—

"Are you always armed?"

Darius refocused and hid his knife away. "Yes. Believe it or not, in my line of work, one comes upon ruffians of uncertain character. The antiquities field is replete with thieves and murderers and worse."

"What could be worse than a murderer?"

"You don't want to know. The dangers and the inconvenience of travel are only two of the reasons I'm happy to be home."

"I would think travel would be fascinating."

"Spoken like a girl who's spent her whole life in Bath with an invalid. Believe me, one can endure only so much sand in one's cracks before the sensation ceases to be amusing."

Pru glared at him.

"I mean the sand betwixt my toes, Mrs. Thorne. What did you think I meant?"

She huffed—she did indignation so very well. "You are impossible."

"Very likely." He took a footstep closer, so close he felt her warm breath between them. "Now, tell me—did you return my dildo?"

Pru's lovely mouth opened, but not even a squeak managed to come out.

"Did you think I wouldn't notice? I do hope you washed it before you placed it back in its receptacle."

"I—oh!"

Her cheeks burned, her eyes glittered, but she was still robbed of speech. She stared up at him, frozen to the hallway carpet.

"I am not judging you," Darius said reasonably. "I hope you found it efficacious in relieving your tension."

"I am not tense! And I didn't—it didn't—blast you, Darius Shaw!"

"It didn't work at all? I didn't think it was too large to accommodate the average gentlewoman easily, but perhaps I miscalculated."

Pru abandoned all pretense but not her pugnaciousness. "I hope you didn't pay too much money for it. It was useless."

Ah. "Perhaps you didn't utilize it in the right way."

"I'm sure I know where such a thing goes. I *was* married, you know."

"And the more I hear about your late husband, the less I think of him. Why would he leave a luscious morsel like you alone and seek comfort anywhere else? He must have been remarkably stupid."

Pru didn't seem to have a retort for his backhanded compliment. She worried her lower lip with a tooth and continued to blush brilliantly. Darius leaned in for the kill.

"I would be happy to demonstrate the proper use of the ivory instrument, if only to assure myself that its purchase was not foolhardy. And if I gave you some little pleasure in the process, it will repay you for the hours you have spent helping me."

"P-pardon?"

Darius watched as she twisted the end of her golden-brown braid. If he was lucky, in a few moments he would free her shimmering hair and relieve her of the night rail that covered her from chin to toe. It was thoughtful of her to creep around his house without a wrapper and slippers—it made his job so much easier. He stilled her twirling hand, covering the ruby ring. A spark of heat spread to his palm—surely the stones should be cold and hard. But there was no time to examine the peculiar sensation in his hand when other parts of him were screaming for priority.

But not tonight. Tonight was Pru's. It was the least he could do.

"Come, Pru. You have admitted your curiosity but

seem uneasy at actually engaging in an *affaire* with me. Very well. I can supply the necessary expertise in assuring that you reach feminine satisfaction."

"I will not sleep with you!"

"My dear, very little sleeping will be involved. But I swear not to take my own pleasure. Tonight shall be all about you—*your* needs, *your* desires. My little ivory friend can probably provide them nearly as well as I can." His fingers slipped into the tangle of hair, and he patiently worked the strands apart. Pru swayed, her eyes wide. Darius felt a bit like an Indian snake charmer—she was rising to his tune, but he'd better catch her before she bit him. He drew her closer to his chest and brushed his lips across her pale forehead.

"Then, when you are alone in your bed at Bath for the next three or four decades, you will be able to replicate what I'll teach you tonight. You should be able to do without men quite permanently right into old age if you don't care to take a lover."

"I don't—you would—I can't," she mumbled into his shirt.

He chucked her stubborn chin. "Of course you can. You *should*. You owe it to yourself, really. There's no shame in self-gratification. Your eyes will not cross and your palm will not grow hairy. If all those old wives' tales were true, every gentleman in the *ton* would be afflicted. Most ladies, too."

She pulled back and he let her go. "I don't believe you."

"About the hair or the other?"

She dropped her lashes, too embarrassed to speak.

"It's true, Pru. Women have the same requirements

as men. If your mother told you otherwise, she was lying. Have you never felt the urge to touch yourself?"

"Never. Well, hardly ever," Pru amended.

"You've gone all this time as a widow practicing self-denial? There have been no men in your life?"

She shook her head. He cupped her cheek—it was warm, soft, white as milk in the flickering hall light. "That's a pity. I think it's time for a change."

"Do you?" she whispered.

"I do."

Darius felt a shiver shoot down his spine. As he recalled, a gentleman spoke those two words in a wedding ceremony. Well, he was certainly not going to marry Prudence Thorne or anyone if he could help it. He was looking for a quiet, restful life now. A wife like Prudence Thorne could not be expected to keep her thoughts and opinions to herself—she was the least quiet, restful female he'd ever met. He'd have been better bringing Sheikh Mahmoud's slave girl Fairuza to London if he wanted obedience.

And if he had, he would not be suffering quite so in his nether regions as he breathed. Pru smelled like a garden of damask roses in the afternoon sun. A man could stand over her hair and bury himself in the wavy strands, drugging himself in her scent. Darius wondered where else the rose scent would pervade his senses—the crook of her arm? The sweet indentation of her navel? Between her white thighs? He groaned, just a little.

"Are you all right?"

"Absolutely. Never been better. So what do you say, Pru? I promise I will not place you in harm's way. Are you ready for a taste of Paradise?"

Chapter Six

Was she ready? She'd been ready since she'd opened the door to the brute, so jealous of her cousin when she thought the man standing before her was Cyrus Shaw she could barely see straight.

No, that wasn't right. She had seen—every tall, delicious inch of him, the dark ruffled hair, the faint stubble at his jaw, the travel-worn, sea-scented clothes. His eyes, green jasper with flecks of gold dust. The curl of his full lip when he thought she was his uncle's avaricious courtesan.

He had cleaned up well, although at this hour his jaw was shadowed again. His disorderly dark hair had been brushed back, revealing surprising sun streaks at his temple. His jacket fit him like Weston had sewn it to his body, and his inexpressibles—well, best not to look there. He had promised that he would not take true advantage of her, which was in some respects disappointing. But since she had so little experience with sin, perhaps it was best to indulge in smallish increments.

"Yes," she said faintly.

"Excellent." He extended a brown hand—the very one that had held the knife to her—and she placed hers in it without trembling too badly.

He led her back into the bedroom, a hideous room so pink it must resemble the insides of one's stomach. Her own was fluttering in nervousness, and there did not seem to be a drop of saliva at all in her mouth. As if he could hear her thoughts, he murmured, "I was going to have some brandy. Will you join me?"

Pru did not drink strong spirits, but now seemed a good time to start. Wordlessly, she nodded her head. Darius dropped her hand and went to a corner cupboard. Sitting on the shelf was a bottle of amber liquid and an odd assortment of glasses. He selected two and splashed the liquor into them with a generous hand.

"Here." He clinked his glass toward hers. "To new experiences."

"Um," Pru said, feeling like a fool. She took a sip, scorching her tongue in the process. "People *drink* this?" she asked after sputtering a minute.

"I allow as this is not the finest representative of its kind. You know my financial circumstances," Darius said, deliberately taking a large swallow from his own glass. "It's not too bad. I've had worse."

Pru could not imagine anything more vile, unless it were camel urine. She placed the drink down on one of the few available surfaces. She had forgotten she was surrounded by perversion everywhere she looked, so she closed her eyes. "Let's get on with it."

"Does the room disturb you?"

"You know it does."

"I have a solution. Lie down on the bed, Pru."

She stumbled toward the bed, a massive affair covered with what seemed to be the skins of one hundred white French poodles. The fleece was soft to the touch and surely not made of dog despite her fanciful description. She caught sight of herself in the mirror on the ceiling—white face, white nightgown on white fur, and shut her eyes again. She flinched when Darius lifted her head and fastened a blindfold over her eyes.

Starch and sandalwood. He must have taken the cravat that had been draped over his arm and tied it around her head. It was better she could not see what was about to happen, wasn't it?

She tried to relax, but every nerve in her body decided to turn Scottish and dance the Highland Fling. The bed dipped as Darius settled next to her. Gently, he unclenched her hands from her stomach and laid them at her sides. She felt his rough thumb at her wrist, like one of Mama's doctors. Her pulse raced as he stroked her arm, pulling up the sleeve of her night rail to her elbow. His fingertip followed her vein, and she swore she felt her blood leap to meet it.

Pru felt hot suddenly, the weight of her nightgown nearly unsupportable. Thank goodness Darius began to unbutton the tiny pearls at her throat, pushing the ruffles from her chin. When she was exposed, his hand lightly splayed upon her upper chest; for one brief moment Pru thought about asking him to touch her a bit lower.

But then he would discover her insignificant breasts, although at present they seemed bursting, the nipples bristling and hard. How embarrassing. Could he tell the effect he had upon her already? He had just touched her arm and her throat, for heaven's sake. What would happen when he—

Oh. She felt his warm brandied breath on her cheek. The stuff may have tasted vile, but the scent was rather pleasant. He cradled her chin.

"May I kiss you?"

Pru swallowed. "Is it necessary?"

Darius chuckled. "I believe so, yes."

"All right."

She wondered if his eyes were closed, whether his mussed hair fell forward across his brow as he bent to her. She licked her lips and felt the shock of his tongue on hers. She wasn't even ready for him! Her mouth was still open! But he didn't seem to mind, merely covering her lips with his and gently pushing her tongue back where it belonged.

But his tongue—it followed hers right back into the cavern of her mouth and *licked* her. Everywhere. So resolute in its exploration she forgot to object and simply held herself open so he could continue. Did she remember a kiss that was ever like this? Perhaps Charles had done just such a thing and she had put it out of her mind. But somehow it seemed extremely foolish and unproductive to think of Charles, so Pru kissed Darius back.

She did not know what she was doing, but what did it matter? The brandy on his tongue was sweeter than hers in the glass, and she threw herself into the kiss with greedy enthusiasm. Her fingers were somehow in his slippery dark (sun-streaked!) hair and smoothing down the fabric of his jacket. He still wore his boots. The French poodle blanket would get dirty. He was wearing far too many clothes, but it would not be part of their bargain for her to ask him to remove them.

He tugged at the hem of her nightgown, and Pru felt the night air at her thighs, followed by one work-roughened hand. She didn't mind the odd friction of it. Somehow it made her feel more alive—she'd had nothing against her skin but silk and satin and the finest lawn, but Darius's hand was so much better. How he could kiss her and manage to see to other parts of her body was quite wonderful. He stroked her legs until she couldn't help but spread them apart ever so slightly. Encouraged, he moved up to her center and toyed with the golden curls at her juncture. He seemed to be *petting* her, and she very much wanted him to do something else.

He broke the kiss. "Am I distressing you?"

"No! Yes." Pru was glad she couldn't see his face—he probably was looking at her as if she was a lunatic. "Aren't you going to use the *thing?*"

"Ah. Of course. The *thing*."

She could hear the mockery in his voice. "The d-dildo. The penis."

"I know what thing you meant, Pru. But you're not ready for it. Not yet."

Not ready? The lower part of her body was on fire. But he probably knew best, versed as he was in the mysteries of the exotic East and surrounded by the prurient artifacts of his trade. His lips descended again and she made do parrying with his tongue while his finger finally—*finally*—slipped into her folds.

She was mortifyingly wet, but she thought that was supposed to happen. Charles had always complained—

No. No more Charles.

Darius stroked her from the very tip of her diamond, thumbing it and her rubies so gently she wanted to scream. He swirled, he seduced, he strummed as his tongue did the very same thing inside her mouth. She had never felt so deliciously *wanton*—blindfolded and spread open, Darius's magical hands causing the strangest sensation low in her belly. Her hand moved from his shoulder to press onto his, holding him harder at her core, wondering if he could feel the sparks of lust that were overtaking her.

"Impatient, are we?" he murmured against her lips.

"Mmph," she responded. Yes, she was impatient. There was something that was about to happen just at the edge of her grasp, and if it didn't soon she would go absolutely mad.

To her disappointment, Darius disentangled his hand from hers and removed his tongue from her mouth. He was sitting up, sliding down the bed.

"Why did you stop?" She knew she sounded plaintive—whiny, even. Did the man not know what she needed? He'd claimed to be knowledgeable about—

Every inch of her responded to what surely was his kiss *down there*. Hot, wet, his fingers helping. Just like what that naughty angel had been doing with the maiden in the painting she had such difficulty carrying up the stairs. Darius was her own naughty angel, and if it meant she was dying and going to heaven, that was perfectly fine with her.

His tongue seemed to have grown inches, so proficient it was in sweeping over her womanhood, sweeping into—oh, good Lord. Wicked, wicked man. And when he took her diamond between his lips and suckled, just as he had threatened to, he turned from angel to devil and she flew straight off the bed.

Wave after wave came. She bit her lip to keep from keening like a wild animal, but she felt wild. And dangerous. Her fingernails bit into his scalp as she held him in place just in case she accidentally knocked him away with her gyrations. Pru seemed to have no control over the lower portion of her body, or her breasts, or her mind. And she was still wearing her stupid nightgown when all she wanted was to be naked under the stars.

This was what Sophy had with Cyrus. No wonder the girl had not cared for propriety. When one had tasted carnal delight, all common sense took a leave of absence.

After an eternity of exquisite bliss, Darius slowed his pace and Pru attempted to move the pieces of her fragmented thoughts into some semblance of coherence. She would simply die of exhaustion if she had to endure the dildo—it was entirely unnecessary at this point. Although tomorrow—

She'd have to stay. There was no leaving Jane Street after this.

With two shaking hands, she pulled the blindfold up over her forehead. It was important to see Darius Shaw's face, see if he could have possibly enjoyed himself as much as she had. He raised his head from his labors and lifted a brow. He seemed unruffled, although his lips were red and there was a sheen of sweat on his forehead.

"Are you all right?" His voice was sin itself, low, languid. Of course he knew she was all right—he could not have missed the response of her body as she vibrated beneath him.

"Quite well, thank you. That was—very pleasant."

His lips quirked. "Very pleasant? That hardly seems an adequate description. Perhaps we should consult *Roget's Thesaurus*. I believe I saw a copy in Carmela's sitting room."

"You were masterful, as you must know." Pru heard the tinge of resentment in her voice. But it wouldn't do to annoy the man if she wanted him to do this to her again, so she affected a wobbly smile. "What exactly was that at the end?"

Darius rolled away and leaned on an elbow. "What did it feel like?"

"I'm not sure I can describe it, even with the assistance of Dr. Roget." Fireworks. Shooting stars. Earthquakes. Volcanic eruptions. Something so strong and sweet she folded in and out like an accordion. Even her nose tingled. She put a hand to it. Still there.

"You've never felt anything like it before?" He seemed inordinately pleased with himself.

"Never."

"It was the little death, Pru. Your crisis. An orgasm."

"Oh." Charles had talked of orgasms, but as far as Pru knew it only referred to the man ejaculating his semen. He would continue on top of her for what seemed like hours, no matter how uncomfortable Pru was in those less-than-seven times, until he spent inside her. She really did have a great deal to learn.

"Well, it was lovely. Thank you."

"My pleasure."

But he hadn't really had any. "Do you want me to do the same thing to you?" She wondered if he would take off all his clothes if she kissed him in such a way. She had seen statues, yes, and, of course, a lot of nude bodies since yesterday, but never a real-life man up close. Cyrus most definitely didn't count, white arse be damned.

Darius's jaw went slack. "Pardon?"

"You know, k-kiss you down there so you can have your own orgasm."

"Ye gods," he muttered once he got over his coughing fit. "I don't think that's necessary, Pru. Respectable ladies usually are not expected to engage in such behavior."

Pru wriggled up so that she had the lace pillows at her back and her nightgown back over her legs. Mostly. "Why not?"

"I'm sure I couldn't say. We abide by rigid, ridiculous rules, which is why places like Jane Street exist."

"So you are saying a courtesan would put a gentleman's *thing* in her mouth but a lady would not."

"That's the general gist of it. There might be some exceptions, of course, if a man got really lucky."

Pru made up her mind. "I came to Jane Street to expand my horizons. This is your lucky night, Darius Shaw."

Chapter Seven

Somehow this starchy, virtuous widow had turned into a courtesan. Darius could not credit himself entirely for her transformation—Prudence Thorne's blood was a stream of sensuality beneath her pale, pearly skin. He'd barely touched her before she came apart, bursting against his tongue like a ripe peach. Tasting like one, too. The scent of Damascene roses had clouded his senses as he feasted. She'd been wasted on that damn fool of a husband.

Ten years was a long time to go without sexual congress. The few months that Darius had trod his own celibate path had not exactly been a picnic. He was as hard now as he'd ever been in his life, but tonight was supposed to be Pru's turn.

He had given her his gentleman's promise, not that he was much of one. But there would be no true consequences if he allowed her to—

A woman like her wouldn't like it. And for some reason he'd much prefer if he could bury himself inside her in the usual run-of-the-mill way, watch her lashes tangle as she cried out, see her small breasts rise and fall, kiss them to peaking pink perfection. Gad, but he was becoming alliterative, a sure sign he'd lost his mind.

Absently he wiped his mouth on the sleeve of his infernally tight jacket. He was burning up. He needed to shrug it off, and where was Malcolm? Suddenly he was so tired he didn't think he had the strength to kick off his boots.

"Darius?" she asked in a small voice. Here she'd made a generous offer, and he was hesitating like a schoolboy. But his head had started to pound just like when he had the summer fever in Alexandria.

Curse it. Not again.

"I—I don't feel quite well, Pru." Damn it. If it wasn't one thing, it was another. First the bout of sneezing, now this. He'd come home to escape the vagaries of Egypt, but it seemed he'd brought his troubles with him.

Her face crumpled. "Do I sicken you?"

"No, no." The wretched pink stripes on the walls wavered.

"Is it your previous indisposition? You are not sneezing."

He gulped for breath. He could not afford any delay for illness—the auction was scheduled for the day after tomorrow. All his invitations had gone out, and the event was already the talk of the town. "No, I'll be fine."

And maybe he would be. Perhaps the ill humors in his body had built up for so long he needed immediate release, and here was Pru wanting to provide it. A good come cured everything, didn't it? At least for a little while. Then it would be a dark room, cool cloths, Malcolm at his side barking at him to drink his broth.

"I accept your offer, Pru. But if at any time you change your mind about it, you may stop."

"I'm sure I'm equal to the task, if you give me some guidance." She sounded like she was getting ready to pluck a chicken or polish the silver. Well, she would be polishing *something*.

"Do you mind if I disrobe? It's rather hot, don't you think?" He tried to stand and quickly thought the better of it. So he divested himself of his clothes sitting on the edge of the bed, slithering out of his breeches until he got to his boots. He pictured himself toppling off the bed onto his head if he bent one inch farther, so dizzy was he.

Damn. Damn. Damn.

He took a breath. "It wouldn't do to wake Malcolm. Can you help me with these?"

Pru scrambled off the bed, an angelic vision in her lace-trimmed, nearly sheer lawn nightgown. Her hair hung in shimmering waves, held back by the impromptu blindfold. When she knelt before him, he fumbled clumsily with the knot. She gazed up at him with such clear trust that his heart broke just a little bit. He was a cad to let her go through with this. If he had a shred of decency, he'd send her up to her room and put her on the first stage to Bath tomorrow morning.

But he was a Shaw. And she was a woman on her knees in his bedroom. And he needed—he needed—

She tipped backward pulling off the second boot. He gave her a hand, but his arm was as weak as his scruples.

"What should I do?" Her eyes were wide, taking in his sun-browned body. He sat up taller. He had nothing to be ashamed of—his life had included plenty of vigorous exercise as well as business cunning. He was, Darius thought ruefully, the total package—brains and male beauty. If only he had some money, he'd be an eligible catch.

But soon he'd have an adequate nest egg. In two days—no, it was past midnight—tomorrow the auction would commence, and by the end of the evening he'd be a rich man.

Rich enough to buy a country property. Rich enough for as many sheep as could bleat. Rich enough to take a wife.

If he was still alive. His vision blurred. His mouth moved, but he couldn't hear himself. Pru pushed him back on the bed, following whatever directions he seemed to be giving. She nodded earnestly and eyed his rampant cock, which didn't seem to care that the man it was attached to was experiencing some light-headedness. He glanced up at the mirror on the ceiling, saw the spill of Pru's golden-ash hair, his own face looking back at him with a rather dazed expression. He watched as she bent over him, her soft hair tumbling onto his thighs. *Sweet gods.*

She began by smoothing him between her small palms, her touch so gentle it might have been butterfly wings.

"I won't break," he grunted. She gripped harder immediately, and he hissed his pleasure. Her hands were cool, strong, very nimble. She explored him with her thumbs, circling the tip of his cock, finding the pearl of moisture and sliding her fingers over it. Sheathed between her hands, he closed his eyes as the room spun. She moved up and down his member as though she'd been doing this every night of her life, and the days besides. One hand drifted down to cup his sac, and the exquisite pressure was enough to make him think he was going to lose all self-control.

He must have made some sort of noise, for her hands stilled. "Should I stop?" she whispered.

Never. "Kiss me," he choked out. "Please."

He could feel the heat of her body as she leaned over him, but he didn't dare open his eyes. There was hardly anything more beautiful than watching a woman pleasure him so, unless it was seeing her secret smile as she came apart beneath him. Or above him. Darius was determined to observe Pru in all ways eventually. Right now he scrunched his eyes shut as her lips hovered over his cock. Soon she would—

And then she did. A tentative tongue swiped over its head. He stiffened even more and sighed.

Encouraged, she became bolder. Soon he was encased in the warm, wet heaven of her mouth. Between her hands and her tongue, she treated him to one agonizingly wonderful sensation after another. For a novice, she was most persuasive in her amorous skills. If Darius didn't know better, he'd believe himself to be in the bed of one of the famed courtesans of Courtesan Court.

But Pru was no courtesan, and would not know what to do with what was about to happen next. With a growl, Darius extricated himself with some difficulty, rolled over onto his stomach, and pumped against the mattress.

He should feel some remorse for spending in an embarrassingly short period of time, but Pru in her artless innocence could not be resisted. And he was not himself. Not himself at all.

"Am I finished?" she asked.

He certainly was. Darius buried his nose in the furry bedcovering. Malcolm would have to clean it tomorrow.

"*I* am finished, my dear. That was—exceptional. Thank you from the bottom of my black heart."

"Did you ejaculate your semen?"

Good Lord, but she sounded like she was reading out of an anatomy book. "I did indeed." He rolled back over, covering his flaccid penis with one hand. To his shock, she brushed it away.

"I want to see."

"There's not much to see now."

Pru squinted down at him as though she was looking at a beetle under a magnifying glass. Her eyes were bright in the lamplight, her face flushed from her exertions. "It looks very different now, doesn't it? How very peculiar men are."

"I suppose we are." He was not about to ask how he compared to her late husband—he knew he had nothing to be ashamed of, even in repose.

"Did I—did I do it right?"

"Absolutely." He took her hand in his, circling her palm. "Are you sure you've never done this before?"

Her cheeks became rosier. "Very sure. Until I came to Jane Street, I had a most imprecise understanding of what can transpire between a man and a woman."

"Thank you for trusting me enough to broaden your knowledge." His voice was rough, his throat dry as dust. "Could you fetch me your brandy if you're not going to drink it? I'm terribly thirsty."

Pru rose, smoothing down her crumpled night-gown. She was delightfully disheveled, so much more attractive than her daytime scraped-back, buttoned-up self. In less than the space of an hour, she looked younger, freer, nearly wanton.

But perhaps he was hallucinating—the fever some-times played tricks on him. Darius prayed to the various deities he'd encountered in his travels that he could stave off the worst of his illness until after the auction.

Pru returned with the tumbler and stood at the edge of the bed. "I suppose I should be going."

"It *is* late. And you'll be leaving first thing." Darius took a punishing sip. "I wish you wouldn't go."

"N-now or tomorrow?"

Had he said that aloud? He must have. "Both. But I'm a restless sleeper. It's best if you go on up to your own bed. If you stayed, though, tomorrow we could finish up the inventory and arrange the items for the auction. I won't touch you again unless you want me to." *Please stay.*

Pru's golden brows knit. "Do you want to? Touch me again, that is?"

"Can you doubt it?" Darius wanted to touch her all over—every nook and cranny of her milk-white skin, every gilt hair, every toenail. He'd not even touched her breasts once—the same breasts that puckered invit-ingly beneath her nightgown. He decided her nipples would be pink, pale, and lovely like the rest of her. The thought of bringing Pru more pleasure was very ap-pealing.

But not, unfortunately, tonight. He would mix Mal-colm's magic powder with the rest of Pru's brandy and sleep until noon if he could.

"Why?"

Darius frowned. "Why what?"

"Why do you want to touch me again?" Her chin had lifted, her spine had straightened.

Gone was the soft girl in the throes of her first orgasm. Whether she stayed or not depended on whatever he said next. He wasn't quite up to a flowery speech, and she would think it false in any case.

"I like you," he said simply. "I don't know why, because you're not like any other woman I've ever been with."

She opened her mouth to reply, but then must have thought the better of it. Instead she remained beside the bed, her fingers working at the blasted ring. He'd forgotten all about it.

The clock on the mantel chimed the hour, startling them both. "Go to bed, Pru," he said gently. "I hope I see you in the morning, but if not, thank you for tonight. I'll never forget it."

She nodded once and was gone, closing the door behind her. Darius sprang off the bed, just in time to vomit up the brandy into the silver bowl Pru had brought up this afternoon.

He rang for Malcolm. At least he had not disgraced himself in front of Pru, although he'd much rather see her face above him as he lay dying—or wanting to— than Malcolm's. She'd claimed to be good at taking care of people, but he would not willingly subject her to the next few hours.

What kind of man was he that he sickened so easily? He was not an eligible catch at all.

Chapter Eight

Judging from the slant of light in her room, Pru had slept the morning away. How wicked of her, when there was work to be done. And perhaps some play.

She'd decided to stay—what harm could another day or two do? Last night had been extremely informative. *Trans*formative. She truly did not feel like her old self. What Darius Shaw had done to her—what she had done to *him*—had been an extraordinary adventure.

He had asked her to stay. Sounded sincere. And did not bother to flatter her with lies to get her to agree. She liked him the better for it—she knew perfectly well she was not the most beautiful woman of his acquaintance, or even in the top ten. He must have been exposed to a great many temptations in his travels, and Pru had little practice with seduction.

Face it—she had no practice at all. The less-than-seven times with Charles had not included any of the things that she and Darius had done last night. Not even the kissing. Certainly Charles had kissed her, but

it was more like the accidental bumping of mouths. He
had never swept in, swept her away, conquered. Pru's
lips tingled with memory. How she wanted to kiss Darius Shaw again.

Would it be too bold to do it over breakfast? But
perhaps over luncheon was more apt—it was quite late.
Pru could not recall the last time she'd slept in. But her
body had been replete, drowsy, languid when she'd left
Darius. She'd stretched on her narrow little bed and
lost consciousness almost immediately.

When she woke up she washed and dressed quickly,
wishing she had something other than a black dress to
put on. Black reminded her too much of her embarrassing widowhood, when she was forced for propriety's sake to mourn a man she wished to perdition. But
she had nothing else—in fact was running low on un-
mentionables. She could not imagine asking Malcolm
to wash her underwear, but later today she needed to do
it discreetly.

She pinched her cheeks and bit her lips, hoping to re-
cover some of the rosiness she had when she had been
blindfolded and bedecked with kisses. Pru opened the
door and listened at the top of the stairs. The house was
quiet, so quiet she wondered if she were the only person home. She moved down to the next landing. Darius's bedroom door was shut, as well as the separate
door that led to the sitting room, and she felt too shy to
knock to see if he was within.

Her rumbling stomach sent her directly to the kitchen.
It, too, was quiet, empty of people, but Malcolm had left
her food on the plain pine table. When she lifted the
linen napkin, she discovered a pretty china plate for her
with a roll, a wedge of cheese, and an apple. He'd

wrapped the teapot in a quilted cozy, but it had long gone cold, proof that she *was* a slugabed. When she pulled out her chair, she saw a grubby square of paper with her name misspelled—Mrs. Throne—in Malcolm's execrable handwriting.

How strange. These must be instructions for her to carry on without him. Pru bit into her apple and unfolded the paper one-handed.

Madamn master is sik. Do not go in!!! Back latter. M.

Well! How shabby of Malcolm to desert Darius in his moment of need. Darius had complained last night of feeling somewhat unwell, but that had not stopped him from bringing Pru to heaven and back. But if he was truly ill today, he probably would not be interested in continuing Pru's sensual journey. Drat and damn.

She hadn't heard any sneezing or gasping or coughing when she hovered uncertainly outside his door, but it would do no harm to check on the man, no matter what Malcolm had said. Pru poured out the cold tea and set a kettle to boil. He'd responded well to tea the other day—tea cured everything, as her old nurse used to say. And she needed some, too, to clear her head and prepare for what might be rejection. Darius had been interested in her yesterday, but hours had passed.

Pru knew she was nothing special—if she had been, Charles would not have died in another woman's arms. Well, in her rhododendron bush. But she was beginning to think Charles was not so special, either. His equipment was nothing—*nothing*—like Darius Shaw's as far as she could recall. Even at rest, the man was impressive. Pru wanted to get her hands on him again, and her lips, too. Darius had made very satisfactory noises as she pleasured him, making her feel a power she did not know she possessed.

Pru knew she was bossy—she'd had to be. But what happened last night was entirely different. Her control over him was nearly her own submission. Pru had liked the odd sensation deep in her belly. She'd felt wicked.

And liked it.

After arranging a tea tray with a cup for her as well, she carried it upstairs, going to the sitting room door first. "Darius?"

There was no answer. Possibly he was still abed. She moved down the hall and pushed the bedroom door open with a hip. The room was swathed in blackness. The French window to the tiny balcony overlooking the garden was draped with a dark blanket, and Pru could barely see a foot in front of her despite the daylight. "Darius, are you awake?"

The lump on the bed groaned. "Go 'way."

"Nonsense. If you are ill, you need caring for. I've brought you tea."

Darius snorted. "Cast it up."

"If you do, I'll fetch you more. What's wrong?"

"Fever. Don't worry. Not contagious. Have it every now and again. Picked up something on my travels and can't put it down."

The poor man. He was right to want to come home then and escape from the dangers of the world. "How could Malcolm leave you like this?"

"Told him to. Need something from the apothecary to tide me over. Auction."

"You cannot possibly go through with the auction!" Pru looked around in the gloom for somewhere to set

the tray but saw nothing but the dreadful objects that
Darius planned to sell on every single flat surface.
There was no place open but the bed, so she placed it
on the poodle counterpane.

"Don't move. Must you be in darkness, or can I air
out the room?"

"Doesn't matter."

Pru pulled the wool blanket down, and the spring
sunlight flooded the space. She threw open the doors to
the fresh air and took a deep breath herself. She'd had
plenty of experience in sick rooms and knew Darius
wasn't faking it from the stale smell of the room alone.
And when she saw his beautiful face gray with fever
and sweat, her heart tripped.

"You're going to have a cup of tea. And then I'll
bathe you."

"Go home, Pru."

He said it without much energy, so either he was too
sick to care or didn't really want her to go. Pru decided
it was the latter.

"Nonsense. I'll stay until you are well. Give me the
list of people you invited to the auction and I'll notify
them that the plans have changed."

Darius struggled to sit up. "No! Has to go on. Parliament is breaking up. Everyone will be in the country
for the summer."

Pru knew this was true. London was about to fall
quiet for the next few months. "All right then. We'll
figure something out. How long do your episodes last?"

"A few days. Sometimes more."

He was shivering now, but Pru did not believe it was
due to the open window. She poured him a cup of tea

and held it to his mouth. "Here, drink a little. Have you eaten?"

"Can't. Please leave me be, Pru. I'm of no use to you."

"But I can be of use to you, you silly man!" Men! So full of ridiculous pride, as if they weren't entitled to stumble a bit along the way. "When this has happened before, what is the most efficacious way to treat it?"

"Bark. C-cinchona tree. From Peru." His teeth chattered against the cup. "So cold."

Pru covered him with the blanket from the window, tucking it up under his chin. No doubt he'd be better lying down, but she had to get the tea into him somehow. He managed to swallow most of it, then with a hunted look in his eye, tumbled off the bed to grab the chamber pot beneath it.

"Oh, dear."

"Told you."

He was naked. And still magnificent even if he was sick as a dog. Pru averted her eyes and carried the basin to the window, where she doused the poor plants below.

"Do you have a nightshirt?"

"Dresser. Top drawer." He crawled back into the bed. "I'll just sweat through it. Really, Pru. Leave this to Malcolm. He should be back soon."

"Not if he has to go to Peru."

Darius managed a grin at her joke. "My disease is common enough. Alexander the Great. Dante. Cromwell."

"But they're dead!" Pru said in alarm.

"Malaria's an occupational hazard in Egypt. I survived the worst of it. No reason to think I won't keep on going, barring a little minor inconvenience every once in a while. We Shaws are tough. You'd better go back to Bath, Pru."

"I don't care how tough you say you are," Pru said stubbornly. "I'm staying until the end."

"Not mine, I hope."

"Oh! Don't jest about such a thing. You must not die. Who else will enlighten me in the sensual arts? After last night, you've quite ruined me for anyone else."

"Why, Prudence Thorne. I believe you're flirting with me, and me on my sickbed."

"I believe I am," said Pru, blushing.

"Then I'll have to get well with all due speed. You've given me a reason to live." He placed a brown hand over his heart, and Pru subdued her urge to climb into bed with him. Instead, she sat at the edge next to him at a decent distance and drank her own cup of tea to steady her nerves.

"If you are not well by tomorrow night, can Malcolm manage the sale?"

Darius grimaced. "Malcolm does the best he can— more than the best—I could not find a more loyal servant in all of Christendom and the Islamic world besides. But he's basically unlettered. Can you see him describing the provenance of my treasures? I cannot. But I suppose he'll have to if I can't pull myself together."

Darius had labeled every object meticulously in his neat handwriting. Pru had been amazed that he remembered their origins and ages, unless he was just making it all up. He'd spoken of forgeries when he first met her, but in her inexpert judgment, the treasures looked real enough. Legitimate. And costly. Precious stones studded a great many things. She rubbed the ruby ring, trying in vain to loosen it. She would simply have to buy it from Darius—it was far too valuable for her to accept it as a gift. She'd just have to wear gloves for the rest of her life.

"I'll do it."

"Pardon?"

"In disguise, of course. That trunk you showed me yesterday with the women's clothing. The veils and whatnot." There had been beautiful dresses from Paris fit for the most flamboyant courtesan, but the exotic Eastern silks had caught her eye, embroidered in gold thread and so splendid Pru had wanted to strip off her ugly black to try them on. A bit of kohl for her eyes and no one would ever recognize her, not that she was apt to know the type of gentleman who collected erotic art.

Darius sat up so straight he looked pained. "I forbid it."

"Don't be foolish. If you're well enough, you can sit right there and guard me. But I can do the persuading. I might even improve the sales."

"Absolutely not. A woman like you—"

She was awfully tired hearing about "a woman like her." No one knew her, nobody. She was beginning to think she didn't know herself. Pru smacked him on his broad chest.

"I will do it and you will like it."

"I will never 'like it,' Pru! You haven't the first idea what my clients are like. They'd take one look at you and paw you to pieces."

"Let them try. I'll stab them with my ring." The raised oval diamond was very sharp—a nuisance when it kept catching on things.

"They'll think you are a Jane!" Darius spluttered.

"All the better. Who would they prefer to buy from? A mysterious courtesan or a grizzled servant like Malcolm? But perhaps you don't think I am attractive enough."

"Of course you are attractive enough! Don't fish for compliments, my girl. I've been dying to bed you almost from the first, and everyone else will want to, too."

Pru grinned like a happy idiot, but inwardly so she didn't spoil their argument. Instead, she glared at the man, who was turning from gray to green in alarming fashion. "You are too ill to make a sensible decision. I am going downstairs to unpack the rest of the boxes. When Malcolm returns, we can ask his opinion."

"I don't give a damn what he says! No woman of mine is going to parade about half-naked in front of the worst of the *ton!*"

Oh, *excellent.* Pru had never been so happy in her life. Darius thought she was his woman, at least for a little while. And that would have to be good enough unless she could figure out a way to make the situation permanent.

For it was clear to her that Darius needed her. And after last night, she would not be satisfied with simple—or complicated—kisses. She wanted much more, and the splendid specimen languishing on the bed needed to make a spectacular recovery soon.

Chapter Nine

Insupportable! To think that Prudence Thorne planned to help him in a way that could only bring disaster upon her. Upon them both. Perhaps he *should* cancel the auction. The Jane Street house would sell fairly fast, and he might live off the proceeds of that for quite some time, even if he had to split the proceeds with his idiot brother.

But if he didn't have an idiot brother, he never would have met Pru.

Darius had gagged on the chicken broth that Pru seemed to think would cure him quicker. He'd drunk the evil stew of ground-up Peruvian bark and managed to keep it down, and had stripped the blankets back off because he was burning up again.

At least she hadn't made good on her threat to bathe him, although the devil knew he needed it. Pru and Malcolm were closeted downstairs removing items from the last of the boxes. Pru had taken his inventory and his notes and wasn't even bothering to consult him. She'd probably mistake the Etruscan bronze for Sumerian, but what did it matter?

Darius lay back down on his damp pillow, feeling acutely sorry for himself. Somehow Prudence Thorne had turned the tables on him. Here was his one chance at happiness, a life of respectability, and it was all in the hands of a bossy little widow who made his cock crazed with need even as he wanted to die. He was not master of his own fate, his own fortune. Instead he was sweating like a pig and keeping close to the chamber pot. At least he wasn't sneezing.

Malcolm had assured him all the straw had been baled up and taken to some rubbish tip. It was Darius's own fault for entrusting his motley Egyptian crew to pack everything for shipping. He should have supervised it, but he'd been on the hunt for tomorrow night's pièce de résistance. But he was very much afraid he knew who the true star of the evening was going to be—his most unlikely mistress.

There was not a doubt in his mind that he had awakened the sleeping beauty inside Prudence Thorne. An awake Pru was a woman to be reckoned with. He almost dreaded her return, for one whiff of her rose-scented body brought him to his knees. He closed his eyes and remembered her taste, her touch, the sound of her cries when he brought her to completion. But they had no future together—she was an heiress and he an adventurer who'd seen and done far too many things to ever win anything more than her lust if she knew the truth.

He was not worthy of her, even beyond the fact that his body betrayed him with this foul disease too often for comfort. And what woman would want to be saddled with an invalid, especially when she'd spent her whole life caring for her sick mother? No, Darius and Pru needed to part ways as soon as the auction was over. He hoped he could rally to spend one last night in her bed, or she in his—or on the carpet. The sofa. The dining room table. It didn't really matter where as long as he could fit himself inside her just once.

Who was he kidding? He smelled like one of Astley's elephants. She'd have to be unconscious to permit it.

With a vigor he didn't know he possessed, he rang the bell Pru had found and placed at his bedside. After an eon, Malcolm shuffled up the stairs, his left leg trailing after him in an exaggerated limp.

"Where's Mrs. Thorne?"

"Out. We finished up and she said there was somethin' she had to do."

Darius felt some misgiving. "You don't suppose she's left, do you?"

"I just said she did, guv. You losin' yer hearin', too? You still look like shit, if I may be so bold."

"As if I could ever shut you up. Where did she go?"

"Damned if I know. Woman's stuff, I imagine. She's got my kitchen drippin' in drawers and shifts. Don't know if I'll be able to cook dinner through all the linen and lace." Malcolm gave him a lazy wink, and Darius was unaccountably jealous. He'd not seen any of Pru's underthings as yet.

"I'm not hungry anyway."

"Sure and there's more than one mouth to feed in this house, guv. Mrs. Thorne has got to keep her strength up for the big night. We've been plannin' between us all afternoon. I say, she's a little firecracker, ain't she?"

She *had* gone off like a rocket last night. "Mrs. Thorne's underwear is not the only thing that needs washing. I want a bath, Malcolm. "

The older man scowled. "How am I to bring up hot water the way I walk? Nope. You'll have to wait for the lady to help you. It will be more fun to have her scrub your back anyhow."

"You old charlatan. You can walk as well as anyone when you want to. Very well. Help me to the kitchen and I'll wash down there. Get me my robe."

"Don't be a fool. You're not up to walkin' all that way yet, and I'll be damned if you take me with you when you fall down the stairs." Malcolm went to the wardrobe anyway and pulled out Darius's Turkish silk robe.

"I'm perfectly fit." To prove it, Darius put one bare foot on the floor. The room tilted and he clutched the coverlet.

Malcolm's lips disappeared in disapproval as he handed the robe over. "Look at yourself. Weak as a kitten."

"I still have claws, Malcolm, and if you do not help me, I'll dismiss you from my service."

Malcolm snorted. "You haven't paid me my full wages for eight months. I'll quit."

"Whatever." Darius sighed, struggling to get his arms in the holes. "Please."

Malcolm untangled a sleeve. "Oh, all right. Lean on my good shoulder."

"Which one is that today? I can't keep up with your lies."

"Coxcomb." Darius heaved himself off the bed, and

Malcolm ducked under his outstretched arm. "Hold on, laddie. I've got you."

Just barely. The two of them lurched down the endless stairs. Before moving on to the basement level, Darius poked his head into the parlor. The furniture had been rearranged to make way for the gilt chairs he had rented for the auction. The adjacent dining room was crammed with objects on display—Pru had been bringing things downstairs all day while Darius drifted in and out of sleep. She must be even more exhausted than he was.

And now she was out who knows where—anything could happen in London. She had told him she wasn't familiar with the city. She had no maid, no escort.

"You should have gone with her."

Malcolm did not pretend to misunderstand. "I asked. She wouldn't hear of me leavin' you alone."

"Damn it. I'm not a baby."

"No, you're a sick man, but you're right about the bath. You stink to high heaven. I'll have to wash meself just from touchin' you."

Darius grinned. They made it to the kitchen with just enough difficulty that he was winded but not totally knackered. He collapsed in a chair while Malcolm heated water and dragged an enamel tub from the back pantry.

Pru's washing hung like wispy ghosts from a string along the whitewashed beams. Darius had seen far naughtier undergarments in his time, but he pictured Pru in them—and then out of them—and his mouth dried.

When the tub was mostly full, Darius shooed Malcolm away and shrugged out of his robe. He wasn't going to be mother-henned by his manservant when there was still so much to do before tomorrow. Malcolm left with a list and almost the last of Darius's funds. But one had to spend money to make money, as his father used to say. Too bad the old boy had not always been able to follow his own advice.

Darius leaned back in the tub and rested his head against an old towel, feeling every year of his age. The Shaws had lived by their wits for as long as Darius could remember. In the case of his brother Cyrus, half-wits might be more apropos. But Cyrus had managed to snag a rich bride, so maybe he wasn't so lacking after all.

Their childhood had been feast or famine. Darius's father would go off, for months and sometimes years at a time, searching the globe for artifacts. He had traded in ordinary antiquities as well, but the real money was in the erotic. When Darius turned fifteen, he began to accompany his father on his jaunts. Why spend money for university when the world held so many educational opportunities for the cost of a ship's berth? He'd been at it now for two decades, and by and large it had been an eye-opening experience.

It was remarkable what some men—and women, too—paid to collect a bit of perversion. Darius had long been desensitized, although he'd tried out nearly every position and proclivity depicted on the objects he dealt in. For the past few years, a distinct pall had fallen over his sex life. Oh, make no mistake—he was capable, but the joy had been lacking. It had taken a certain widow to remind him of his innocence.

He was innocent no more. And should be ashamed of himself for leading a virtuous woman astray.

But he was not.

Darius grabbed the bar of soap Malcolm had left on the chair and scrubbed the worst of his odor away. He was beginning to feel nearly human again, though the waves of hot and cold had followed him right into the bath. At present he looked a bit like a plucked chicken, goosebumps marching up and down his arms. He knew that in ten minutes or so he'd be hot and sweating— best to just stay where he was and wait it out in the water. Malcolm would not be too long at the wine shop. When he got back, he could help Darius back upstairs and change his bed linen besides. There was no point in cleaning up if one were to lie back down in the filth.

By Darius's reckoning, this was his eighth or ninth recurrence of the malaria he had contracted half a dozen years ago. Not so bad, really. He could suffer from gout instead, if only he ate and drank to excess. That had definitely not been his problem. Alcohol was damn difficult to get hold of in Moslem lands, and there had been long stretches when he and Malcolm were lucky to share a bowl of couscous. But his luck was about to turn, if only he could get through tomorrow night.

He lathered up his lank hair and plunged down into the tub to rinse. He needed barbering, from what he'd seen at the club last night. Short hair *à la Brutus* was all the rage—he must look like the savage he was to the *ton*. But they were not above bidding at his auction. Darius had held several successful auctions over the years after returning from his buying trips since he'd closed his father's shop, usually in rented halls. Tomorrow would be a change of pace, hopefully more conducive to sales. There would be wine.

And there would be a woman.

Slicking his wet hair away from his face, he lay back in comparative peace. The knives had eased in his stomach, his head was not pounding, his skin not completely shriveled in the cooling water. For the first time in some hours, he felt almost well. He might have fallen asleep if the front door didn't slam upstairs.

It wouldn't be Malcolm—he'd return the way he left, through the tradesman's entrance. Darius sat up as he heard the light footsteps tripping down the kitchen stairs. *Pru.* At least he smelled more appetizing than he had a short while ago. He pasted on a smile and hoped she wouldn't flee once she caught sight of him au naturel. He hadn't counted on her coming home to find him in such a compromising position, but was damn glad she didn't get lost in London. Even in daylight, anything could happen, even in the most civilized city in the world. He dreaded to think about Pru on the streets of Cairo.

So intent was she on pulling down her washing that she didn't see him in the corner. Darius cleared his throat, and Pru dropped a snowy white chemise onto the kitchen slates.

"Oh! I wasn't expecting to find you downstairs. Are you feeling better?"

She stood her ground, wasn't a bit missish about coming upon him naked in the bathtub. Of course, the enameled tin was deep and only his upper torso was exposed. She'd seen—and touched and kissed and suckled and licked—it all before anyway. To Darius, their night felt like a lifetime ago, long enough at any rate for him to have recovered and begin to stir again beneath the soap bubbles.

"Now that I'm seeing you. You are a sight for sore eyes." He watched Pru's cheeks color becomingly. "Once in Egypt," he said, "I contracted opthalmia, and I couldn't see anything for days. It was frightfully inconvenient for an antiquities dealer to be unable to distinguish a clay pot from copper."

"How dreadful. I've read about that. It struck Napoleon's soldiers and scientists, did it not?"

Darius was surprised she knew of it, and regretful he'd brought the subject up. She'd think him a total weakling, prey to every disease known to mankind. Next he'd break out in hives and erupt in warts.

"Yes. But I'm totally cured. Totally. Where did you go?"

She smiled. "Out." She turned back to her clothesline, efficiently stripping it of her unremarkable underwear. Darius covered his erection with a washcloth.

"Out where?"

She sat at the table, smoothing and folding her clothing into neat squares. "You'll see. I thought I might do kind of a rehearsal for tomorrow night after dinner."

Darius shifted in the bath. "I am much improved. I don't think I shall require your assistance after all."

"Pooh. From what Malcolm tells me, your indisposition can last for days, and it comes and goes willy-nilly."

"Pay no attention to Malcolm. He's an old fraud."

Pru nodded. "That may be, but he does seem to have your best interests at heart. No, I'm determined to help you. Looking forward to it, in fact." She bundled up her clothes and rose. "I presume Malcolm is somewhere about to help you back upstairs?"

"Nearly. He's due back any minute."

Pru frowned. "I told him not to leave you alone! Stupid man!"

Darius was not sure to whom she was referring, but decided not to take offense. He had been demonstrably stupid on numerous occasions. He was being stupid now lusting after Prudence Thorne in a basement kitchen. It wasn't as if he could do anything about his inconvenient desire. A chill prickled down his spine and he realized the water was stone cold. He really should try to get out.

But not in front of Pru. He still had some pride, and she didn't need to see him stumble up the stairs, if he could even get to them on his own.

"You're turning blue. How long have you been sitting down here?"

She stood over him like a stern schoolmistress, not that he'd ever had one. There had been male tutors and a short spell at Eton until it was discovered what his father did for a living. Darius had defended the family honor with his fists until he purposely flunked out.

"I'm all right." He clenched his teeth to keep them from chattering.

"I'll fix you a cup of tea."

She flew around the kitchen as if his very life depended on a hot cup of India tea. Watching her made him dizzy again, so he shut his eyes to keep the walls from wobbling. Blast, but he hated this feeling of helplessness. He ignored her scolding and sank back into the water. When the room turned mercifully silent, he knew she was near and opened one eye.

"Can you manage to hold it yourself?"

"Damn it, Pru. What do you take me for?" Darius meant to growl, but somehow sounded more like a puppy than a dog. He grasped the mug she held out with two shaking hands and took a sip.

Her cool hand swept across his forehead, and she clucked her disapproval. "You should never have gotten out of bed."

"I had to. I stank."

"Well, you smell lovely now. But you would have been better off to wait for me to give you a sponge bath."

The tea scalded his throat. "Delightful as that sounds, it is hardly appropriate." Not to mention damned embarrassing. Pru would make someone a comforting mama, but he was not her child.

"Does your head hurt?"

He shrugged. She slipped behind him, massaging his temples as he tried to hang on to his tea. Her fingers were magic, and he wished with all his heart they would move somewhat lower.

"Where did Malcolm go anyway?"

"The wine merchant in the next street. There will be refreshments tomorrow night, the better to part our guests with the contents of their wallets."

"Very clever. You've done an auction before?"

"Not quite like this. But what we lack in space, we'll make up for in amenities."

"And I'm one of them!" she trilled, sounding altogether too happy about rubbing shoulders with the most disreputable lechers in London. Darius would have to lock her in her room.

Chapter Ten

Darius had eaten some of his supper and was feeling almost fit. He'd been spared the indignity of Pru helping him back to his room before he was encased in ice by Malcolm's return. His sheets were still fresh, his hair still fluffy, his resolve unwavering. Pru could not participate in tomorrow's events—if she was discovered, the scandal would indelibly stain her for the rest of her days. Darius could not hold himself responsible for the ruination of a lady—he may have been a bit casual all his life, but damn it, he did have some honor. She might think this all a lark, but the auction was serious business.

He should be unconscious after Malcolm's sleeping draught, but he was far too restless, and too determined to get Pru into his bed again. The pages of the book he'd selected went unread as his mind kept returning to Pru. Pru, pale against the sheets. Pru bent over, her voluptuous bottom waiting to be worshipped. Pru above him, riding him to oblivion. Three days ago he did not know the woman existed. There was something very wrong with him, besides the malaria, to be so fixated on his brother's cousin-in-law.

Cyrus had come calling tonight, and Pru had flashed upstairs to hide and hadn't yet come back down. His brother hadn't stayed long once he discovered Darius naked in his sickbed. Cyrus had never been much good with any unpleasantness, and a few artful groans from Darius guaranteed he'd go back to his bride. All was apparently well on Rex Place, which should soothe Pru. Despite her irritation at the elopement, he knew Pru cared for Sophy's happiness. God help Cyrus if he ever took a step wrong, for Pru was a force to be reckoned with.

It certainly wasn't because she was physically imposing. She wasn't tall or especially beautiful—she was more wren than cardinal. But from the moment she'd lectured him thinking he was his brother, he had felt an unexpected flicker of desire for her. And now that he'd tasted her, the flicker had turned to full-fledged conflagration.

What was keeping her? She knew he wanted to speak to her. Wanted much more. Cyrus had been gone a full hour. Darius could not wait much longer—his cock tented the bedcovers.

A tinkle of metal against metal outside his door had him rearrange the pillows over his erection. There was a gentle knock. *At last.*

"Come in."

The door pushed open, and Darius's mouth fell open along with it. A barefooted houri garbed in midnight blue silk stood in the doorway. She was veiled, her hair completely covered, kohl-rimmed blue eyes to match her ensemble the only aspect of her face visible. A bandeau across her breasts barely covered them—the snow-white mounds spilled over the gold-embroidered edges. Her harem pants hung low on her hips, revealing a flat stomach. A raft of gold and silver bracelets covered her wrists, and the maharajah's ruby and diamond pendant encircled her throat, dipping into her suspiciously sudden cleavage.

"P-Pru?"

"I am Fairuza, master. Your love-slave." She spoke with an indefinable accent, breathless and buzzing and basically absurd.

Damn Malcolm and his penchant for gossip! Darius and Sheikh Mahmoud had not quite seen eye-to-eye about the disposition of Fairuza. Darius had purchased the girl solely to set her free, and numerous aspersions cast against his manhood had resulted in a hasty exit from Alexandria. The sheikh had felt tricked, but it seemed to Darius that no fourteen-year-old girl should have to submit to sexual degradation. Mahmoud was not a nice man.

"Good God! Aren't you cold?"

"My master will warm me," Pru said as she jingled and clinked her way across the carpet.

"I see what you're trying to do, and I won't have it! You can't go around half-naked like that at the auction. And besides, your skin is too white to pass for Egyptian." White like roses. White like fresh snow. White like pure innocence, but somehow packaged as sin.

"I am Circassian, stolen from my village. My father earned many chickens for me." She paused. "And gold, too, of course."

"Rubbish. I am serious, Pru. Rigged out like that, you'll cause a riot tomorrow night."

Pru leaned invitingly over the bed. Her breasts were barely contained in the flimsy embroidered bodice she wore. "I distract the rich men, no? Or would it be yes?"

Darius flipped away from her tempting bosom. "Get dressed this instant."

Pru tiptoed around the bed, but her bracelets betrayed her. Darius squeezed his eyes shut.

"I good girl. But I can be bad."

Darius flipped again. It was he who was a chicken—on a spit, turning from his greatest temptation. "What if your ruse is discovered, Pru?" he asked into his pillow. "You'll be ruined. Bad enough when I thought you meant to be a regular Jane, in a mask or something. But this—this! Words fail me."

"Is good. How you say, the cat has got your mouth." She giggled. "I have better plans for it."

Darius opened his cat-gotten mouth to object, but the jangling alerted him to the fact that Pru was crawling next to him on the bed. He rolled over to the edge, as far as he could go away from her sinuous body without falling on the floor.

This was unfair. He couldn't escape her—he could barely stand up. The only thing capable of standing was his cock, which had burrowed into the bedding in fruitless relief. This was not how Darius wanted her their first time—he didn't want Pru in disguise, but as her fresh-faced, sharp-tongued self.

"I do whatever master says," she purred.

"Get up and go wash your face. You look like a raccoon," he said cruelly.

"Is the custom in the harem."

Ha! He had her now. He rolled back over. "Then I

presume you've removed your nether hair. Sheikh Mahmoud's women—all women in the East—do so."

Her eyes widened. He bet she was blushing under the blue silk.

"Oh," she said in a deflated voice, absent the accent. "You don't want me."

He'd gone too far, bastard that he was. He took her slender form in his arms. "Pru, Pru. I don't want to bed you as someone else. You are perfectly fine as you are. Better than fine. Beautiful, like a white English rose." He wiped a tear streaking through the kohl. "God, Pru, I've been lying here for hours wanting you. Days. It was all I could do last night not to finish what we started."

"You were ill."

"No man could ever be ill enough to resist you."

Somehow the veil headdress unwrapped and Pru's hair tumbled onto the pillows. Darius encountered a crackling sound as he explored the luscious mounds peeking from the silk bandeau and pulled wads of tissue paper from beneath her breasts. He balled them up and threw them weakly in the corner. "You are perfect as you are. Perfect." A sweet peaked nipple worked its way into his devouring mouth, and he tugged and suckled like a greedy child. He could feel Pru melting beside him, heard her gasps, felt her shivers of pleasure. Her hands and lips were as busy as his, stroking and nipping his bare flesh. Her every touch left a brushfire in its wake.

He couldn't wait for her to wash her face and moved up her blushing throat to her unstained lips. She needed no artifice to deepen their natural pink. Her kiss was clean and honest—there was no trace of shyness or hesitation. Her costume had emboldened her—waspish Mrs. Thorne had disappeared. Pru was nothing but velvet skin and slippery silk and knowing eyes.

He'd lied about the raccoon business. The kohl turned her eyes into aquamarines—clear, bright, dazzling. They were the most beautiful eyes he'd ever seen, and he'd seen a lot of beautiful eyes.

But no one had ever looked at him as Pru had—by turns hopeful and trusting, defiant and determined. She seared him with her gaze as she kissed him, choosing to watch him make love to her until his own eyes crossed.

He might not be able to return her stare, but his body would show her what he felt.

He unhooked the scrap of fabric over her breasts and returned to nuzzle. Her breast fit neatly in his palm, as small and perfect as a peach half tipped with raspberries. He ignored the rush of blood in his ears as he licked and laved, Pru's fingernails grazing his bare back. He could taste every inch of her and never get enough, but he knew what they both wanted tonight. What they both needed.

His hand slipped beneath the loose ribbon of her Turkish trousers and found nothing but warm skin and damp curls. Her bud pulsed against his circling thumb and her nails dug deeper. Further exploration told him she was wet but very tight, too narrow to accommodate his raging erection.

Darius could not bear to hurt her when she had waited ten years to give herself to another man, unworthy as he was. Stroking gently, he continued to caress and kiss her breasts until her body grew rigid with need. Her hands ripped into his back and her breathing grew ragged. He knew when she spun into her bliss, convulsing and crying his name.

Trembling, Pru curled into him as if she wanted to share his skin, her eyes bright with tears. Happy ones, he hoped. Her hands came to rest on his face, cupping his cheeks.

"I want you. Inside me," she whispered.

"That's where I want to be. But you're not quite ready."

"Then make me ready."

He couldn't stand up to walk. How would he manage the rest?

He kissed the tip of her nose. "There's a vial in my top dresser drawer. Fetch it for me."

Pru scrambled from the bed, bunching her trousers at her waist. Her rounded arse was deliciously visible through the sheer fabric. She looked as if she was having difficulty walking, too—he hoped he'd weakened her knees and shattered her modesty. She struggled one-handed with the drawer-pull of the tallboy, then with a sigh allowed her pants to fall to the floor. Darius thought his heart would stop.

She kicked the silk from her ankles. She was alabaster in the lamplight, an exquisite statue come to life. Her hair fell to her angel's wings, clipped straight across. Her bottom—well, her bottom was a perfect pear, and Darius wanted to take a bite although he knew it might shock her. Pears, peaches, raspberries— he was thinking like a bad poet.

Pru rummaged through the drawer, then held up the green glass bottle. "This?" she asked, turning. A single curl fell over her forehead, and she brushed it back. It was a pity she trimmed and pinned her tawny hair back—Darius would like to entangle himself in its rose-scented strands.

"That."

She removed the stopper and sniffed. "Oh! It smells so—so—decadent!"

"How would a woman like you know what decadence smells like, Pru?" Darius said with a smile.

"I know what I know." She padded back to the bed, her lovely front on display, her nipples still swollen and pink from his attention. "What do you mean to do with this?"

"It will smooth my way inside you, Pru. You're very tight."

Her face clouded. "There's something wrong with me."

He pulled her back down on the bed. "There is nothing in the world wrong with you. You're finely made, that's all, and I—not to brag, but take a look, my love. I'm rather large."

Pru's smudged lids dropped in embarrassment. His cock had never seemed bigger. Pru had had that effect on him nearly from the beginning. He supposed his months of celibacy could be blamed, but he was damned anxious to bury himself in Pru's tight, sweet passage. But not before she was prepared to receive him.

"Relax. Come lie with me."

She settled back down in the crumpled linens, gripping the bottle. Darius gentled it away from her and poured a stream of the heady oil into the palm of his hand, setting the bottle down safely in the crook of her elbow. He covered his cock with the tingling liquid, stroking himself slowly to impossible stiffness. Pru watched as he pleasured himself, eyes wide. A cloud of

fragrance invaded his senses—dark, spicy, and decadent, just as Pru said.

"Should I be touching you?"

The friction of his own practiced hand was bad
enough—if she put hers on him now, he'd lose control.
He shook his head. "No, love. But I want you to touch
yourself. Coat your fingers and play."

"I couldn't!"

"If I can, you can."

Pru lifted the bottle from the bed and dabbed a little
on her fingertips.

"More, Pru."

She frowned but followed his direction. Shutting
her eyes, she lay back against the pillows and thrust her
fingers into her curls.

Pru was already wet—he'd made her so, but she
grimly poked at herself, feeling like a fool. Darius had
brought her to climax with patient, well-placed strokes,
but her own hand seemed clumsy and counterproduc-
tive. When she lifted her eyelashes a smidgeon, she
found him staring at her center, his hand still working
his rod. She closed her eyes again and bit a lip, trying
to recreate his earlier rhythm, pushing away the awk-
wardness she felt to be so exposed.

Pru startled as a drop of oil fell on her belly, followed
by Darius's hand. He leaned over her, spreading the aro-
matic fluid from navel to crease. When he mounted
her—*if* he mounted her—he'd likely slide right off.

She stopped rubbing. "I'm sorry. I can't do this.
Why should I do it when you are so much better at it?"

Darius chuckled. "It's very erotic for me to watch

you touch yourself, but you look like you're puzzling over a difficult mathematics problem. I just thought you might be a little more delicate than I in lubricating yourself. Someday you may learn what your body needs."

"What it needs is you!" she said in frustration. Why couldn't he just stick his *thing* in as Charles had done?

No, not Charles. Charles had never kissed her and fondled her and made her crazy. Charles had never looked at her as Darius did right now, as though he was both amused and very, very amorous. As though he wanted to eat her up without a spoon.

"And so you shall have me, Pru. Hold yourself apart for me."

That she could do. Another trickle of oil dripped over her nether lips, and then still more. Darius slid his fingers over and under her folds, teasing her opening. Pru supposed kissing her again down there was out of the question with all of the slippery liquid, and sighed. But soon she was making do very nicely with one of his fingers, then two buried deep inside her.

The oil made his touch feel entirely different. He skimmed and smoothed, continuing to drench her with the contents of the bottle—on her belly, on her thighs, even her buttocks. Warm, wicked, wonderful imprints raced across her skin. The knot of tension at the base of her spine loosened, and she was nearly in the flying state she'd been in when he'd kissed her breasts and pressed her bit of magical flesh into her pubic bone.

Her diamond. And she'd been wholly unaware of it before. In three days Darius Shaw had taught her more about her own body than any medical text.

He said one day she'd enjoy touching herself. She

supposed she might, if it meant that Darius looked at her with the hunger she'd seen through her lashes. As though he loved every inch of her.

Not love. Lust. Desire. Need. They were enough tonight.

Darius withdrew his fingers so gradually she almost didn't realize it. He took one of her hands from her task and toyed with her fingers, oiling them as his were. Then he covered her hand with his and forced her to discover her swollen center, impelling her to circle under his expert pressure. Her hand was weightless, caught in Darius's current, swirling and drawing her flesh to a hard peak. Pru was on the verge of her crisis, caused by her own hand as Darius's fell away.

"You'll want to keep your hand between us, love," he said, his voice raspy. "My God but you're beautiful."

Pru couldn't argue. She felt beautiful. Wanton, too. Her breath hitched. She was close. So close.

And then he was over her, his heavy cock poised at her entrance. She held herself open with one hand as the other continued its elliptical journey around her diamond. She knew there was another name for it, but diamond would do. Darius made her feel precious. Many-faceted. Sparkling. She was not plain old Pru, but a woman of the world, who touched herself with no inhibitions and waited for her lover to claim her.

He fisted himself and edged in, filling her with none of the discomfort or dismay she remembered. Pru watched him as he looked at their joining, dark hair to fair, her hand still busy. His face was a mask of pain.

"What's wrong? Are you ill again?" she asked anxiously.

His rueful grin assured her. "No. Never better. *Never* better. You are so tight around me. It's heaven. But I may not last long. You are a witch."

Pru's heart gave a little flip. Darius was a man who had known many women—not that he'd confided that inconvenient fact to her. But working for days with Malcolm had expanded Pru's acquaintance with Darius Shaw's past. She was no femme fatale, even if it had been fun dressing the part tonight. But she *did* seem to have an effect on him, even if it was spurred on by his illness. Lord knows, he had an effect on *her*. She was so distracted by his exquisite gliding in and out she almost forgot to touch herself.

It felt so *good*. Good was an entirely inadequate word. Her body was alive with electricity, from the tangled hair on her head to her toes. The toes that were curling as she felt a pull to her groin, a hot ripple across her breasts, her mouth drying. And then she was lost. Darius grabbed her shoulders and kissed her, flooded her, held her so close that her hand was crushed between them. Her diamond pulsated under her fingers, jumping like a live thing. Heat washed over her, the fragrant oil now absorbed in every pore. There was nothing in the universe but Darius, who was still kissing her as though she was the last woman in it.

When his lips left hers, he wasn't finished. Her temple, her blackened eyelids, the bridge of her nose—all were feathered lightly with his kisses. He tumbled her over on top of him to ease his weight, and she lay drugged and breathless atop him.

"I am sorry," he murmured, placing one last kiss into the corner of her mouth. "I forgot myself at the end. I should have withdrawn." He paused, searching her face. "But I don't think I could have. You really *are* a witch."

Pru was perversely pleased, although the thought of a child should not make her feel quite so happy. But she had never conceived with Charles. Of course, they had only had sex less than seven times.

"Don't worry. I am probably barren."

He brushed a smudge from her cheek and his thumb came away sooty. She must look a fright. "You can't know that."

"I'm old, as you said."

Darius snorted. "Not that old. But you'll tell me if there are consequences, won't you?"

Pru's euphoria ceased as if it had never been. He was telling her good-bye as she lay on him like a slippery, stained rug.

She nodded, not that she had any intention of doing so. She had plenty of money and could see to a child on her own without tying herself to a man like Darius Shaw. She darted away from his hold. "I'm terribly tired, Darius. You should try to sleep as well."

For a moment, she thought she saw a flash of disappointment, but then he arranged a bland smile on his face. "I suppose you're wise not to want to sleep beside me. Good night, Pru."

She gathered up her bits of blue silk in a hopeless effort to cover herself as she ran up the stairs. Her experiment was over, and the day after tomorrow she would leave Jane Street and its temptations—most especially Darius Shaw—forever.

Chapter Eleven

Darius had dragged himself out of bed and was inspecting the furniture arrangement when Pru came downstairs, late. She'd had a difficult, near-sleepless night, reliving each kiss and stroke until she'd been compelled to touch herself again with surprisingly successful results. She had managed quite well without Darius—as he'd said the other night, once she got the hang of self-gratification, she'd never need a man again. It helped that she imagined him in her narrow bed, whispering his wicked nonsense. Charles had never spoken.

She wore one of her black dresses, as was fitting. The sapphire-blue slave girl had danced off the stage, and practical Pru was back.

"Why are you out of bed?" She couldn't disguise the disapproval in her voice.

Chastened, Darius sat down abruptly on a spindly gold chair. The chairs, lined up like rigid soldiers, must have been delivered this morning. Darius was expecting quite a crowd—there was not an inch between the rows to spare. All of the treasures were set cheek-by-jowl on the dining table and makeshift display tables. Carmela's naughty paintings were joined by Darius's—he would sell whatever would bring him a profit from the Jane Street house. Let its next owner collect his own particular accessories to *amour*. An auctioneer's podium, also rented, stood in the double doorway between the parlor and the dining room.

"Good morning, Pru. Are you all right?"

"Quite. Are you?"

"I've been better. But there are a few last-minute details to attend to."

He made no mention of their night, gave her no lustful, warm looks. In fact, he appeared gray and tired.

"I can help you."

"No, you can't. That's what I want to talk to you about. I've made arrangements to get you back to Bath today. I don't want you here when my guests turn up."

He really was done with her. She'd been stupid, thinking one night would change everything. *No woman of mine.* Pru guessed she didn't belong to him any longer. She was back to being *a woman like you.*

She had too much pride to beg to stay. Let him fall flat on his face.

And then, before she could wish it so, he did.

Darius slipped from the chair, knocking several over in his faint.

"Malcolm!" Pru screamed.

For once Malcolm moved like a youth half his age. He was in the parlor in seconds, clucking over his master like a nervous grandmother.

"I told him to stay upstairs, the young fool. Och, how are we going to manage tonight?" Malcolm loosened Darius's tie and patted him gently on his white cheeks. "Out like a light. We'll just have to postpone the auction. He has a list. Could you write notes before you go?"

"I'm not going anywhere," Pru said. Fairuza would come to the rescue.

In Pru's opinion, the evening was progressing well. The parlor was packed—some gentlemen even spilled out into the hallway because there were too few chairs. Malcolm had set up a cashbox and wrapping station by the front door. Darius had been very clever. The auction was by invitation only, but it also cost the invitees a pretty penny to simply enter the Jane Street house to view the collectibles. They had milled around the two display rooms for a quarter of an hour perusing the objects, making ribald jokes. Pru was grateful she was veiled, in scarlet this time, so they wouldn't see her blushes. She did not recognize anyone but discovered that perverts came in all ages, shapes, and sizes.

Pru had finally managed to settle the men down by shaking her bracelet-clad arms and banging on the gavel on the podium.

"Where's Shaw?" someone shouted.

"My master, he is indisposed. Is I, Fairuza, his love-slave to do honors."

"Honor me, love!" Raucous laughter followed. She tapped on the gavel to no effect.

"See here, gents," yelled Malcolm from the hallway, "you quiet down and let Fairuza do her job or you'll answer to me." Malcolm had a fireplace poker between his hands and looked suitably ferocious.

Pru pointed to her left. "I begin with painting of

vestal virgins and large red devil, Italian circa sixteenth century. See large titties. What bid?"

The room was dead silent. Pru touched the wicked necklace that matched her costume so beautifully. She stroked the diamond, larger than the one on her ring, circling slowly, then dipped her finger down into her cleavage. The tissue paper felt quite damp beneath her breasts.

"One hundred pounds!"

"Two!"

After more shouting, Pru made her first sale, squinting down at Darius's list of reserve prices. The painting had gone for more than he'd estimated.

Her confidence soared, and she sold off a few more pieces. As she ticked the last off from her paper, a hush fell across the room. She looked up to find Darius striding down the aisle, white as a sheet and looking thunderous.

"Fairuza, you may go upstairs now and await me."

Knowing chuckles followed his words. Pru thrust out her chin, although Darius could not see it beneath the scarlet silk. "I stay to help."

"No. You will obey me."

"I show treasures."

"Let her stay, Shaw! We paid good money to see her treasures!" There was general consensus from the roar in the room.

Pru was now nose-to-nose with Darius. "You woke up, I see," she whispered.

"Blast it, Pru," he whispered back. "How could you put yourself at risk like this? You look like—a—a—"

"Love-slave?" she asked sweetly. "The auction is

going very well. I've exceeded your reserve prices on six of the items. You may conduct the rest of the sale, but let me stay. If you fall ill again—"

"Fuck," Darius said, most explicitly.

"Please. I truly think I can help you." She twirled and jingled around and bowed deeply to the crowd, hoping her breasts would not spring forth from their scanty confinement.

"All right. But at the first sign of trouble, run, don't walk upstairs. I will deal with you later." He turned to his guests. "Good evening, gentlemen. Forgive my delay. I expect Fairuza has taken good care of you?"

"Not as good as she's taken of you! You look half-dead, Shaw. She must be a tigress in bed."

"You don't know the half of it," Darius drawled. "Now then, Fairuza, make yourself useful. Fetch the silver chalice from Jerusalem. Now here's the *real* Holy Grail, my friends. Or should I say Unholy?"

Pru had to admit Darius was skilled at disposing of his collection in record time. A few of the guests left early, happy with their purchases, but Darius kept promising a rarity that had never yet been seen on England's shores as the final item up for bid. At last there was nothing left but a long painted papier-mâché box propped up against the wall that Pru had not noticed before.

"Here is the pièce-de-résistance, a one-of-a-kind object. Fairuza, lift the lid and show our guests this prize."

She did. And swallowed hard. Inside the box was a doll. A naked doll, with enormous glass eyes. Pru's eyes grew as huge as the doll's. This was no antique, but an exquisitely hand-crafted stuffed velvet doll the size of a small woman, perfect in every detail from the lines on its fingers to the enormous cocoa-brown nipples on its enormous breasts—breasts that certainly defied gravity and nature's laws. Its gleaming jet hair—real, she was sure—fell straight to the small of its back. Some poor girl had sacrificed a lifetime's growth of her crowning glory. The doll's eyes were made of almond-shaped blue glass, ringed in tiny black stitches meant to be kohl. Like hers right now, Pru reflected. Longer-than-was-ever-possible feathered eyelashes and arched eyebrows made the toy look perpetually surprised. Its plush embroidered red lips were held open in an O, and pink velvet lined an indentation large enough for an object to be inserted.

Pru was pretty sure what that object might be.

Darius moved next to her as she froze before the thing and picked it up himself. Pru's eyes swept downward, past a pert little bellybutton in a rounded stomach. The doll had no matching black hair at the apex of her thighs. Darius had said women in the East made themselves hairless there, and was even at this moment spreading the doll's slender legs to point out one of its other available orifices, equally as pink as its mouth. An ankle bracelet of gold coins, the doll's only "clothing," jingled when he flipped it over and parted the arse cheeks. There was a great roar from the crowd, and the bidding started even before Pru could parade the doll up and down the aisle, not that she wanted to touch the obscene thing. This was somehow worse than everything else that had gone before it.

Pru felt light-headed. The doll stared back at her with sparkling tip-tilted blue eyes. If this was all a man wanted out of life—a beautiful soulless, voiceless re-ceptacle—Pru was doomed. She took it from Darius's hands as if it were a dead rat.

Darius kept up his auctioneer's patter, extolling the virtues and rarity of every hand-stitched bit of thread and fabric. It may not be old, but it was destined to be a classic, he said, a one-of-a-kind work of art. Sea glass eyes from the Mediterranean made of ancient Roman wine carafes, hair of a Chinese concubine, Egyptian velvet skin softer than a woman's. Pru stifled a snort—velvet was damned difficult to care for. Excessive use and one was bound to flatten the pile and permanently wrinkle it. A few nights under a fat balding lord and the beauty of the doll would be history. Nevertheless, she held its mammoth breasts against her own inadequate-but-padded ones and glided down the row between the gaping men. Hands inevitably shot forward to touch the doll or her, she wasn't quite sure—until she felt a deliberate pinch to her bottom. She stopped midstep and the doll jingled.

"Give us a closer look, love."

Pru turned to the pincher, a cadaverous fellow who leered at her with no shame.

"But of course, sir," Pru said in her fake accent. She thrust the doll's left nipple into his right eye.

"Ow! Blasted wench! What kind of a show are you running here, Shaw?"

"Forgive Fairuza, Lord Pomeroy. She's dreadfully clumsy. Apologize, my dear."

"I will not. He put hands on gluteus maximus."

"Did he?" Darius's face darkened. "You may touch the merchandise, Lord Pomeroy, but not my love-slave."

"I'll buy her from you, Shaw. Teach her a lesson. It's a wonder you can stand her impudence."

"My master insists upon my impudence, Lord Pomeroy. Every morning. Every night. Sometimes at luncheon, too." Laughter rippled around the room.

"Fairuza," Darius said, a warning note in his voice. "I'm afraid my love-slave has an imprecise understanding of our language, gentlemen, which is why I asked her *not to speak*."

Pru resisted the urge to rip off her veil and spit in Lord Pomeroy's face. Instead, she lowered her eyes. "I will do as my master says. Always. Many times."

"Forget the doll, Shaw. What will you take for the fair Fairuza?" This from a drunken buck who looked much too young to be present. Murmurs of approval from his party emboldened him. "One thousand pounds!"

"Two!" came from the back of the parlor.

Darius pounded his gavel but could not bring the room back to order. Bids on her were coming in fast and furious. For the first time this evening, Pru felt some misgivings about the game she played. She looked helplessly at Darius, who had turned very pale at his podium.

"Be the quiet, all of you!" she shrieked. "I not for sale. I love my master and would scratch out the eyes and tear off the balls of you English pigs."

This did not bring her the results she hoped for. True, a hush had fallen over the room as she began her tirade, but the men's moods turned ugly at the insult to their heritage.

"How do you know she's not a heathen spy, Shaw? Why, she could be planning your murder right now!"

"I kill no one, only the chickens in my village," Pru

said. "I no spy." She clutched the hideous doll tighter, as if it would come to life and defend her.

"She's probably as ugly as a pig herself," Lord Pomeroy said. "No wonder she has to wear a veil."

Darius rapped the gavel so hard its head flew off into the front row, narrowly missing Baron Davies. "Gentlemen, gentlemen. Calm yourselves. I assure you Fairuza is not worth your astronomical offers, and you are right—she is as ugly as sin. No man can look at her face and live, which is why I have to put a sack on her head when we are impudent. Now then, back to this exceptional doll, which promises only pleasure and no pain of ever listening to a tiresome woman's complaints. Fairuza, step back up here so all our guests can have an equal opportunity to inspect this masterpiece. *Now!*"

Pru flinched at the order, but had to believe he wanted her near to protect her from the near-riot she'd started.

And she'd told the whole room she loved him, whereas he'd said she was an ugly pig. She'd spoken the truth. Had he?

When she got close enough, Darius snatched the doll away from her and propped it back in its box. "What in God's name are you thinking?" he asked through clenched teeth. "We're almost home free."

"A sack over my head?" Pru countered.

"Do you want them to beg to see you, you stupid woman? You were a hair's breath away from being stripped!"

"So what if I was? I'll never see these wretched men again!"

"No you won't. I won't permit it. When we marry I'm going to lock you up!"

"Lock me up?" Pru's mouth snapped shut. *What* had he said?

"And throw away the key. Maybe I'll let you out for Christmas."

One of the men rose from his gilt chair. "Shaw! I've got a pretty whore waiting for me. Let's get on with this."

"Then what do you want a rag doll for, eh? Why, the man who buys this might as well take out an advertisement in the *Times* that he can't get a real woman," sneered Pomeroy.

"Bloody hell," Darius muttered. "Now look what you've done. They're thinking with the wrong head."

Pru stood frozen next to Darius as he tried to spin his auction out of its grave. She heard snatches of "convenient" and "loyal," but paid them no mind. He wanted to *marry* her? If she was not entirely mistaken, he had just proposed in a rather threatening manner. She had not as yet accepted, however.

"And so, even if this magnificent work of art simply sits in a darkened closet, know that you have shown yourself to be a man of impeccable taste and perspicacious acumen. The ancient coins alone on the ankle bracelet are worth something," Darius said with mounting desperation.

"Two pounds, and that's my final offer," said the elderly Marquess of Huntington. "A man my age is lucky to dip his wick into a knothole in the wall. This doll will do as well."

"Sold," Darius said, tapping the gavel stem against the podium. A cheer went up and then it seemed all ell broke loose. Darius held her arm as the men disappeared noisily into the night, clutching Malcolm's inexpertly wrapped brown parcels. Pru surveyed the wreckage of the room—overturned spindly chairs, broken wineglasses, smoking cigar butts in ash trays. Each one of Darius's fingertips was burning into her bare arm.

"We need to talk."

Pru extricated herself from his grip. "*You* need to go to bed. You're dead on your feet."

"Not. Dead. Yet. No thanks to you." Darius swayed and reached out to his auctioneer's block.

Pru caught him before he went down, squeezing him against her artificial breasts. He was too large for her to hold up for long. "Malcolm! Come help me!"

Malcolm emerged from the hallway, moving so quickly he must have forgotten he had a bad leg. "I've got him now, Mrs. Thorne." He wrapped his arm around Darius's back. "Come on, laddie. I've got a bucket full of pounds and all the I.O.U.s you could ask for. It's time to relax."

"I want to count it all," Darius said stubbornly.

"And so you shall, once you're safe in bed. Mrs. Thorne, bring up the cashbox."

Pru tore off her veil and followed the men as they lurched up to the bedroom. Her eyes were beginning to water from the makeup, but she didn't have time to scrub her face. She could, however, dispose of the padding in her bodice, and left a trail of crumpled tissue paper all the way up the stairs.

Darius fell into bed as if he were pole-axed. Malcolm removed his boots and loosened his neckcloth while he lay almost insensate on top of the poodles.

"You should have never come down," Pru scolded.

"And if I hadn't, you would have been carried off into some lord's harem, Fairuza."

"Nonsense. Englishmen don't keep harems. And anyway, Malcolm would have protected me."

The valet cum butler cum cook nodded and lit more lamps. "Aye. And so I would have. But you must admit the guv here has a way with words. Squeezed those toffs for every penny and then some."

Darius gave a lopsided smile. "I'd count myself, but I don't think I can sit up. How much did we make, Pru?"

She didn't miss the "we," but didn't trust herself to speak yet of their apparent engagement. "Malcolm, perhaps you should bring Mr. Shaw something cold to drink. *Not* champagne. Some fruit juice perhaps? And something light to eat. A scrambled egg. One for me, too. This love-slave business is hungry work."

"Comin' right up. You'll call for me if you need me?"

Pru nodded. When Malcolm closed the door behind him, Pru sat on the bed and unbuttoned Darius's shirt. She laid a hand on his throat. And frowned. "You're very hot again."

"More than you know. What's happened to your chest?"

"I am back to normal. Or abnormal."

"There is not a thing wrong with your breasts. They're lovely. Perfect."

"You *are* ill."

"I am, but there's nothing wrong with my mind. Unlike my customers, I know good value when I see it. That doll should have fetched more than two pounds," Darius grumbled.

"It was an abomination. I could not have slept in his house knowing it was here."

"It's been here the whole time you have, Pru."

"In its coffin. When you took it out, I was absolutely appalled. Wherever did you get it?"

"An old Egyptian woman made it for me."

"You commissioned it?"

"I thought it was a good idea at the time. A bit of a lark—a silent, pliant woman. A true rarity."

Pru shuddered. "Well, if that's what you want, why did you ask me to marry you?"

"I did, didn't I? I apologize if I wasn't on bended knee. I don't believe I could have gotten up once I got down."

"You were serious?"

"I believe so. I've never asked a woman to marry me before."

"You didn't precisely ask. Though you did mention imprisoning me."

"Some women feel that marriage is a cage." Darius took her hand, absently fingering the diamond on her ring. "I would never clip your wings, Pru. You'd keep your own money—that's why tonight was so important. If I'm going to take a wife, I need to support her. I'm not a fortune hunter like my brother."

"What about the sheep?"

"Oh, I hope there will be enough left over for a lamb or two. Will you, Pru? Will you marry me? I must warn you—I'll probably get sick again. Malcolm says I snore." He took a deep breath. "I've done things I'm not proud of. Slept with too many women, but you're the only one I want for the rest of my life."

"Now is not the time for honesty, you stupid man."

She bent to kiss him and do a little bit more, and stopped only when the eggs arrived.

"Well?" asked Malcolm as he dropped the tray next to the bed. "How much is in the kitty? I want my back wages."

Pru was as warm as her fiancé. She straightened her loose bodice and folded her hands in her silk-clad lap. "I'm afraid we haven't gotten around to counting it yet."

"What have you been doing all this time? Ah!" Malcolm slapped himself on his forehead. "I'll just go then, shall I? You young people have your fun. But don't kill him before he makes an honest woman out of you, Mrs. Thorne. The lad's still sick."

"He *has* proposed, you know."

"So I expected him to. He always knows which shell holds the pearl. See you in the mornin'." Malcolm whistled as he left, no sign whatsoever of any limp.

Pru glanced down at Darius's beaming face. "I haven't said yes yet."

"But you will."

"I might not."

Darius struggled up on an elbow. "What if I tell you I love you?"

Pru unfolded a napkin from the tray. "I might not believe you. We only met four days ago. Eat your eggs. They'll get cold."

"It's past midnight. That makes it five days."

Pru bit a lip. He was oh so tempting, but she had rushed into one marriage, and look where that had led her.

Well, it had led her here, with a gorgeous, half-

ndressed man, a plate of untouched scrambled eggs in
er lap. "It's still too soon."

"Then we'll have a long engagement. But I want us
o live together. On my farm."

"We'll shock the sheep, living in sin."

"The sheep won't notice. We'll stay indoors. In
ed."

She picked up an egg-laden fork and put it down.
"here was no way in the world she could eat now, with
er heart hammering like Darius's gavel in her chest.
There's more to marriage than sex, Darius."

"I don't doubt it. And I expect you to school me in
ll of its rules and regulations. You're a very organized
woman, Pru. A woman like you could make something
ut of a man like me."

Tears blurred the pattern on her plate. "I thought
ou were the teacher in our arrangement."

"I've done my job. You're in flames I kindled. You'd
nake any man a wonderful wife. But I want you for
nine."

"Oh." She put the plate back on the tray. "I'm
fraid, Darius," she whispered.

"So am I. We can be afraid together."

He pulled her into his arms and held her close. She
could feel the erratic beating of his heart and the heat
of his body. "You're ill. Not rational. You might be hal-
ucinating and regret what you said in the morning."

"I might. But I don't think so. When I thought those
nen would get their hands on you tonight, I felt some-
hing rather primal. You belong to me, even if you don't
now it yet."

"I do?" she asked doubtfully.

"You do. But I'll give you all the time you need. I

can't promise to be a model citizen always, but that' probably best—you'll get to know me, warts and al. Just don't leave me, my love. I really couldn't bea that."

Pru pictured them in a tidy manor house, rose creeping over the studded doorway. Sheep on the fron lawn. A garden in the rear, fenced so the bloody ani mals would not eat her prize specimens. A child, if they were lucky. A friendly sheepdog at the very least.

"I'll give you six months to woo me."

He was so quiet she thought he had fallen asleep She lifted her head to see his eyes closed, a satisfie smile on his face. The wretch! Here she was, giving he heart away again, and he—

And then he spoke, the smile still in his voice "That sounds reasonable. We'll have a Christmas wed ding. At least I won't forget our anniversary."

Pru settled back into his arms. "I wouldn't let you."

"No," Darius sighed happily. "I'll be hen-pecked near to death."

"And you'll like it."

"I believe I will."

Epilogue

Six months later, Mrs. Prudence Jane Thorne, née Prescott, and Mr. Darius Alexander Shaw of Rosenn Farm, Piddletrenthide, Dorset, were married by special license in All Saints Church after the Christmas Eve service, the only witnesses their butler Malcolm and housekeeper Lottie Eldridge. The vicar rushed through the secret ceremony, shocked as he was to discover his new neighbors had deceived everyone in the county, dismayed that the anticipation of their wedding vows had resulted in a very voluminous bulge to the new Mrs. Shaw's skirts, and already exhausted from thinking about preaching again tomorrow.

The newlyweds had gone about this all wrong in his opinion, but then the world was full of sin, ensuring he'd have his work cut out for him forever. But Mr. Shaw had offered money for the repair of the church tower, and Mrs. Shaw arranged lovely flowers and greens from her garden for the altar, and it was Christmas, so he was in a forgiving mood. Better late than ever, and they did seem sincerely penitent for their re-

luctance to wed and awfully lovey-dovey—their dev
tion was almost unnatural.

God moved in mysterious ways. Almost as myste
ous was the unusual ring Mrs. Shaw wore to pledge h
troth, which had caused a few local tongues to wa
when they first saw its size and sparkle. But the woma
was fond of her flowers, and claimed the design w
some exotic plant her husband had seen in his travel
It was a bit garish for a gentleman farmer's wife, but
really was none of the vicar's business.